STAGE
FRIGHT

DIANE L. KOWALYSHYN

This is a work of fiction. Names, characters, places and incidents are either used fictitiously or are a product of the author's imagination, and any resemblance to business establishments, events, locals, or actual persons living or dead, is completely coincidental.

Stage Fright

Copyright © 2022 by Diane L. Kowalyshyn

Cover Art by *Christine D'Abo*

First Edition, 2022

Trade Paperback ISBN 978-1-7779747-2-5

Digital ISBN 978-1-7779747-3-2

For Hunter, Bob and Eleanor—because they're patiently waiting to be reunited.

ACKNOWLEDGMENTS

This book represents a beginning of sorts—my first self-published work. I'd like to thank those people forthcoming with advice and information to make this new journey less convoluted. To Magda Gold, Judy Malcolm and Tim Simmons, my early readers, who stuck it out. The idea for this book began with the death of a dear aunt. When I went through her belongings, I discovered she'd had a mastectomy—something she'd never shared with family members. I couldn't imagine surviving such a devastating surgery without the support of loved ones. This book grew out of her solitude and my overwhelming need for happily ever after.

Chapter 1

"I love you."

Pansy Parker's pronouncement hung in the silence of the darkened bedroom until Rex Bugsbee moved from beneath the cotton sheet and reached for the pants he'd tossed on a nearby chair.

She held her breath. "Did you hear me? I said I love you."

Head lowered, he buttoned his shirt, then swiped his hand across a whiskered chin. "I heard."

Pansy's heart sank. His slumped shoulders said more than she wanted to know. Wrapped in the rumpled bed sheet, she knelt on the bed. "I told you I could accept this arrangement, but somewhere along the line, my feelings got in the way. I don't want to be friends who meet once a week to have great sex. I want us to be together. See each other exclusively." Even as she spoke, she could see him distancing himself.

He collected his phone. "A casual relationship is all I can handle right now."

She loved Rex's voice, dark and silky like his beautiful hair. Now, though, it sounded rough and tight and not in the least like a man in love. Pansy could convince him. She had to. "I don't understand. Why are you so spooked?"

Anger flared in his eyes. "I'm not afraid. I don't have any more time to give you."

"But that's the beauty of becoming a couple." Pansy jumped off the bed, dragging the sheet with her. Rex pulled on his socks and dropped onto all fours to search for his shoes. "It'll make things easier. We'll share the chores. I'll shop and cook, and you do the dishes. You'll have time to relax, go play basketball with the guys."

He ignored her and gathered his coat from the oak rack near the entrance.

Pansy hurried to the door and slid in front of him, blocking his exit. "I'm sorry. I take it all back. Nothing has to change. Things can stay the way they are."

He reached for the doorknob.

"You were honest with me and I blew it." She tried to slow her breathing. God, she sounded frantic. She balled her hands into fists and focused on not crying.

Rex straightened and exhaled.

"What's wrong?" she asked, stepping closer to slide her arms around him. He didn't resist—a good sign. The familiar smell of his woodsy cologne lingered in the smooth fabric of his Oxford shirt.

"I can't do this anymore either," he whispered.

Oh, thank God. Pansy smiled. He knew. They'd be good together. He did love her. She snuggled closer.

"You have nothing to apologize for," Rex said, sadness edging his tone.

She didn't understand. It sounded like he'd lost his best friend, not like he planned to say the three little words she desperately wanted to hear. Her heart tightened again, beating faster.

"I haven't been honest with you," Rex said, his arms finally going around her. "You deserve so much more."

Pansy's heart thumped in her ears. "Whatever it is, we'll work it out together."

"We can't." He released her and stepped back.

With shaking hands, she cinched the sheet across her chest. "Why not?"

"Because I'm already married."

A hush blanketed the theater.

Skye Andrews stood on her mark with Pansy Parker's horror plastered on her face. She froze. The lights dimmed, the curtain dropped, and the applause started. In seconds, stagehands surrounded her and disassembled the set for the second act.

Skye rushed into the wings and ducked into a quiet alcove to change into her next costume. The stage manager, Talbot James, followed her. Some might find his puppy-dog admiration annoying, but she thought it was kind of sweet.

"Fabulous scene," Talbot said. "Each time I see it, I find myself hoping Pansy can convince him."

With her index finger, Skye motioned for him to turn around. She needed to strip out of one outfit and put on the next.

He spun. "You make me root for her every time."

"Thanks," she said. She smoothed her hair with her palms. "I get caught up in her emotions too. I get lost in the part."

God, Skye loved acting. As long as she could remember, she'd been pretending to be someone or something she wasn't. She thought of herself as a glass-half-full gal. Her reviews touted her as a spunky Emma Stone look-alike, with more curves.

Tonight's performance of *The Married Man* had glowing accolades, the crowning glory of the graduating class. In a few short days, the company would disperse and take jobs with theaters across the country—some performers would travel to different continents. Jason Hansome, the leading man and a close personal friend of hers, had taken a post with a production company in Edinburgh, Scotland.

"Almost your cue," Talbot said, putting a hand to his headset.

Skye tugged the fabric of her form-fitting dress across her hips. She took a deep breath, squared her shoulders, and waltzed back out on stage as the insensible Pansy Parker.

The show continued without a hitch, and soon the entire troupe stood on stage, arms linked, to take a collective bow. The applause persisted and they bobbed another two times. In this business, three curtain calls sent a message to the entire crew that their efforts had not gone unnoticed. After the ovations, the curtain dropped and stayed down so the farewell party could get underway.

Jason Hansome, aka Rex Bugsbee, scooped Skye into his arms and swung her around. "What do you say we get naked and celebrate our independence in my dressing room with a bottle of bubbly?"

Skye laughed, her hands resting on his broad shoulders. "That might be a little difficult considering neither one of us has a dressing room. Besides, champagne gives me the mother of all headaches."

He grinned at her, eyes mischievous. "In that case, how about I grab us a couple bottles of beer?"

"Make mine a light," Skye said, giving him a peck on the cheek. He lowered her and hurried off in search of suds.

Skye and Jason had once tried to dangle their feet in love's deep end, but they quickly realized their relationship lacked that special something—the racing heart, sweaty palms, and sexual attraction that stole breath and cart-wheeled stomachs. She and Jason had an unusual bond; she loved him, but in a brotherly, *best friends forever* kind of way. And since her best friend had plans to move halfway around the world, the fangs of separation anxiety had left teeth marks on her ass.

Tonight, during the second curtain call, Skye put her upset over Jason's imminent move aside and vowed to enjoy herself. Why not? She deserved it, and Jason had all but promised a theater would extend an offer to her before graduation.

He wove through the cast and crew toward the fridge.

"Miss Andrews?" A small voice came from behind her. Skye spun and saw a striking young woman with red-chili-pepper hair. She had a tentative smile and wore the tightest jeans and top Skye had ever seen.

"I'm Cassandra. My brother's part of the lighting crew," she said. "I begged him to let me come to the party to meet you. May I have your autograph? I've seen all your plays. You're my favorite actress."

Skye may have been Cassandra's favorite actress, but her favorite actor drew her eye like metal to a magnet. She couldn't stop staring at Jason's backside, and since he'd been Skye's leading man in the last two out of three shows, Skye guessed she'd really snuck in to see him. Skye reached for the program held in her tight grip.

"Sorry." Cassandra startled and passed it to her.

Jason sidled over and held Skye's beer while she finished personalizing the program. He seemed mesmerized with Cassandra's impressive cleavage until Skye elbowed him in the ribs upon the return of said program.

Skye made introductions.

"Oh, Mr. Hansome," Cassandra simpered. "It's such an honor to finally meet you." She held out her slender hand. Jason took it, gallantly bowed, and kissed the back of it.

Skye shrugged. Jason would never let an opportunity to get lucky slip through his fingers. She loved him, but sometimes she didn't like him much. In no time, she'd be the proverbial third wheel, and since she lived in the spare room of her Aunt Bessie's apartment, she took leave sooner rather than later. "Give me a rain check on that beer," Skye said. "Promise we'll get together before you leave?"

Totally distracted, Jason nodded.

Skye thanked a few other members of the cast, said her so-longs, put on her hat and coat, and walked a couple of blocks to the nearest T station. Ordinarily, a bunch of the crew would make their way to the train together. Not tonight. Not with the after-party in full swing. She hurried along the cracked sidewalks beside a string of vacant storefronts.

Over the past few years, there had been a distinct refurbishment in the theater district, but there were still some seedy spots. The streetlight overhead flickered and cast eerie shadows along the way.

Skye swung the strap of her purse over her head and across her shoulder to ensure a solid grip. One of the lighting techs had been mugged in this area a few weeks ago. Head down, she beat a hasty path to the corner.

Cars sped past, and she could hear not only her own footsteps but others echoing behind her.

The pedestrian light turned green, and when she stepped from the curb, she glanced around.

No one was there.

She'd been hearing things.

Again.

Over the last few months, she'd been plagued with feelings of being watched or followed, but on each occasion, she'd been proved wrong—talk about being a drama queen.

Skye picked up her pace in the next block, and just as she reached the stairs to the underground, someone placed a hand on her arm and yanked.

She shrieked, and the fright almost jettisoned her into the atmosphere.

"I'm sorry I frightened you, Ms. Andrews," a deep voice broke over labored breathing. "I had to run full tilt to catch you."

She struggled to calm her own heart rate. "Uh, have we met?" she asked.

"No, not yet we haven't. I wrangled an invitation to the after-party to introduce myself. One minute you were mingling with everyone, and then *poof*, you were gone. My name is Jeremy Steel."

Skye reached out and shook his hand. "Nice to meet you, Mr. Steel," she said. "I don't want to be rude, but I have a train to catch."

Jeremy stood his ground. "Might I take a moment of your time? I have a business proposition."

Skye glanced at her watch. If she missed the eleven o'clock, she'd jump on the eleven twenty. "I can spare a few minutes."

"Great," Jeremy said. "I saw your performance this evening. Very impressive."

"Thank you. It's nice to be appreciated."

"Do you know who I am?" he asked.

"Should I?" Suddenly she wished she'd not been quite so accommodating.

"I'm a producer," Jeremy said. "I think you'd be perfect for the lead role in my next show."

Skye's heart jumped. "Are you with the Opera House?"

"No. I'm not associated with any of the Boston houses," he said. "I'm from Gershwin's in New York."

CHAPTER 2

TEN YEARS LATER

Armed with a double non-fat macchiato latte, Skye entered the office of the Commonwealth War Graves Commission, the CWGC, in Maidenhead, England. She snagged a slip from the beak of the ticket dispenser perched like a vulture on the edge of a desk and took a seat in the crowded room.

Number twenty-seven.

The CWGC had only been open for a half hour, and yet twenty-six people were ahead of her.

Damn.

Her plan to visit the commission in person to expedite approval suddenly seemed like a ridiculous idea. She noticed the filled wickets and realized she'd better make herself comfortable. She'd have to be patient and wait her turn. The overhead LCD sign flashed number nine, so she settled in.

Why wouldn't the commission be busy?

Would the war in the Middle East ever truly be over?

Was there anything more devastating?

Skye couldn't imagine burying a son or daughter. Such abominations went against the natural order—burying her elderly aunt seemed difficult enough.

Solemn, sober faces dotted the waiting room. When she finished her coffee, she dug out the leather journal Aunt Bessie had left her from her bag. It had been three weeks, and Skye still hadn't been able to read the journal her aunt bequeathed her. The small, flowing cursive strokes were fashioned into unusual letters and characters of some sort of strange tongue, perhaps Gaelic. Each time she sat down to read, the words swam across the page, frustrating her. She held the bound book in her hand and thought about her dear aunt.

Skye cried like a magpie in the ICU during her aunt's final hours. Loneliness and an atrophied body had claimed her. Bessie had developed mobility, hearing, and sight issues since Skye's last visit to Boston about a year ago. Bessie had digressed to the point where she used a cane, wore a hearing aid, and had lost sight in one eye due to failed cataract surgery. If only Skye had listened more closely during their weekly phone calls to hear the desperation in her aunt's voice.

Skye sat and rubbed the cover of Bessie's journal. The soft leather felt warm and comforting in her hands, and somehow, she connected with her aunt whenever she held it.

"Last call for number twenty-seven," a voice on the loudspeaker bellowed. She'd been so engrossed in her thoughts she'd forgotten all about the queue.

Brain cells fired.

She jammed the journal inside her bag, sprang to her feet and, without a forward glance, slammed full tilt into a uniformed man with a cane.

Like a pinball, she ricocheted off the solid wall of his chest. His cane and his briefcase skidded across the floor, and he teetered on shaky legs.

Skye recovered first—probably because as a klutz she'd had lots of practice over the past ten years. She often thought of herself as a modern-day Calamity Jane.

She reached out to steady the military man. "Let me help you," she said. He put his hand up and leaned away. Maybe he thought she might finish him off by clubbing him with her fist.

"You've done more than enough." He barked the words as he struggled to maintain his balance.

Rebuffed, Skye backed away and set about collecting the papers spilled across the floor from his briefcase. She placed them on the closest chair.

For as long as she could remember, disaster surrounded her. Leave it to her to run down a decorated and wounded soldier. She picked up his cane and held it.

Taut eyebrows scored his handsome face and hinted at the pain he suffered. His color waned. He limped to a chair and sagged into it. Sweat beaded his brow, and with his eyes tightly closed, he seemed to wrestle his ragged breathing back to normal.

"I'm so sorry," she said. "What can I get you? A glass of water? A gun to shoot me with?"

His eyes sprang open.

In that moment, Skye got her first clear glimpse of his seriousness, his troubled and yet determined brow. Short, tight brown hair curled beneath his regulation British Forces cap. His black jacket, buttoned to his square chin, lay smoothly across his chest. Medals gleamed on his breast pocket.

And her knees nearly buckled. Her heart raced and her hands became sweaty. She could barely catch her breath, and she thought she might throw up.

"I've seen enough death and destruction to last a lifetime. Besides, all you did was mortally wound my pride."

The pain must have abated because he no longer appeared pale.

Warmth spread from her core to fingertips.

"No harm done." He reached over to collect his papers and shoved them back into his briefcase. He plucked his cane from her hands and straightened.

Skye moved closer. "Let me help." She reached for his briefcase. "Lean on me."

"I don't need your help." The killer glare nearly vaporized her.

She backed away. "I'm sorry. I didn't mean to…"

The voice on the loudspeaker called number thirty-two.

"Oh, crap," she said. She crumpled the numbered ticket in her hand. "Wouldn't you know it? I missed my turn."

For the second time in the last nine months, Captain Dalry sensed the imminent danger moments too late. The sweetest little missile he'd ever laid eyes upon targeted and took him out.

Once upon a time, he would have noticed a striking woman on his radar. Iraq changed everything—a fact that frustrated him more with each passing day. He wanted to disregard her. Shut her out. Keep her at arm's length so he wouldn't have to deal with his new limitations. But a good soldier remained fluid. He improvised—worked with whatever resources were available.

Of course, she needed to wear a flashing yellow light to warn all oncoming traffic. She seemed to be a hazard not only to herself but to everyone around her. When her bottom lip quivered, the ice around his heart instantly melted.

"Don't worry about missing your turn. There is more than one way to skin a cat," he said. "And if you promise not to mother me anymore, I'll get you past this line and upstairs. Deal?"

"Really?" The smile on her face stole his breath. Which didn't help his cause because she put her hands on him all over again. "Are you certain you're okay?" she asked.

"Did you hear what I said? Stop fussing over me." Every time the woman touched his arm, the instant heat made him think he'd been prodded with a hot poker.

"Aye, aye, Captain." She gave him a mock salute.

"We'll take the elevator."

"Are you really a captain?" she asked. She grabbed her bag and fell into step beside him.

"Uh-huh. Captain Jet Dalry, at your service." He set his briefcase on the floor and pushed the call button.

"Jet? Are you a pilot?"

"No." He chuckled. "Jet's short for Jethro. I prefer Jet."

She stuck out her good hand.

He hesitated.

"For the record, a handshake is a greeting and should in no way be considered mothering," she said. "I'm Skye Andrews."

They shook.

Her hand felt soft and smooth, unlike his clammy paw. Pain from their collision spiked his heart rate and body temperature, or so he hoped that's what she would think. The elevator doors shut, and the car lurched heavenward.

"Do you work here, Captain?"

"Call me Jet, and no, I don't work out of this office. I visit every couple of months. I'm the military liaison officer. I provide the commission with all the names of our lost forces."

"Sounds depressing."

"It can be, but without me, our fallen heroes wouldn't be able to gain access to a commission cemetery."

"My aunt's father is buried in a commonwealth cemetery in Kilmarnock."

Jet eyed her. "Then you know how important it is to keep accurate records."

"Believe me," Skye said. "I'm painfully aware."

Jet stepped back. He must not have heard her correctly.

The lift jerked to a stop and the metal doors slid open.

They stepped out of the elevator into a neat gridwork of a dozen or more desks. A stringcourse of closed offices lined the far wall.

"What brings you to the UK, Skye?"

"What makes you think I'm a visitor?"

He came to a stop and stared at her.

"Okay. I came here to bury my late aunt's ashes. Soon after I arrived, I realized I couldn't add another inscription to the headstone without permission from the CWGC."

"I see," Jet said. "Where are you from?"

"New York."

"The city or the state?"

"Both."

"I guess your aunt never had any children of her own?"

Skye's brow creased. "No, she never married. It's a long story. She was actually my real aunt's sister-in-law."

Jet set off through the maze of desks and Skye followed. "You're not really her niece then."

"I'm the only niece she's ever known, my dad's sister didn't have any children either."

They continued until they came upon an office. The nameplate on the door read John Smilie. "You're doing her a great service. It's very thoughtful of you."

Jet noticed a tear in her eye.

"A better person would have been there for her while she was alive, not after she passed."

Jet didn't want to reach into that particular snake pit, so he ignored her last comment. "If John can't help you, no one can."

"And how, pray tell, do you know John has time to listen to me plead my case?"

"He has time."

"How do you know?"

"Because he's expecting *me* to walk through this door, and you're a heck of a lot prettier."

Chapter 3

John's gentle disposition put Skye at ease straight away.

The redheaded gentleman stood until she took a seat after Jet made introductions. Then Jet excused himself and disappeared down the hall.

"What can I do for you?" John asked, settling behind his desk.

"When I arrived in the United Kingdom, I headed directly to Kilmarnock to visit the Grange Manse church to make funeral arrangements for my late aunt."

"I'm sorry for your loss," John said. He leaned forward and pulled open a drawer. He lifted out a Rolodex and placed it on top of his desk. "Don't laugh. I don't advertise it, but I still embrace some of the old ways."

Skye smiled. "My aunt did too. She always said, 'If it's not broken, don't fix it.'"

"Wise woman." John pulled out half glasses and placed them on the end of his nose and spun the wheel. "Ah, here it is. You need to speak with Reverend Colin Taylor. He will help you make all the necessary arrangements."

"Yes, we've already met. He was a lovely man. He took the time to give me a tour and tell me the history of the old church."

"What did you think of the beautiful stained-glass mosaics and the walnut and ivory pipe organ?"

"I've never seen anything like either of them before."

"So I've been told," he said.

"You've never been?"

"It's on my list," John said. "The pipe organ is supposed to be one of the largest in the county."

"It's well worth the trip," Skye said. She took a deep breath and got back to the reason for her visit. "In the late '80s, Reverend Taylor met with my aunt to help her commit her mother's ashes. He told me the difficulty lies in obtaining permission from the Commonwealth War Graves Commission. He said your organization owns the headstone."

"I see," John said.

Skye dug out a letter and unfolded the papers. "The reverend wrote a letter explaining the situation, and he even ran a copy of the original letter he penned forty years ago."

"May I see it?"

Skye handed John the paperwork and sat quietly while he read both.

"My late aunt Bessie wanted to be laid to rest beside her mother and father, and I'm hoping I can have another inscription added to the headstone."

"Let's see what we have on file." John swiveled his monitor and pulled out his keyboard. He scanned the letters again. "Your aunt's surname is McDougall?"

"That's correct," Skye said.

"Do you know what her father's initials were?"

"W. P." While John busily inputted information, Skye kept thinking about her chance meeting with Jet. She kept glancing out into the hall to see if she could catch a glimpse of him.

"Which war did Bessie's father serve in?"

Skye spun around. "World War I."

"You wouldn't happen to know his year of death?"

She did. She'd come across all his paperwork when she cleaned out Bessie's apartment. "He died in 1918."

"Do you know what force he served with?" John asked.

"He was a Royal Scot."

"Nationality?"

"I believe he was born in the United Kingdom."

John Smilie finished typing and pushed the search button.

Information filled the screen. "Private William Patterson McDougall, Kilmarnock Cemetery, K261."

"That's correct." Skye's aunt never threw anything out in her ninety years, and she found the original registration of sale for Bessie's father's lair purchased by his widow in 1918.

John's forehead wrinkled, and he scrubbed his hand across his chin. "This doesn't tell me much." He flipped to the copy of the older letter. "Maybe if I punch in Bessie's mother's information." John filled in fields, and suddenly an attachment popped up under the alphanumeric code CEM 268. He clicked it open. "Here it is. A representative from this office went out to determine if there was enough room on the headstone to add another inscription." John scanned the report. "Unfortunately, this document states there was only enough room for one more inscription. I'm sorry, but based on this information, I'm going to have to decline your request."

The bottom dropped out of Skye's stomach. It never occurred to her that her application would be denied. Especially since Skye had gone to the cemetery to make her own assessment.

All the military graves comprised Section K of the cemetery. The headstones were like soldiers at roll call—uniform and straight, row upon row of fallen heroes. The late afternoon sun had warmed her path, and her footsteps released the peaty fragrance of freshly cut grass. The inscription on Bessie's father's grave had weathered over the years. Skye bent over and used her finger to gauge whether another inscription would fit.

"I've been to the Kilmarnock Cemetery and checked out the headstone. There's plenty of room."

"It's not that I don't believe you," John said. "But you have to understand, I have to follow commission rules. I need documentation to engage a stone mason."

"I took some pictures of the headstone with my phone, would that work?"

"It might. May I see them?" John asked.

She dug her phone from her pocket, and when she tapped the screen, nothing happened.

Her phone was dead.

Sometimes she thought Murphy's Law applied to her and her alone. She rooted in her bag and found her charger. She inserted the cord in the base and passed the plug to John. "I didn't have time to juice up this morning. Would you mind?"

John ducked beneath the desk.

Her screen lit up.

She opened her photos and scrolled through the file. "Here they are. There's four or five, so just swipe to see them all." She passed him the phone.

He took his time viewing all the photos, pinching the screen, zooming in and out. "Would you mind sending a couple of these to my email?"

"Not at all," Skye said. She confiscated the phone and highlighted the photos, while John dictated his email address.

John started typing an email. "I concur with your assessment. There's plenty of room for another inscription. I'll get the ball rolling at this end, and once everything is in order, I'll send the paperwork over to the local stonemason in Kilmarnock to add Bessie's inscription. I assume you want the inscription to follow the same format as the other two?"

"That would be perfect." Skye had written down Bessie's date of birth and death and she handed the paper to him. "I'll be dropping in on relatives in Southampton from here and then I'll be staying with a friend in Edinburgh for a few weeks."

"I'll try to expedite the process for you, but it will likely take three to four weeks. I'll shoot you an email when everything is in order for your aunt's committal."

John unplugged Skye's charger. She stuffed it back in her purse and she rose out of her seat. "That should work out very well then. Thank you for all your help. I've taken up more than enough of your time. I'm sure you and Jet have much to discuss."

"Sadly, yes," John said. "How do you know Jet?"

"I don't, really. We've only just met." She held up her hand. "I'm a bit of a bungler, and I nearly knocked him over this morning not paying attention."

Skye fidgeted in her seat and searched the corridor. "Do you know where he might be? I'd like to thank him as well." She didn't make eye contact because she thought he'd see right through her feeble excuse for wanting to see him again.

John took a moment and walked to the end of the corridor and back. "I don't know where he's gotten to."

Skye tried not to let her disappointment show. Of course, she knew it was better this way. It's not like anything could come of them—she'd be returning to the States once all the repairs to Gershwin's theater were completed.

"Would you like me to give him a message when he surfaces?"

"Yes, please," Skye said. "Thank him and tell him I'm sorry."

Chapter 4

In the basement exercise room of the CWGC, Captain Jet Dalry tried to erase the image of Skye Andrews from his mind.

He used the gym whenever he visited Maidenhead. In the change room, he'd stripped off his dress clothes and headed to the gym floor. This particular gym had all the typical amenities and pungent aromas—treadmill, weights, exercise bike, and the trademark rancidness of overripe socks.

He climbed onto the recumbent bike and rode. His iron will stemmed from months of work. He'd spent hours watching the wheelchair brigade work their upper bodies at the veteran's hospital, and he never stopped pushing himself.

No pain, no gain.

The doctors were wrong.

He worked long and hard, and the months of physio finally paid off when he'd gotten back the use of his legs.

Before his deployment to Iraq and the explosion, Skye Andrews was exactly the type of woman he'd been attracted to. Her easy-on-the-eyes appearance complimented her bubbly and bewitching personality. Unlike every other aspect of his life, his taste in women hadn't changed.

Desire and defeat stabbed deep. It made him wonder if he would ever smile again.

Way beyond his normal workout, Jet began his cool down regime. His heart beat like a barrel drum, and sweat slickened his skin. He got off the bike and retired to the men's change room where he jumped into the shower and ran a bar of soap over his rippled and puckered skin—five plastic surgeries and he still remained horribly disfigured from the waist down. He dried and dressed and went back upstairs mad as hell.

"There you are," John said, his head lifting from his computer screen. "Where did you get to?"

"I went down and grabbed a quick workout."

"No wonder I couldn't find you. I never would have thought to check there."

"Was there a problem?" Jet asked.

"Not at all. Skye Andrews asked me to thank you."

"She's gone?"

"About thirty minutes ago."

Finally, Jet could relax.

He couldn't stand another dose of that woman, especially since he'd spent the better part of an hour exorcising her.

He dug several files out of his briefcase and passed it to John. "Here are the latest fatalities."

After being denied active duty, Jet had taken on the task of record keeping. The desk job proved to be all he could handle right now. Not at all what he'd had in mind when he enrolled in the officer training program a few short years ago.

"How many this quarter?"

"A dozen," Jet said.

John shook his head, grabbed the cache of information, and flipped through it. "What's new with you?" He set the file down on his desk.

Jet kneaded his thighs. With the tissue loss and damage, massaging the area seemed to be the only thing to relieve the pain and improve the circulation. "Our division is having our big reunion next weekend."

"Sounds like fun."

"The following week I'll be attending the memorial service for Private Graham."

"The soldier injured in the same mortar blast as you?"

Captain Jet Dalry nodded. He cringed and swallowed the bitter lump that instantly formed in his throat. "He lost both of his legs and died from a massive infection a week ago."

"Is his information included in this package?"

"It's on top."

John Smilie opened the folder and began reading. Mere moments into the file he stopped and regarded Jet with wide eyes.

"What? Something wrong?" Jet asked.

"Private Graham's interment is going to be in the Kilmarnock Cemetery in Ayrshire County."

"That's right."

"Would you mind doing me a favor while you're there?"

Jet shrugged. "Sure."

"I need someone to jump-start the process in Kilmarnock. They take their time if you don't keep on top of them. It would be a big help to me. It's easy to disregard an email but not a personalized visit."

"No problem. I'm going to be there anyhow. All I need is the lair number and the particulars."

John Smilie jotted the information on a separate sheet of paper and handed it to Jet.

"Anyone I know?" Captain Dalry asked, examining the particulars.

John Smilie sat back in his seat. "It's Skye Andrew's great uncle."

Chapter 5

Since Skye arrived in the United Kingdom, nothing had gone as planned—the story of her life. Actually, things began to spiral out of control the moment her aunt's will had been read. In the past ten years, not once had her aunt mentioned she wanted to be buried in the family plot in Scotland, or that there were rings and necklaces to be delivered to family members. Once the shock of her aunt's death and the edict for the unanticipated transatlantic trip abated, Skye realized there had not been any time frame mentioned. It might be a few years before she'd deliver the ashes and jewelry, certainly not until her current production had run its course. Unfortunately, the universe and Aunt Bessie had other designs. She'd put her career before her family for too long. And to what end? She'd been working steadily in New York, and yet she still wasn't a household name. Aunt Bessie's death had been a wake-up call. She needed to have a good hard look at her priorities because, as of this moment, she'd been racing down the same road as Bessie. If she didn't change her ways, she would end up single and alone.

Skye had it all planned. She'd lay her aunt to rest in Kilmarnock, deliver the estate jewelry in Southampton, and travel to Edinburgh to visit with Jason. But nothing went as arranged. There were hoops she had to jump through first. Lucky for her, the CWGC in Maidenhead wasn't too far out of her way. She'd simply have to return to Kilmarnock to bury her aunt's ashes before she returned to the States.

With Bessie's ashes still tucked safely inside the bronze urn in her suitcase, she left the CWGC, collected her luggage from the storage locker at the train station, and hopped on another train—this one to Southampton station.

In her mind, she kept replaying her meeting with Captain Jet Dalry. She'd never been so instantly attracted to someone of the opposite sex before. The man had gotten under her skin. Plenty of men had tried, but none ever seemed to be quite so successful. His ornery demeanor suggested he could barely tolerate her—maybe his lack of interest beguiled her.

Nearly knocking him on his ass hadn't been her finest moment.

To rid all thoughts of him, she tried to focus on her cousin, Moira Buchanan. Skye had emailed her a week ago and told her she'd advise her when she knew more. She called from the station.

"You're here? Already?" Moira asked.

"I'm en route to Southampton now," Skye said. "I should arrive midafternoon. I'd like to drop by this evening if you're free?"

"That sounds grand. Have you found a place to stay?"

"Not yet," Skye said.

"I'll make up the spare room then," Moira said.

"I don't want to trouble you."

"It's no trouble at all," Moira said. "You're family."

"In that case, I accept."

The train ride had been short, and when she exited the station, she hailed a cab and handed the driver Moira's address. She strode up the drive and stood at the door marked Entrance□

She tried the knob and found it open, so she walked into what appeared to be a waiting room. There were chairs, magazines, a closed interior door, and an intercom.

Skye pressed the button. "Moira, it's me, Skye."

A voice warbled through the speaker. "I'll be with you in ten minutes."

The chilly instructions baffled her. It made her wonder if maybe she'd made a mistake agreeing to stay here. Maybe she should make hotel reservations elsewhere. While she waited, she rifled through her bag and withdrew her AAA Travel Guide. She pinpointed the nearest hotel and switched on her cell.

Still dead.

She made a decision. Once she gave Moira the jewelry, she'd make her way back to the station and book herself on the next train bound for Edinburgh.

When the door finally sprang open, a black woman with piercing gold eyes sailed right past her and paused at the outside door. Another woman followed on her heels—this one had salt and pepper hair. Skye recognized her immediately from the photos she'd seen in Bessie's apartment. It was Bessie's second cousin.

"I'll see you same time next week," Moira said waving good-bye to her client. When she faced Skye, her smile lit her round face. She wrapped her arms around Skye. "It's so good to finally meet you. I'm Moira."

"I thought so," Skye said hugging her back, her apprehension instantly evaporating. "I didn't know you were a doctor."

"I'm not an MD," Moira said. "I'm a hypnotherapist. I wear the lab coat because it adds a measure of professionalism to my work. Some people think hypnotherapy is a circus act."

"You mean you don't swing a shiny gold fob on the end of a string and ask people if they're getting sleepy?"

"Hardly," Moira said. "I use relaxation techniques to destress and detox my patients."

"Where do I sign up," Skye said. "I've been running on empty for weeks."

"And you're still recuperating," Moira said. "Did you get your stitches out?"

Skye parted the hair on her head. "The day before I left for the UK. I'm used to it. I'm kind of accident-prone. You might want to rethink my staying in the spare room. Speak now or forever hold your peace."

"Nonsense." Moira said.

Skye steered the conversation away from herself.

"Do you have any more patients this afternoon?"

"No. I cleared my schedule when you said you'd stay. It's not every day a famous New York actress comes calling," Moira said. "Why don't I show you to your room so you can freshen up? Then I'll put on a pot of tea, and we can sit and get to know each other a little better."

A half hour later, the two women sat in the kitchen chatting like old friends.

"Aunt Bessie thought the world of you," Moira said, refilling Skye's cup.

"I should have spent more time with her."

"You did the best you could do."

"Did I?" Skye had been second-guessing herself ever since she got the phone call asking her to make a decision regarding Bessie's perforated ulcer.

"Bessie said you called every week."

Skye shrugged. "I should have made a point of visiting."

"You've been starring in back-to-back productions. You went whenever you could. You're being too hard on yourself."

Skye wiped a tear from her eye. "What's done is done." She sat up a little straighter. "Do you know why I'm here?"

"I assumed you needed to deliver something."

Skye lifted her purse onto the table. "Were you familiar with Bessie's wishes?"

"Are you kidding?" The get-real expression on Moira's face told the tale. "Bessie was the most secretive woman on the planet."

Skye chuckled as she dug a velvet jewelry sleeve out of her purse and unrolled it on the table. "Bessie left these to you." A blood-red sapphire ring with matching necklace, an exotic emerald pendant, and a gold filigree oval bracelet were nestled in the black velvet.

Moira covered her mouth with her hand. "Oh my. They're lovely. I had no idea." A blush colored her cheeks.

"I have to say I'm really glad I'm not the only one who's been kept in the dark all these years," Skye said.

"Bessie was a recluse," Moira said. "She never really talked about herself." She glanced over at Skye and stilled. "What's wrong?"

"She wrote a journal," Skye said, biting her bottom lip. She dug it out of her bag and placed it on the table beside the other heirlooms. "Only, I'm not sure I'll ever be able to read it. Maybe you can interpret it."

Moira flipped the pages of the leather-bound journal. "That's Bessie's handwriting all right. But I haven't a clue what language it's written in or what it says."

Skye huffed and sat back. "How is that fair?" Bessie left you her fancy jewelry and me her undecipherable secrets."

CHAPTER 6

Once the dinner dishes were cleared and washed, Skye charged her phone and jumped online to book train tickets to Edinburgh the following day. "Are you certain you don't mind dropping me at the station in the morning?"

"I want to take you. My first appointment isn't until ten," Moira said. "It's the least I can do after all you've done."

Skye navigated the site, and she saved the boarding pass to her phone. "All right then. I think I'm all set. If you take me at nine, you'll have plenty of time to return home." She glanced at her watch. "Oh my, is it eleven o'clock already?"

"I'm afraid so." Moira stood and stretched. "Time for me to turn in."

Skye retired to her room, put on her pajamas, and slipped between the sheets.

But sleep eluded her.

Wide awake, she switched on the small lamp on the bedside table and pulled Bessie's journal from her bag. In the low light, shadows were cast across the book's leather cover. It revealed a pattern she'd never really noticed before. Swirls and indentations came together in a recognizable fashion—a pattern resembling the keepsake given to her by the man at Bessie's service of remembrance a couple of weeks ago.

The Luckenbooth.

She dug deep into her suitcase and pulled out the brooch to compare them. They were the same. She opened the journal with the brooch clutched tightly in her hand and the strangest thing happened. The script on the page began to shift and move into legible sentences—sentences Skye could read and understand.

Her heart pounded and her palms slickened. Not wanting to jinx anything, she began reading and instantly fell into something akin to Harry Potter's pensieve. She'd been transported back in time to the days immediately following Bessie's death.

A small table draped in burgundy satin stood at the front of the church. A bronze urn sat upon the cloth accompanied by a framed eight-by-ten photograph of Bessie, behind which stood a beautiful spray of flowers. At Skye's request, the florist had added heather and Scottish thistle to the bouquet. A wonderful, fresh highland aroma filled her nostrils.

Skye sat in the pew beside her mom and dad and listened to the reverend as she said a prayer and read the opening scripture. Several different church members took their turns talking about Bessie. The choir sang her favorite hymns. When the benediction and grace was over, Reverend Margy MacLean invited everyone for refreshments in the basement hall.

While the church patrons thinned and headed downstairs, Skye took a moment to collect her thoughts. She was about to join everyone below when a little old man in the third pew summoned her.

"How do you know Bessie?" he asked.

Despite the thick Italian accent, Skye understood the question. The elderly gentleman had a full head of snow-white hair and deep wrinkles lined his face.

"I'm her niece," she said. No point in explaining further.

He nodded. Then he reached inside his jacket and removed an envelope from his breast pocket. He waved Skye closer.

"I'd like you to do something," he whispered.

Skye, thinking he needed her assistance getting out of the pew, moved beside him. "There's an elevator you can use to get down to the hall," she said, offering him her hand.

"That won't be necessary. I won't be staying. I'm returning something Bessie gave me years ago. I want you to lay it to rest with her. She once told me it had special power—that long ago, parents attached similar pieces to their children's shawls to protect them from evil spirits." The man's hand shook as he passed Skye a white envelope. She took it from him and helped him to his feet. He grabbed his cane and walked away.

She held the envelope in her hand, not sure what to make of it. From the other side of the rectory, a woman from the auxiliary group called to her. "Ms. Andrews, everyone is waiting for you."

"I'll be right there," Skye said. When she looked over her shoulder, the man was already at the door. Skye hurried after him. "What's your name?" she asked.

"Aldo Genovese," he said.

At the entrance of the church, Skye saw him descend the granite stairs and climb into a sleek black stretch limousine. Without so much as a wave or a backward glance, he shut the door and the car sped away.

She put the envelope in her purse, and with everything else going on, forgot all about it.

During the week that followed, Skye worked full tilt emptying Bessie's apartment. She'd only been able to wrangle two weeks away from her current production in New York to handle Bessie's affairs. She came across it on her return flight to New York when she was searching for her phone charger in her purse. She ripped open the white envelope Aldo Genovese had given her and shook the contents into her hand.

It was a brooch, approximately the size of a silver dollar. A brilliant blue stone sparkled between three intersecting hearts, corralled inside one larger crowned heart.

She squeezed the pin. It felt warm—no, scratch that, hot in her hand. In fact, so hot it slid out. The moment she dropped it, she'd been catapulted back into Moira's spare room. While she blew on her fingers to cool them down, she noticed the handwriting in the journal shifted back into a series of unintelligible marks.

What the hell?

How could that be?

And how the hell had Bessie been able to write about something that happened to Skye when the incident in question didn't even occur until after she passed away?

A mystery, to say the least.

Skye had to be suffering from sleep deprivation. She'd been averaging four, maybe five, hours a night since Bessie died, and Skye put it down to lack of sleep rather than the alternative.

But then, Bessie had always claimed to be able to see things. Skye always put her aunt's eccentric claims down to harmless exaggeration. Now, she didn't know what to believe.

Skye was certain of one thing. Bessie penned the journal. Both she and Moira recognized her handwriting.

What if Bessie could see things?

Skye pressed a finger to the brooch. Since it had cooled, she grabbed the journal with the idea of putting both back into her suitcase when once again, the words on the page aligned, and just like before, she toppled headfirst into another memory.

Skye walked the tree-lined street beside the nineteenth century townhouses of Greenwich Village to the corner coffee shop called Java Joe. Tired from taking the red-eye from Boston to New York, she needed to dose up on caffeine to stay awake for the rest of the day. She'd been a wreck in Boston. Guilt ridden for not making more time for her aunt when she was alive. She put her maudlin feelings out of her mind and smiled, happy to be back in the Big Apple, and got into the long line.

She stared straight ahead, but her eyes saw something altogether different than the coffee queue.

Her peripheral vision faded.

Darkness engulfed her.

All but a solitary beacon of light.

When she gazed lower, she noticed a hand clad in black leather gloves holding the tubular body of a flashlight.

The light brightened the shadows and illuminated everything it shined upon. It darted back and forth, making her stomach lurch. Dust motes floated and sparkled in its bright beam.

She knew this place. It was backstage at the Grand Olivier theater.

The flashlight rested on the rung of a step ladder. Its beam lit up the wires of a fly prop. Sawing reverberated.

Metal chewing metal.

When she followed the swath of light, she noticed the same leather clad hands grating a bow back and forth across the fly lines.

"Miss Andrews?"

She catapulted back to the coffee shop. She'd never had a nightmare when she was awake before and quickly put it out of her mind because her life had never been so off-the-rails before.

The Java Joe barista spoke. "Would you like your usual?"

Skye jerked to attention. "Yes, please." She stepped up to pay the cashier and waited while her double non-fat vanilla latte brewed. She scooped the cup from the counter and beelined onto the subway.

The city yawned and slowly awakened.

Vendors busily restocked their corner stalls and trailers. Food trucks sizzled and smoked in preparation for the morning rush.

Skye intended to throw herself back into her current production. Right about now, her work was about the only aspect of her life she had any control over.

Over the last ten years, she'd starred in a handful of shows. Each and every show had a good long run, and her current, *Ruby Slippers*, had been one of the box office favorites for the last year and a half.

The Grand Olivier, an old vaudeville theater, had seen troupes come and go over the past hundred years. The theater had been renovated in the eighties and had been slated for a retrofit once *Ruby Slippers* closed, which she hoped wouldn't be for at least another year. She hurried backstage and into her dressing room. She startled when she opened the door and noticed Amy, her understudy, sitting up to her mirror, reciting lines.

"You're back? Already?" Amy asked. "I thought you'd be busy for at least another two weeks."

Skye swallowed the grief welling in her throat. She didn't want to talk about it. The loss was still too raw. "You're here early."

"Just trying to do a competent job while you're away," Amy said. "Does Hershey know you're back?"

Hershey Goldblatt produced *Ruby Slippers*. He and Amy had an on-again, off-again relationship, which must have been off at this particular moment. "Not yet," Skye said. "I thought I'd surprise everyone."

Skye had followed the online reviews this past week while tending her aunt's affairs in Boston, and Amy had done a decent job filling in. Ever since Amy had been cast as her understudy, she'd been after Skye's job. It seemed that she didn't like her very much. They weren't close. She'd never even expressed any sympathy or condolences for her or her aunt. If Skye had to guess, Amy considered Skye's absence her big break. This business could be cutthroat—someone always stood in the wings waiting to swoop in to steal your job and the limelight.

"I guess I'll give you some privacy," Amy said, excusing herself. Her flashing eyes nearly vaporized Skye.

By noon, the entire troop of cast and crew were warming up their voices and running lines for the two o'clock matinee. The curtain rose and the show went on without a hitch.

Until the twister scene.

With Toto tucked in her basket, Dorothy darted across the stage from visiting with Professor Marvel in the Gypsy Caravan and hurried to the farmhouse.

"Aunty Em?" Skye shouted in Dorothy Gale's character. "Uncle Henry? Where are you?" She crisscrossed the set, and once she hit her mark on stage, the flyman cued the special effects, which simulated a storm outside her bedroom window. From stage left, a large fan blew tumbleweeds across the stage. Then came the larger items—the breakaway scenery.

Soon the window in the bedroom set vibrated and broke free of the frame and created a very dramatic and unexpected climax. Skye's movements were choreographed down to the second. She lifted her arm to protect her head from the window careening stage right into the flies.

Only this time, it didn't.

The lines holding the pane, invisible to the audience, broke and dumped the window right on top of her.

Time splintered and she floated in and out of consciousness.

People rushed and shouted all around her.

"Ms. Andrews?" a male voice said. "We're transporting you to Allen Hospital for an MRI and an x-ray on your wrist."

Strapped on a gurney, an EMT pushed her through hordes of people who'd gathered on the street. Her head pounded, and one arm had been immobilized in a splint. She lifted her hand to remove the oxygen mask.

"What happened?" Her voice sounded like it had been pressed through a vegetable grater.

"One of the props malfunctioned and caused a chain reaction after you were knocked out. The window's counterweight fell on the lighting equipment, which started the fire. You've got some smoke inhalation, so you need oxygen." The EMT adjusted the mask on her face and slid her gurney inside the ambulance.

The next time she opened her eyes, she was inside an examination room at the Allen. A nurse handed her a Styrofoam cup with water. "The MRI came back normal, but you're going to need a stitch or two for that bump on your head.

"What about this?" Skye asked lifting her splinted arm.

"It's sprained, not broken. The doc on call will stitch up your head and tensor wrap your arm shortly."

The nurse adjusted Skye's bed so she could sit up.

"Can I take this mask off now?" Skye asked.

"That depends. How does your throat feel?"

"Better."

The nurse removed the plastic mask and tubing and hung the gear on the wall behind her head.

"How long do you think the doctor will be?"

"Shouldn't be too much longer," she said. "There's someone in the waiting room who'd like to see you. Would you like some company?"

"Do you know their name?"

The nurse narrowed her eyes. "I think he might be your producer."

"Hershey Goldblatt?"

"That's right. Do you want me to send him in?"

Skye wondered why Hershey wanted to see her. Probably wanted to tell her Amy would be picking up the lead while she recuperated. "Sure, might as well. I'm not going anywhere."

The nurse left and before Skye knew it, a knock sounded at her door.

"C'mon in," she said.

"You gave everyone quite a scare," Hershey said, walking into the room. "How are you feeling?"

"Like I was caught in a twister."

"Ha. I'm just thankful yours was the only injury. I mean other than the Grand Olivier. Everyone got out safely. There were about a dozen cases of smoke inhalation, but everyone's been discharged."

"I'm confused," Skye said, probably the bump on her head. "The EMT's said the firefighters got the blaze under control quickly and the theater sustained only minimal damage."

"That's right, but unfortunately the fire destroyed most of the stage. With no stage, there's no production. All it means is that the renovations to the theater will begin sooner rather than later."

"How long do you think they'll take?" Skye asked.

"Anywhere from three to six months," Hershey said. "We've already got contractors in place, so we're ahead of the game."

"Will you reopen with *Ruby Slippers*?" Skye asked.

"Maybe. It depends. If everyone is still available, we will," Hershey said. "It's too soon to make that call."

Another knock sounded at her door and Talbot James, the stage manager, entered the room. His face a mask of despair.

Hershey found his voice first. "What are you doing here? Wasn't today your day off?"

"The fire is all over the news," Talbot said.

Skye had worked with Talbot on many productions, and they were sort of friends.

"Are you okay?" Talbot asked Skye. "I thought you were still in Boston. When I heard the lead had been injured, I assumed it was Amy. When I heard you were back, I dropped everything and came right over." Skye thought he might cry.

"I'm okay," she said. "Good thing I've got a hard head."

"The only reason she still has a head is because she deflected the window with her hand."

Talbot's attention shifted to her wrapped hand. "Is it broken?"

"No, thank goodness. Once they tensor it and put stitches in my head, they'll cut me loose."

Just then, a doctor in scrubs pushed into the room. He moved past Hershey and Talbot and over to Skye. He examined the wound on her head and did an about face and addressed the men. "I'm going to close the curtain while I stitch up Ms. Andrews." He reached for the fabric and drew it across separating the room.

"I'm going to take off," Hershey said. "I have several calls to make. Will you be able to make it home by yourself, Skye?"

"No," the doctor said. "She'll need a ride. I'm going to give her some pretty strong medication for the pain."

"I'll make sure she gets home," Talbot said.

"Don't be silly," Skye said.

"I'll put you in a cab then."

Then Skye's recollection of events and Aunt Bessie's version veered in completely opposite directions. At the time of the accident, Skye had been in pain when the doctor stitched her head. This retelling gave her the luxury of separation. This time, she could hear the conversation between Hershey and Talbot on the other side of the curtain. It was surreal because she could also hear her groans and squeals behind the curtain.

"I spoke with some members of the audience who were in the front row," Hershey said in hushed tones. "They saw wires snap simultaneously. What are the chances of two fly wires breaking at the same time?"

"Slim to none," Talbot said.

"That's what I thought." Hershey paused, and she imagined him running his hands through his hair the way he did when he was trying to figure something out. "I spoke with the fire marshal who examined the fly lines."

"And?"

"He said the cables weren't broken."

"What are you talking about?" Talbot said. "If the window dropped on Skye, they had to break."

Hershey pitched his voice even lower. "The lines were cut, nearly clean through. The weight of the window caused them to snap during the performance."

Talbot wheezed. "Are you saying what I think you're saying?"

Hershey took a deep breath. "I'm saying it was no accident."

The brooch had heated to the point where Skye couldn't hold onto it any longer, so she dropped it onto the open journal. Just as before, the cursive writing withered and atrophied into hieroglyphs.

What the hell?

She remembered being zoned out in the morning at the coffee shop, but she hadn't remembered seeing someone in the act of fixing the lines so they'd break during her performance. All this time, Skye thought she had the world's worst luck—she was a walking, talking accident waiting to happen. According to her aunt's journal, that didn't seem to be the case in this particular instance.

Skye had been targeted, not cursed.

When Skye thought about Aunt Bessie sitting and writing these pages, documenting what unfolded on one of the worst days of her life, she no longer believed her aunt had been prone to fabrication or exaggeration. Bessie had absolutely no way of knowing what happened on the set of *Ruby Slippers*. And yet she clearly did. Not only had Bessie seen what happened, Skye had too, only she'd blocked it out for whatever reason. Skye saw and documented something else—something that sent shivers skittering down Skye's spine.

Bessie always said their lives were connected. She said she *could* see into the future. After reading and reliving these few journal entries, Skye's eyes had been opened. The possibilities put her mind into overdrive. For any of this to happen, Bessie must have known Aldo would give Skye the brooch, and she'd figure out its role in deciphering the journal.

And if all that proved to be true, then Skye needed to concede that Bessie had given her another curtain call with these events—to send a message or show her something she'd missed or hadn't seen or connected the first time around.

Things of great importance.

Unnerving things.

Someone wanted her out of the way.

Chapter 7

Skye tossed in bed that night, unable to get her head around what had happened at the Grand Olivier Theater. There had only been one person who had both the motive and the means.

Amy.

In hindsight, Skye doubted Amy wanted her dead. But Skye didn't doubt for one minute that Amy wanted her hurt badly enough for her to assume the lead. Too bad her plan backfired and wound up shutting the entire production down.

At this juncture, Skye would never know beyond a shadow of doubt. Before she left New York, the fire marshal said he'd notify her if any evidence came to light in the ongoing investigation. Weeks later, there'd been too much water under the bridge to expect answers.

At first light, Moira drove Skye to the train station. While Skye wrestled her bag from the boot, Moira got out to say good-bye.

"I'll call you when I finalize Bessie's arrangements," Skye said. "Maybe you can clear your schedule for a day or two and attend the service."

"I'd like that very much," Moira said.

The two women hugged, Moira got back into the car, and Skye waved before she went into the station.

A half hour later, Skye got off the first train and transferred to the second in Maidenhead. She moseyed through the car hoping to spot an available window seat. A man in uniform, two rows up on the right, caught her attention. The broad shoulders and uniform drew her eyes like a magnet.

She gave herself a shake.

Was she going to do this every time she saw a military man? The same soft brown curls made her mouth water. She plodded along. Oh, my. Could it be?

Skye cleared her throat. "Is this seat taken?"

He turned.

And there they were—those teal blue eyes. Skye would never grow tired of the exotic color. "I didn't get the chance to thank you for introducing me to John Smilie, so I followed you here."

Jet opened his mouth to say something, but no words came out.

"I'm kidding," she said. "What are the chances? This has to be one in a million." She glanced at the window seat. "May I sit with you?"

Jet shoved papers into his briefcase and stood. "Please."

Skye went to swing her carry-on into the overhead compartment. When she couldn't get the proper leverage, Jet reached up to give her a hand.

At the very same moment, the train lurched forward.

One second she was standing with her arms in the air and the next they were wrapped around Jet's neck. His hands sliding comfortably around her waist.

Skye closed her eyes and tried to swallow the lump in her throat. Her body tingled inside and out. His chest was a solid wall of muscle. He smelled like lemon-lime. She licked her lips and tilted her head for a soul-searing kiss.

The next thing she knew she'd been set aside.

"Another close call. I had to maneuver quickly to avoid getting clubbed," he said.

She opened her eyes. He stood adjusting her bag on the overhead rack. When he finished, he stepped aside and motioned for her to take the window seat.

Slightly embarrassed, she squeezed past him and sat down.

He'd been checking her out at the CWGC. She'd gotten enough attention from the opposite sex to know when she'd caught a man's eye. Unfortunately for her, those signals had all but disappeared.

It made her wonder what had happened to change his mind?

Maybe he was married or had a girlfriend, and his conscience got the better of him. She didn't think he was married; he didn't wear a wedding band, but that didn't mean anything nowadays. She needed to find out before she made a complete fool out of herself.

"Where are you headed?" she asked. A good place to start.

"Home," he said.

"You're not from around here?"

"No. Edinburgh is home base right now. I'm from Peebles originally."

"Peebles?"

"A small town south of Edinburgh."

"Does your family still live there?"

"No."

Still no mention of a girlfriend or wife. Skye nodded and faced the window. The train left the city limits and streamed across more rural areas.

The landscape became a patchwork quilt of color—parcels of land separated by bramble hedges and uneven piles of fieldstones. Lush pinkish-purple wildflowers edged the track, along with thistle, heather, knapweed, and foxglove.

"What about you?" Jet asked. "Where are you headed?"

"To Edinburgh. My best friend lives there. He's an actor with the Raverse Theater. We went to school together. I haven't seen him in ten years, but we've kept in touch."

"Are you an actor too?"

"Yes, I am." She gazed out the window.

Jet opened the file he'd closed when she first arrived. "I hope you don't mind, but I have work to do."

Skye figured he wanted her to leave him alone. "Go right ahead," she said. "I might try to get some shut-eye. I didn't sleep well last night."

Shock slowed Jet's thought processes to a crawl.

Talk about rotten luck. One in a million? Try one in ten million.

Last night Skye had plagued his dreams. This morning, when he saw her standing beside him, he thought he'd go straight to hell. Reality crashed in on him when he rose to let her take the window seat.

Damn train.

One moment he'd been helping her stow her bag, and the next she'd nestled in his arms, and he'd been a nanosecond away from kissing her.

She'd fit perfectly in his arms.

When he'd faced her, her chocolate eyes had closed and the tip of her tongue ran along luscious lips that were the color of Sister Anne's raspberry tarts.

He needed oxygen.

He set her aside and willed himself to breathe normally despite his racing heart and clammy hands.

Of course she was an actress. With a face and body like hers, she could be a model.

He made some lame excuse about having to do paperwork. He checked his files to make sure they weren't sitting upside down on his lap. It took all his powers of concentration to appear to be reading the report he'd hidden behind.

Very soon her breathing deepened, and he stopped pretending.

He shook his head. Hadn't he suffered enough in the last few months?

The road to recovery had been riddled with potholes. There were hours of physiotherapy and the excruciating pain that went with it. He'd refused to take the meds the doctor prescribed because he didn't want to become dependent.

Enter Skye Andrews.

Now his limitations dwarfed his physical accomplishments.

She'd never be able to see him naked and not be put off by his scars. He'd be lucky if she didn't upchuck. Anger blurred his vision. He wanted to curse and pound his fists, but such behavior wasn't befitting an officer. The return trip to Edinburgh would only take a matter of hours. He figured he could tolerate that.

He needed to focus and practice the psychotherapy he'd learned—various mind over matter techniques. He squared himself in his seat, closed his eyes, and began deep breathing.

Without much effort, he tumbled into the darkness of his dreams—a treacherous abyss since Iraq—a place where he relived all the horrors and mistakes, every time he fell asleep.

Very soon war encompassed him. Bombs exploded, machine guns reverberated, AK-47s boomed and bumped as he toed the threshold of an unspeakable hell.

"C'mon sweetie," a female voice said. "Please wake up."

Cool hands doused his flaming skin.

Was it a nurse or his medical evac?

He tried to hold onto the voice. "It's all right," she crooned. "You're safe now. You're on a train headed for Edinburgh."

In the next second, he jerked violently in his seat and bolted upright. Sweat trickled off his brow and he breathed heavily. He clutched the armrests of the seat so tightly his knuckles were bloodless and white.

Not a nurse.

Skye Andrews.

"You were having a bad dream," she said. "I could see your eyes moving back and forth beneath your lids and I didn't know what to do. I've heard it's not good to wake a person in the middle of a bad dream."

"A bad dream?" Jet's voice cracked under the weight of those words. "I wish with every fiber of my being that's all it had been."

Chapter 8

Skye's heart went out to the man sitting beside her. Worry lines creased his brow, and his distant eyes robbed her of breath.

Their conversation stalled.

Not wanting to pry, she quieted. He needed a few moments to collect his thoughts. She figured he'd break the silence when he reclaimed his control, but the minutes compounded. Soon, she realized he had no intention of talking. In fact, Skye thought if he could have crawled into a hole, he would have.

To fill the void, she pulled out her phone and texted Jason.

Skye had called Jason as soon as her production was canceled. Her arm and head injury had been the catalyst for her to take some much-needed time off, and she decided to make the most out of it and visit her BFF. Jason had done very well for himself. He'd worked his way up to producer, and when she told him her plans, he made some lame excuse that he could use her expertise to coach and mentor some of his newer actors.

Though Jet tried to act indifferent, Skye knew he'd been watching her through a fringe of eyelashes. All he had to do was open his mouth and she'd tell him who she messaged and why.

Now they both had unanswered questions.

An hour later, the train pulled into Waverley station. Jet stood up and helped her remove her carry-on from the overhead bin. "I'm sorry," he said. Then he exited the train.

Skye wanted to run after him and ask why he'd apologized. For no longer being interested? For getting caught up in a painful memory in front of her? For not talking? She'd never know because she'd never see him again. He barged out of her life as gracefully as she barged into his.

Thank God for Jason.

He'd been a stalwart friend. Whenever things got her down, she could always count on him to make her feel better.

She exited the terminal and sat down on her luggage at the curb, right where he told her to wait. Before long, he screeched to a halt in front of her.

He flew out of the car and enveloped her in a bear hug.

She wrapped her arms around his waist and squeezed. "Wow. Guess you missed me, huh?"

Jason rained kisses on the top of her head. "More than you know." Before he released her, he buried his nose in her hair and inhaled deeply. "You smell even better than I remember."

"Thanks, I think," she said. Skye turned her head to see a woman standing beside them.

The woman stuck out her hand. "I've heard so much about you," she said. "I feel like I know you already."

Skye couldn't seem to spit out an appropriate greeting, so she shook the woman's outstretched hand.

"I'm Tammy," she said. "I work with Jason. We've been together, I mean, we've been working together for the past eighteen months."

Jason and Skye talked at least once a week for the past ten years, and not once in all that time did he mention anyone named Tammy. Tammy didn't seem like Jason's type. At least not the type she remembered. Perhaps his tastes had changed. Actually, when Skye thought about it, Jason hadn't talked about dating anyone in a very long time.

He grabbed Skye's bag and stowed it in the boot. "C'mon you two. Get in. I'm double parked and I don't want to get a ticket."

Tammy climbed into the back of the Mini Cooper. "Our rehearsal had just finished when you texted Jason," Tammy said. "Since he usually drops me at my flat on his way home, I came along."

Jason drove the little car through a maze of inner-city streets. He came to a stop in front of a row of refurbished Georgian Terrace flats—the classically simple and symmetrical designs featured a series of same-sized windows floor upon floor. He got out and pushed the seat forward so Tammy could get out.

"See you tomorrow," he said.

Tammy squeezed out.

"I suppose I'll get a chance to talk to you at the pub after rehearsal tomorrow night," Tammy said to Skye. "Jason wants you to meet the whole gang."

"That's right," Jason said. "I plan on keeping her very busy while she's here."

Tammy waved, then darted up the steps and went inside as Jason pulled out into the street.

Skye noticed Jason's demeanor change as he shifted into second gear. "How come you never mentioned Tammy before?"

Jason kept his eyes straight ahead. "There's nothing to tell really. She's a great kid and a very talented actress."

"A kid?" Skye burst out laughing. "Not with those curves she isn't."

"You know what I mean. She's half my age."

"Not quite." Skye thought for a second. "That's never stopped you before. Don't tell me the great Jason Hansome has finally met his match."

"It's not like that."

"Oh really? Since when? When you lived in Boston, a girl like that would have been nothing more than an afternoon snack."

"She would not."

Skye shook her head. She didn't want to argue.

Neither of them were the same people they used to be.

Jason parked in front of a black brick building. "This is my place. I know it's dark and dismal. The building used to be a tavern at the turn of the century. Originally the inn had ten rooms. The contractor who purchased the place renovated it into five flats."

"And yours is the loft, right?"

"That's right," Jason said. He grabbed her bags and led her around the side and unlocked the door.

Stairs towered upwards.

As she climbed the slanting risers, she knew how Jason maintained his washboard abs and muscular physique. He opened another locked door at the top of the landing, and Skye walked inside the large open-concept room and struggled to catch her breath.

The view of the old city out the windows distracted her. New York had its fair share of century-old buildings. Here, the buildings were ancient—erected in the seventeenth or eighteenth century. Modernity wasn't a concept embraced here, and the history humbled her.

She twirled a slow circle. "I can see why you love this place. It's a simpler way of life, with a ridiculous number of stairs and no elevator access."

"You can have the bed. I'll sleep on the couch," Jason said, hanging his coat on the hook beside the front door.

"Over my dead body," Skye proclaimed. "I'm a lot smaller than you. I'm fine on the couch."

"Fine. Arguing with you has always been pointless. Are you hungry?"

"Famished."

A threaded iron rod ran the entire length of the apartment and held the building square. Jason hung his clothes from it. The makeshift closet had no walls, but it adequately separated the bedroom from the living room. He handed her a stack of hangers. "You unpack, and I'll go and grab us fish and chips for dinner." He headed for the door.

"Wait," Skye said. "Where the heck is the loo?"

"Oh," he said. He put his hands on a full-length mirror on the wall beside the kitchen and it slid sideways. A mirrored door on a rail.

"Mind if I jump in the shower to freshen up?"

"Sure thing," Jason said. "Towels are in the cubby. I'll be back in a half hour or so." Then he left.

Skye unpacked.

She placed Bessie's urn on the coffee table.

When she sifted through her suitcase, her eyes came to rest on the journal and brooch, which she carefully removed one by one and set them beside the urn. After her shower, she changed into clean clothes and sat down on the sofa to wait for Jason.

The loft suited Jason's personality. It was eclectic. The old brick walls were juxtaposed by modern LED lighting hanging from the rough-hewn beams. The pipes and wires were exposed and painted to blend in with the brick.

One entire wall was a collage of frames. It showcased every single show Jason had ever performed in or produced—from grade school to the present. There were programs and box office bulletins, banners and newspaper columns, and several photos—mostly candid shots taken backstage—some from before graduation, others well after their university days. She couldn't help but smile, thinking about the last project they starred in together.

The Married Man.

Those were fun times at the beginning of their careers.

Suddenly, her stomach cartwheeled.

As she surveyed the mosaic of photos, one thing became painfully clear.

There was only one other person's picture up on that wall.

Hers.

Chapter 9

The door of the flat opened, and Jason bounded inside with a brown paper sack. "Alf makes the best fish and chips in the village, even rivals Ernie's from the old days in Boston. Remember Ernie's?" Jason asked, ripping open the bag and filling a couple of plates.

"How could I forget?" Skye said.

Jason carried the plates into the living room and placed them on the coffee table next to the urn. "Is that Bessie?" he asked.

"Yes," Skye said. "I can put her back inside my bag if she bothers you."

"She's fine," Jason said.

She would have loved to tell him about the journal and the brooch, but he might think she'd lost it if she told him how Bessie had reached out from beyond the grave.

After dinner, Jason disappeared to the other side of the clothes rack and came back holding a dog-eared sheath of papers. "Here's the play I told you about. I'd like you to read it and tell me what you think."

Skye and Jason worked nonstop for the next couple of hours. After eleven, they packed it in for the night. Jason went to bed and Skye scrubbed her face, put on tights and an oversized sweater, and crawled between the sheets she'd tucked over the couch cushions.

And she did everything but sleep—she admired the shadows dancing on the flat's ceiling and listened for the sounds of passing cars outside. With no hope for some blessed shut-eye, she took a deep breath and steeled herself. Then she grabbed Bessie's journal and the Luckenbooth brooch, and for the third time toppled, body and soul, into the script.

Skye stopped to read the instructions outside of Boston General's intensive care unit before she picked up the phone on the wall and dialed. After a brief introduction, she was told to enter. She pushed the silver paddle, which automatically unlocked and opened the doors. She wiped her sweaty hands on her jeans. The pungent odor of disinfectant bothered her nose, and she thought she might sneeze. A bottle of antibacterial gel stood on a lone table in the short hall. She pressed the plunger and scrubbed her hands.

A dozen cubicles surrounded a central nurses' station. At the foot of each patient's bed stood a podium with a chart posted on it.

A man in hospital greens worked over Bessie. He waved her over. "I'm Dex," he said. "I'm your aunt's nurse."

"I'm Skye Andrews," she said.

"We've been waiting for your arrival. I'll page your aunt's doctor so you can have a word with him. I'll be right back."

Aunt Bessie had always been a fairly large, robust woman, but not anymore. She appeared very small and frail lying motionless on the bed—tangled snow-white hair, a breathing tube in her throat, and feeding tube in her nose. The IV shunt protruding from her arm made tears sting Skye's eyes.

"Aunt Bessie?" she said. "It's me, Skye." She ran her fingers through her aunt's bangs to straighten them.

Skye had made arrangements for the trip to Boston as quickly as she could, and as a result, she'd been awake for close to thirty-six hours. She put her hand on top of Aunt Bessie's and laid her forehead on top of both.

In the hazy place between being awake and asleep, Skye felt someone touch her shoulder.

"Ms. Andrews? Skye?" a deep masculine voice soothed. "I'm Dr. Saunders."

Her eyes sprang open, and she lifted her head, eyes blinking to bring her vision into focus. "I'm so sorry. I must have nodded off. I've been awake since yesterday morning." She took a steadying breath and sat up straighter. "How is she doing?"

"Your aunt had a perforated ulcer. I repaired the perforation and inserted a tube for feeding. It's regular protocol for an ulcer. I don't want her trying to digest anything for approximately a week to give the stomach an opportunity to heal. I also inserted a port on her arm for administering her medication."

"Why is she's so out of it?"

"She was very agitated, so I gave her something to keep her settled and administered three antibiotics."

"That sounds like a lot."

"There was spillage when the ulcer perforated. Three are necessary to battle the infection she's fighting. Her condition right now is guarded but optimistic."

Skye pushed herself out of the chair and shook Dr. Saunders hand. "Thank you," she said. Bone deep exhaustion made her stagger.

Dr. Saunders reached out to steady her. "Your aunt will be out of it for the next six hours or so. I suggest you go and get some rest."

The doctor was right. She would be no help to Bessie as the walking dead. "That's a good idea. I don't want to be comatose when she regains consciousness."

Skye rode the T to her aunt's apartment. In the lobby, she'd pressed the call button for the elevator when Dorothy Hutchins, Aunt Bessie's neighbor, sidled up beside her. Skye held the door for the elderly woman, who busily maneuvered her walker inside. "Good to see you again," Skye said. Then she pushed the button for the fourth floor.

Startled, the elderly woman honed in on her. "Skye Andrews, is that you? Well, aren't you a sight for sore eyes. Your aunt's not here, you know. I haven't seen her in a while."

"Bessie's in the hospital. She had surgery to repair a perforated ulcer yesterday."

Dorothy inhaled sharply.

"She came through the surgery and has to heal."

"Are you going to be staying at her place for a while?"

"I'll be here for a few weeks, until she's back on her feet."

"That's good. She's been lonely. A lot of our friends in here have moved into retirement homes. We're the only holdouts. Be sure to keep me posted," Dorothy said. The elevator doors opened, and Dorothy got off and headed across the hall into her apartment.

"Will do," Skye said as she continued down the hall. She jammed her key into the lock and pushed inside.

Aunt Bessie had always been a creature of habit, and she kept her apartment neat and orderly. In all the time Skye had lived with her, every stick of furniture and each knickknack on the shelf stood solid and sure.

Skye couldn't wait to hear the chimes from the antique clock on the wall—one gong for every hour. She tossed her keys into the top drawer of the mahogany wall table beside the door and discovered the usual assortment of pens and stationery were missing. In fact, the drawer was empty except for a slip of paper with the name "Colleen" written upon it. When she opened the bi-folding closet doors to hang up her jacket, empty hangers clattered.

A chill slithered down Skye's spine.

The melodic clock on the wall had been left unwound and had long since stopped. A wedge of folded tissue in the bottom of the case secured the pendulum.

Skye went into the living room. The two peacock-patterned chintz loveseats were pushed against the wall and the oval coffee table that used to be positioned in the center of the room had disappeared. Aunt Bessie's teal chair sat in the corner within reaching distance of the TV. Skye plunked into it, grabbed the remote, and pressed the on button.

Sound blasted from the speakers. Quickly, she lowered the volume. Why hadn't the other tenants called the superintendent to complain about the noise? Suddenly, Skye began to understand how Bessie's health had declined. Bessie couldn't see or hear the TV unless she sat on top of it. The coffee table and end tables had been moved to make navigation with a walker easier.

Skye continued to scan the room. From the chair, she could see the dining room table and hutch. Aunt Bessie had always proudly displayed her fanciful Hummel figurines in the upper display case, but the shelves were void of any fine bone china. She hurried into the kitchen and opened cupboards and drawers.

Mostly empty. All that remained was a cup, saucer, plate, and silverware.

Service for one.

The only food, other than a half loaf of bread and a jar of jam was half a dozen TV dinners in the freezer.

Why hadn't Aunt Bessie said something to her? Had Bessie been selling off things to make ends meet? Skye thought back to their telephone conversations. She never once heard anything but positive things from Aunt Bessie. When they talked, Bessie's only concern had been for Skye. Bessie told her there was more to life than a career. If she didn't hurry up and find a man, she'd end up like her—completely alone.

Upset, Skye called her mom to see if her dad knew anything about Bessie's financial picture. When Skye's mother answered the phone, the increased volume on the phone nearly blew out her eardrum. She adjusted it for their conversation, but essentially neither of her parents could offer her any explanation for Bessie's unusual behavior.

Skye hung up and decided to turn in. On her way down the hall, she peered in Aunt Bessie's room. The coverlet of the bed stretched across the mattress without so much as a wrinkle, and the top of her dresser was void of the usual disarray.

She stood in front of the spare room and shook her head in confusion. When she opened the closed door and went to step inside, she slammed into a solid wall of boxes, stacked four and five high. Each box had a list of contents, and some even had a name attached to it.

Bessie must have known the time had come to move into long-term care. Bessie never did leave anything to chance. She'd taken it upon herself to begin the process of packing boxes.

Over the next few days, Skye trekked back and forth to the hospital, and with each passing day, Bessie's prognosis worsened.

The stone in the brooch had gone from hot to scalding, which forced Skye to drop it. And just like the previous forays, the cursive writing transformed into an illegible scrawl yet again.

Everything Bessie wrote in her journal had happened exactly as Skye remembered.

It made her wonder what she'd missed.

Skye's first two readings had shown her something she'd overlooked the first time around.

She jumped up and paced.

She checked the clock. Two a.m. and she was still wide-awake.

Plenty of time to read another installment.

Remembering Jet's words from the other day she said, "There's more than one way to skin a cat."

She pulled her sleeve over her fingers so she could pick up the hot brooch, then carried it into the kitchen and popped it in the freezer.

Chapter 10

In less than a half hour, Skye sat down with the lukewarm Luckenbooth and her aunt's journal and dove in where she left off.

When Skye arrived at the hospital the next day, Bessie still had not regained consciousness, but the ventilator had been removed. One step forward and two back. In no time, fluid settled in Bessie's lungs, and the cocktail of antibiotics Dr. Saunders prescribed to fight infection proved as ineffective as slapping a Band-Aid on a hemorrhaging wound.

A CT scan and x-ray ruled out an abscess—which confounded Dr. Saunders because an abscess would explain why the antibiotics weren't lowering the high white blood cell count. A diuretic was administered to remove the water from her lungs, and soon after that, a blood transfusion to boost her system back to health.

Both failed.

The sterile green walls of Bessie's hospital room were closing in on Skye.

Aunt Bessie regurgitated fresh blood.

And not just a little, a lot.

The amount frightened Skye. Dr. Saunders requested a consult from another doctor.

Dr. Chin introduced himself, examined Aunt Bessie, and went over her chart.

Skye wrapped her hands tightly around her waist, physically trying to hold herself together. "What's wrong with her?"

"It might be a bleeding ulcer undetected at the time of the surgery, or it could be a new ulcer," he said. "Or there might be a problem at the site of the surgical repair."

"What can we do?" Skye's eyes teared. She distinctly remembered the instructions Bessie had given her when Skye agreed to be her power of attorney. Bessie wanted every and all lifesaving measures to be taken.

"An endoscopy would be most effective in determining what we're dealing with," Dr. Chin said.

"What is an endoscopy?"

"It's a procedure where we insert a tube-like instrument with a light, camera, and laser on it into your aunt's mouth to see what we are dealing with. Ideally, we use the laser to blast the bleed with electro-coagulation."

Bessie wanted all lifesaving measures to be taken. "When will you do it?"

"I don't think you understand the gravity of the situation. An endoscopy is an invasive procedure.

In your aunt's weakened state, I'm not sure she'd survive. It's risky. Sometimes the telescopic tube can rupture the stomach wall."

Her aunt wanted measures to prolong her life not end it. "What's the alternative?" Skye asked.

"Drug therapy," Dr. Chin said. "We'll run a drug at the same time to stop the production of stomach acid."

Better safe than sorry.

And it worked.

A little.

Aunt Bessie didn't throw up any more blood, but test results revealed she had not stopped bleeding internally.

The blood loss had weakened Bessie even more, and Dr. Saunders ordered more whole blood to keep up her strength.

Later the following day, Bessie turned septic. Her incision smelled like rotten eggs. Skye covered her nose and swallowed hard. She watched the nurse solemnly change the dressing.

Dr. Saunders materialized at the end of the day. He stood at the foot of Bessie's bed and tapped her chart with his pen. Skye stood gazing out the window. She'd been knee deep in self-recriminations when the doctor came up behind her.

"I'd like to have a word with you out in the hall," he said.

Skye turned and followed him outside the room.

"I think we've reached the point to draw the line," Dr. Saunders said.

Skye's stomach bottomed. What? No. "I realize Bessie hasn't done as well as you'd hoped, but surely there's more you can do."

Dr. Saunders leveled his eyes on Skye. "We've exhausted all our options. Our treatments aren't working." His eyes softened with compassion. "I want to stop the blood infusions and remove her feeding tube. I'll order medications to keep her pain free and comfortable."

Even out in the hall, Skye could hear her labored breathing and phlegm rattling in her chest.

Dr. Saunders remained still, his voice soft and unassuming. "Ms. Andrews…Skye. Your aunt is dying."

Skye went back to physically holding herself together with her hands. Skye hadn't followed her aunt's express wishes, and the inaction had brought all this on.

Dr. Saunders continued. "I need your permission."
There was abject silence.
Skye dried her eyes and nodded.
"It's the right thing to do," Dr. Saunders said. He gave Skye's shoulder a squeeze and went to the nurse's station to issue the new orders.

Skye dragged the chair over beside her aunt and watched nurses disconnect the feeding tube and remove the blood infusion. A cocktail of medications was then injected into the port on her arm.

Once they were alone, Bessie's breathing did improve, and she seemed less restless. Skye picked up her hand and held it in hers. "I'm sorry, Aunt

Bessie. I failed you. I was afraid to do what needed to be done." Skye closed her eyes to shed the tears that had collected. Skye remembered sitting with Bessie for about an hour before she passed.

This time around when Skye put her head down to kiss her aunt's hand, the strangest thing happened. Her aunt squeezed her hand. The movement made Skye sit up.

Bessie opened her eyes and spoke. "You're much stronger than you give yourself credit for," she said. "I'm tired, dear. I'm packed and ready to go. I don't want to keep mother and father waiting any longer. It's time for you to get on with it. There's more to life than a career." Then her aunt's eyes fluttered closed, and she was gone.

Skye's tears splashed and sizzled on the hot brooch. She let the pin slip through her fingers and onto the journal, then she found herself sitting on the couch in Jason's loft.

For the first time in weeks, Skye's mood lightened.

The guilt she'd been carrying around for giving the order to end Bessie's life dissipated like an early morning fog.

She had done the right thing after all.

Bessie didn't want her to wallow in guilt for not insisting on an endoscopy or for removing her feeding tube. Skye did exactly what Bessie wanted her to do. Bessie's mother had been dead for twenty years, and her father had been gone for eighty.

Bessie wanted Skye to let her go.

Bessie had given Skye this recapitulation to put her death into the proper perspective.

Bessie hadn't packed up her belongings to move into long-term care like Skye had originally thought—Bessie boxed and tagged everything because she'd seen the end of her life.

CHAPTER 11

"No. No. No," Hans Gruber, long time director of the Raverse theater group, said.

From the darkened seats, Skye listened to him give Tammy instructions for the female lead in their upcoming feature, *To Her With Love*.

Hans bellowed commands, and Tammy appeared close to tears. Hans threw up his arms and stomped off the stage. For whatever reason, Tammy didn't understand his vision for this production.

Skye seemed to have a sixth sense when it came to interpreting the written word. For as long as she could remember, she could read a script and, within a matter of moments, knew exactly how a scene should be played—she'd pictured it, like a movie on the big screen. It was a gift—a gift making her one hell of an intuitive actress.

She kept her eyes on Tammy. Since the other cast members were having a costume fitting and were otherwise preoccupied, Tammy started to cry.

Skye weighed her options carefully. She could keep quiet, stay low and not comment, or help Tammy understand the part. Her professionalism won out. She got up out of the seat and climbed on stage.

Tammy spotted her immediately and dried her eyes. "I suppose you saw the whole thing, huh?"

Skye nodded.

Tammy sniffed. She rubbed her already red eyes. "I can't ever seem to make Hans happy."

"Let me tell you a little secret. All directors are on a power trip. The trick is not letting them intimidate you. Stand your ground. Tell him you don't understand."

"I don't think I can do that."

"Why not? Often times a healthy collaboration between the actor and the director produces the best performance."

"You think so?"

"I know so. Now, what do you think Mia's motivation is in this scene?" Skye asked.

Skye helped Jason with his lines last night and had skimmed the rest of the play this morning while she sat in the seats behind the orchestra. This was a typical boy meets girl love story. Boy leaves town and meets another. Later, the girl returns and messes everything up.

"Mia is crazy jealous and heartsick. Do you think Mia is simply going to stand aside and let this other woman take her man?" Skye ignited a fire inside of Tammy.

"Hell no," Tammy said.

"That's exactly right. She needs to turn it on, walk the walk. Work it. Not be a submissive who stands aside."

At that moment Jason sauntered on stage in costume. "Behold Marcus," he said. "I'm the chump who can't make up his mind."

"Try playing the part like this." Skye thrust her shoulders back and held her head high. She sashayed over to Jason and circled him, wearing the character of Mia like a comfortable shirt.

"What do you want me to do?" Skye drawled in Mia's syrupy voice. Her hips gyrated left and right. "Give you space? I won't be waiting around for you while you make your decision. And this is what you'll be missing."

Then Mia kissed Marcus.

Abruptly Skye pulled away.

Jason lost his balance and nearly fell.

"*Brava. Bellissima.* Now that is exactly my vision," Hans said. He strode onto the stage from behind the curtain clapping his hands.

Skye motioned to Tammy. "Now you give it a try."

The rehearsal lasted for another couple of hours.

Hans wanted to do a final run through of the play from start to finish. Skye stood in the wings with the behind-the-scenes crew while they fine-tuned the lighting, costumes, and scenery.

She spun around when someone tapped her on the shoulder. "Talbot?" she said. "What are you doing here? Talk about a small world."

"I thought it was you," he said, leaning in for a hug.

"When the Olivier closed, I heard there was an opening here. I've never been to the UK, so I applied."

"Are you and Jason back together?" Talbot asked.

"We were never together, not even back in the day. We've always been good friends," Skye said. "I had some family business to attend to over here, so I came to visit. He asked me if I wouldn't mind helping out."

"Quiet!" Hans blasted them a fiery order from center stage.

"We'll catch up later," Talbot whispered, right before he disappeared.

She paid close attention to the actors on the stage. Very soon, Skye realized Hans was one of those directors who would never be happy. Even if the performances of his actors were perfect, he'd find something to complain about.

Tammy's portrayal greatly improved from the first run of the day. She had good instincts once she understood the part. She had a knack for intonation and pacing, except in those scenes with Jason. Skye sat in the darkened seats and recognized the problem and knew how she could fix it, but right now was neither the time nor the place.

With precious little time left before opening night, all the cast and crew members went to relax afterward at the Backstage Pub, their regular haunt, across the alley from the Raverse. Skye and Tammy sat at a table in the rear and noticed Jason at the bar engaged in what appeared to be a heated discussion with Hans.

"Oh no," Tammy said. "There's trouble on the horizon."

"What do you mean?" Skye said.

"I've only ever seen Jason drink hard liquor on one other occasion."

Skye noticed the shot in Jason's hand. "I've never seen him drink liquor."

"Last time it took me two days to sober him up," Tammy said. "You're going to have your work cut out for you."

"Did Hans do something I don't know about?"

"Not that I'm aware of."

"Do you remember what caused the problem the last time?" Skye asked.

"Yeah," Tammy said. "You."

"Me?" Skye said. "What did I do?"

"I'm not really sure. All I know is he thought you were hot and heavy with some guy in New York. I think his name was Beau."

"Beau? I can't even remember Beau's last name. We dated over a year ago. It took me two minutes to discover what the jerk wanted."

"All I know is Jason went off the deep end. He thought you two were getting married."

Married? She might have mentioned Beau to Jason, and maybe she said something to the effect that he could be husband material. But she forgot to tell Jason the guy was a jerk until they talked a couple of weeks later.

Hans wormed his way over to their table. "What's up with Jason? He's been ragging me about going too far. He said I've upset you." Hans pointed at Tammy. "And that I've screwed everything up. Whatever that means. He's had one too many, so I confiscated his keys. Who's going to do the honors?" He shook the keys at Tammy.

"I may have been responsible for the last bender," Skye said. "But this one appears to be all your fault. That makes us even don't you think?"

Tammy rolled her eyes and snatched the keys from Hans. "Right. Jason is our responsibility. Good thing, really. It's going to take the two of us to get him up the stairs into the loft."

"Just two more steps," Skye said as she tugged a very drunk Jason up the loft stairs.

"Have I ever told you I love you?" Jason slurred.

"About ten times in the last hour," Skye said, pulling with all her might. She leaned around him to see Tammy. "Push, will ya?"

"How did I get this end?" Tammy asked.

"I've got the door key, remember?"

"Well hurry and open it so I can get the hell out of here and leave you two lovebirds alone."

"Tam?" He perked up. "Is that you? What are you doing here?"

"Trying to get you home safe and sound."

"You're the best."

"The best what? Pusher? Friend? Actress?" she muttered.

"Okay," Skye said. "The door is open. We're almost there. One final shove and I think we've got it."

With a momentous effort, all three spilled inside the door of the loft. Jason slipped down the wall and onto the floor. Skye plunked into the nearest chair, and Tammy bent over with hands on her knees to catch her breath.

"I'm getting a glass of water and then I'm outta here," Tammy said. She straightened and stepped over Jason.

"We can't just leave him on the floor," Skye said. "You have to help me get him into bed."

"Why?" Tammy asked.

"'Cause we need to talk."

"What if I don't feel like talking?"

"C'mon, Tam. I'm not the enemy. Maybe we can figure out what the heck is going on."

"Oh, all right," Tammy said. She shrugged out of her jacket and rolled up her sleeves. "This time I pull and you push."

After a struggle, Skye and Tammy got Jason flopped onto the bed. Then they went into the kitchen. Skye fixed them a cup of tea, and they sat on the stools at the counter.

"I tried to hate you, you know. But you had to go and be nice and mess everything up." Tammy sipped her tea. "Jason thinks you're the perfect woman. Every time he mentioned your name I'd want to puke."

"You're not my biggest fan," Skye said. "What I don't understand is why you two haven't gotten together?"

"I used to send out all the signals, but it's pointless. He's still in love with you." She shrugged. "He wants you. Hell, he only told you ten times on the way over here."

Not in a million years had Skye suspected Jason was in love with her. Then the photos on his wall popped into her head. "He said he loves me, but I can assure you he's not *in* love with me. There's a big difference. We dated for a while when we went to Boston U, but it didn't last. There was no magic."

"That might have been the case for you."

Sometimes people see only what they want to see, unless you happened to be Aunt Bessie. Skye always thought Jason had made a snap decision when he took the job at the Raverse. Now she wondered what actually transpired ten years ago. Maybe Bessie had something to do with it. "Did Jason ever mention having a conversation with my Aunt Bessie before he left the States?"

"Your aunt? What does she have to do with anything? Does she have a crystal ball?" Tammy laughed. "Maybe you should ask her if Jason is still in love with you?"

"I wish I could. She's dead. I came to the UK to lay her ashes to rest."

"Oh, I'm sorry."

Since last night, the pain Skye felt with every mention of Bessie's name had become curiosity.

"Jason talks about you twenty-four seven. Have *you* ever told him you're not in love with him?" Tammy asked.

"Not outright." How odd. Could Jason, the consummate ladies' man, be celibate? "He hasn't been on a date in how long?"

"Since I came to work at the Raverse."

"That's been what? Eighteen months?"

"'Bout that. Apparently, he used to be quite the flirt before I arrived. The actress I replaced forewarned me."

"How long have you been in love with him?" Skye asked.

"Oh, bloody hell," Tammy said. "Is it that obvious?"

Skye didn't miss a beat. "Not really. I simply put two and two together. You're having trouble at work because the play you're performing closely shadows real life. My advice still stands. If you want him, you need to get in there and fight."

"Am I in competition with you?"

A vision of Jet, dark-haired in his captain's uniform, popped into her head. She tossed Tammy the keys. "Jason and I are friends, and I'll make sure he's on the same page. You're the one who needs to stake a claim. You can start by picking him up and taking him to work tomorrow morning."

Tammy huffed and clip-clopped down the stairs. Skye stood at the window until she saw her get into the car.

Had Tammy been right? Had Jason been in love with Skye?

She went into the bathroom, washed her face, and brushed her teeth. On her way to the couch, she stopped and gawked at Jason sprawled across the bed, snoring like a truffle-foraging pig.

She had only assumed both of them had moved on. She had. But had he?

CHAPTER 12

S kye changed into her tank top and boxers and made up the couch but, once again, couldn't seem to fall asleep. After making animal hand shadows on the ceiling for ten minutes, she snagged the Luckenbooth brooch and held it in her hand. Bessie wrote about Skye forgiving herself and her death. She'd packed her life into boxes to be distributed amongst her friends and relatives. It stood to reason Bessie knew Skye sat here tonight unable to sleep because of some burning unanswered questions.

Every time Skye sat down with the journal, she learned something new—something she hadn't seen or something she'd misconstrued. Skye didn't have a clue how the magic worked, only that it did. The journal seemed to impart these secrets at the very moment Skye needed to know. Of course, this was all speculation on her part at this point. But the theory would be easy to put to the test.

Right now, she needed to know if she'd been blind all these years. Was Tammy right? Had Jason been in love with her? Was he still in love with her?

Skye opened the journal and squeezed the Luckenbooth. She closed her eyes and, once again, fell topsy-turvy down the rabbit hole—the action unfolding in her mind like a movie on the big screen.

The clock rewound ten years, and Skye found herself watching Jason a few hours before their final performances of the *The Married Man*.

Jason sat on the brocade sofa in Bessie's living room, and Bessie sat perched in her favorite blue chair. "Skye's really upset. Are you sure you won't reconsider coming to the last performance of *The Married Man*? She thinks she's done something wrong."

"She'll get over it. Besides, I have other pressing matters. I have a very important appointment this evening with a director from New York."

"Why didn't you tell her that?"

"Because it would ruin the surprise. And it was the only way to get her out of the apartment. She's not here because she's mad at me. That reminds me, I have something for you."

"What? Me?" Jason asked.

Aunt Bessie stood at her dining room hutch and pulled an envelope out from behind a plate standing on edge. She opened the letter, lifted the glasses hanging on the string around her neck, and placed them on her nose. Then she passed it to Jason on her way back to her chair.

"What's this?" Jason asked.

"It's an offer from the Raverse Theater in Edinburgh," Bessie said.

"But how? I didn't even apply," Jason said. "They want me to come for an audition—they say I was one of the top three actors they were considering for the lead."

"I know. I sent them your headshots and a copy of your current show BU videotaped for its archives. I included a dozen or more reviews from the shows. They said they loved you."

Jason's expression fell. "I don't know what to say. I mean, it's a terrific job opportunity. But it feels kind of like running away."

"It doesn't sound like you're very excited," Bessie said.

Jason scrubbed his hand across his chin. "Did Skye tell you what happened between us?"

"She said you two went on a date but decided you both were better friends than lovers."

"*She* said we were just friends, I didn't. I'm in love with her, and I don't know what to do about it." He popped up from the couch and paced the living room. "*She* keeps telling me I'm her best friend, but I ache to be so much more. I can't handle just being friends."

"You'll learn to be her friend," Bessie said.

"Maybe. It's not like it'll happen if I stick around here. Maybe in Scotland, I'll be forced into it, won't I?"

"Yes, you will."

Jason folded the job offer and put it into his coat pocket. "Why did you do this for me?"

It was Bessie's turn to be pensive. "I know what it feels like to be hopelessly in love with someone."

"You do?"

"It's another reason I can't go to the show. Even the title dredges up too many unhappy memories."

Jason's eyes locked on Bessie's. "You were involved with a married man?"

"You seem surprised. I used to be quite the dish once."

Jason blinked several times. "I bet you were."

Bessie smiled warmly. "Your charm will see you through this rough patch. Believe me. The pain will dull and recede. I promise. There were times when I doubted too. Being in love is a force unlike anything else in this world. It can turn a saint into a sinner. It's an all or nothing proposition. There was no one else for me, but that isn't true in your case. Your soul mate is overseas waiting for you."

"What if this soulmate shuns me too? I'm not sure I'll survive another rejection. It's too painful."

"Next time," Bessie said. "Your fear will be the only thing standing in your way."

Skye closed Bessie's journal and placed the warm pin on the cover.

Wow, just wow.

The pin and journal had passed her test brilliantly.

Why was she so surprised?

Bessie always said their lives were entwined. Once in a while, Bessie knew what Skye had been thinking; she'd even finish a sentence Skye started.

But never did Skye suspect Bessie could perform a damned mind meld.

Tammy nailed it.

How could Skye not have known that Jason had been totally and helplessly in love with her?

Now, in retrospect, it made perfect sense.

Now the stream of Jason's female conquests right after she proclaimed them nothing more than friends made perfect sense. Jason had a different date on his arm every night, affirmation he could get anyone he wanted—anyone except Skye. He was a cad, and they went out with him anyway.

Skye guessed Jason carried a torch for her right up until about eighteen months ago—when he met Tammy. If memory served, he stopped talking about his dating habits around the same time Tammy began working at the Raverse.

Tammy was Jason's soul mate.

It did make perfect sense. Tammy and Skye were competent actresses, and their physical attributes were a great deal alike. They also shared many similar personality traits. And being in love certainly would explain his protectiveness of Tammy at the bar earlier tonight.

Which brought Skye to her stage kiss with Jason today.

If Jason still had a thing for Skye, he would have reacted much differently. Instead, he pulled back. His movements were mechanical, languid. His body language choreographed his shock and apprehension. Right afterward, he faced Tammy to see her reaction.

What Tammy thought mattered to him. A lot.

Jason may have been in love with Skye once, but not anymore. The only obstacle holding him back was his acute fear of being rejected again.

Skye had her head in the sand ten years ago, but her eyes were wide open now. She'd talk to Tammy. Maybe Tammy could ask Jason out? If not, Skye would do everything she could to get them together, even if it meant playing matchmaker.

With a plan of attack for Jason and Tammy, she thought about the other intriguing factoid Bessie's journal had imparted.

Skye never would have guessed Bessie had been in love, and with a married man, no less. Skye had always wondered why her aunt never came to her final performance of *The Married Man.*

Immediately, Skye pictured Aldo Genovese—the man who had given Skye the Luckenbooth brooch at Bessie's service of remembrance—a man who, by her own admission, she loved till her dying day. What kind of man could tempt a church-going woman into an affair? She imagined it would be one heck of a story.

Skye's curiosity had been piqued the day she met Aldo, and she yearned to hear all about it.

Chapter 13

The following morning, Skye sat in Jason's kitchen thinking about her late-night foray into Aunt Bessie's journal. She'd managed to grab an hour of shut-eye despite it being fraught with restlessness.

Skye kept thinking about Aldo Genovese, and Bessie likely knew Skye wanted to know more. She lived with her aunt for four years while she went to university, and yet she never really knew her aunt. Not really.

Bessie had chosen to live her entire life alone.

A week ago, Skye would have been all right with being a spinster. Her Broadway career had sustained her. Suddenly, an image of Jet flashed in her head.

Damned man had spoiled her.

Maybe her aunt would show her how to exorcise him from her mind the way she gotten Aldo out of hers.

Jason stirred in the other room.

Skye sat at the kitchen table and placed the journal beside her purse. She'd already made a decision to go sightseeing today rather than spending the day at the Raverse. Jason wouldn't be happy. He wanted

Skye to help out at rehearsal, but she had other plans. Jason and Tammy needed time alone, without Skye's interference.

Once she said her piece.

Since *To Her With Love* was set to open the following Thursday night, the next few days would be hectic. And Skye would refuse to let Jason show her around town when she could do it at her own pace. She'd already mapped out her day: Edinburgh Castle, the Royal Mile, and Holyrood House.

She peeked over the kitchen counter and saw him sprawled across his bed, dead to the world. To get to the theater by nine, he would have to be showered by eight thirty, but when he'd passed out last night, he'd neglected to set the alarm.

She put down her cup of coffee and marched over to his bed. "Wakey, wakey, Sleeping Beauty. Time to get up and face a few facts."

Jason groaned. "What time is it?"

"It's ten after eight."

It took all of one second for the numbers to penetrate. "What the…" He sprang into a sitting position. "Why didn't you wake me sooner?"

"Because I didn't want to give you too much time or you'd come up with an alternate plan."

"What are you talking about?" He headed toward the bathroom taking off his shirt along the way. "I have to jump into the shower."

"In a minute," Skye said. "What happened last night?"

"I had too much to drink, is all."

"But, why?"

With unwavering focus, he barely blinked. He never could lie to her.

She pushed harder. "I know why," she said. "You're in love with Tammy and it scares the shit out of you."

He huffed and his mask of indifference slipped only for a second, but long enough for Skye to see the truth.

"I don't have time for this." Jason shuffled into the loo.

A moment later, she heard the water running in the shower. She picked up her coffee and had nearly finished her toast when she heard Tammy on the stairs. She opened the door and hushed Tammy by raising a finger to her lips.

"Bugger me. Jason isn't still asleep, is he?" Tammy asked in a whisper.

"He's in the shower," Skye said shaking her head. "I just wanted to say you were right. Jason may have been hung up on me once, but then you came into his life. Now, he's in love with you."

"Did he tell you that?"

"Not in so many words, but he is."

"He's got a funny way of showing it."

"He's afraid you're going to hurt him the way I did." Skye didn't know if Tammy believed her or not. "I'm going to keep myself very busy for the next couple of days to give you guys a chance to get it together."

Tammy eyed her warily.

"I'm not leaving town, I'm just going to do some sightseeing."

"I thought he'd planned to spend the afternoon with you today doing just that."

"He did. But I've made other arrangements."

Skye collected her bag and travel guide. "You better get a move on if you don't want to be late for rehearsals." Skye bounded out the door and down the stairs.

Armed with her Edinburgh travel guide, she ventured out, sitting on the bench at the end of the block to wait for the next bus. She pulled out the book that held her enthralled—Bessie's journal and the Luckenbooth.

Oddly enough, the brooch didn't seem to be generating the amount of heat it had when Aldo first gave it to her. The stone had always seemed warm to the touch, but since she'd been pairing it with the journal, it had lost a good portion of *oomph*. She opened the journal, squeezed the brooch, and the flowing cursive script became a live video feed.

Blackness engulfed the Rag Time Boston Theater. The camera zoomed in on Bogie and Bergman.

"Ilsa, I'm no good at being noble, but it doesn't take much to see the problems of three little people don't amount to a hill o'beans in this crazy world. Someday you'll understand that."

Tears spilled down Bergman's porcelain cheeks.

"Now, now. Here's looking at you, kid."

The theme music swelled to a crescendo, and a young and vibrant Bessie pulled a handkerchief out of her sleeve and dabbed her nose with it. She leaned over and whispered into the ear of a woman sitting beside her. "This movie keeps getting better every time I see it. Thanks for coming with me."

"What are friends for?" Mima said. She tilted her head and sighed. "Rick's so dreamy. I just don't understand how he can say good-bye to her."

Bessie sat back in her seat. "He can do it because it's only a movie."

The lights in the theater came on. Theatergoers began filing out.

"I know, I know. Say, how did you manage to get past your mother? Isn't this your third time seeing Casablanca?"

"She's been really busy with Bart and Jane's wedding plans. She doesn't even know I'm here. Tonight, she's having Jane's parents for a sit-down dinner."

"How did she manage that?"

"She's been stockpiling our rations and food stamps for weeks. Neither of us drive, so she traded some of our gasoline stamps with the lady on the corner and stood in line for a couple of hours to get a decent cut of beef. It's ridiculous the effort she's making. Bart should have taken Jane to city hall and tied the knot, like everyone else. I tell you, this war won't be over soon enough for me."

The house lights came on and Mima stood. "Did you want to go to the roller rink to see what's shaking?"

"I can't tonight," Bessie said, trailing behind the crowd. "I told mother I'd be home early. I have to stand up in church tomorrow to read a letter she received from a second officer in the Merchant Marines."

"What kind of a letter?"

"A thank you. About a year ago, the women's auxiliary in the church got together and assembled care packages for the fighting troops. Each man received a hand-knitted sweater, scarf, balaclava cap, and gloves. Apparently they were very well received because the entire company had been under clothes rationing."

"What was the name of his ship? Was he on special assignment?" Mima asked, wide eyed.

"He couldn't give specifics because of the censor, but he said he's seen a lot of 'Fritz' down their way. They engage fire in the black of night when their searchlights spot enemy aircrafts. He said one of their sister ships carries the wing of a bomber they shot down by ack-ack fire."

Mima and Bessie hurried through the reception area of the cinema, past the concession, and outside where they parted ways.

Days flew past.

The following weekend, Bessie and Mima went to the Roller Garden. It's what all the young folk did. They tried to push the world's problems aside by going to the movies, the dance hall, or roller rink.

Music blared through the loudspeakers from the local radio station. The song "All or Nothing at All," the latest smash hit from crooner Frank Sinatra, echoed in the arena.

Bessie and Mima sat on the bleachers and tied their skates. "My brother, Bart, and Jane have set a date," Bessie said. "Jane's asked me to be one of the bridesmaids."

"That's wonderful," Mima said. "I love weddings."

"My mother obviously doesn't. She pressed Bart for a longer engagement."

"Why? They've been together for a couple of years already, haven't they?"

"Three."

"I don't think they'd still be together if they weren't right for each other."

"It's not about that," Bessie said. "Mother doesn't want Bart or me to ever leave home."

"Really? I know she's a widow, but Bart's in his twenties, isn't he? Don't you think it's time he struck out on his own?"

"Most definitely. It's time he took a wife and started his own family."

"What about you?" Mima said, pulling her laces tight. "Have you ever thought about getting your own place?"

"That would really set Mother off. No, I think I'll let Bart make the first move. Weren't your parents sad to see you leave?"

"Just the opposite. Sometimes, I think they paid Bob to take me off their hands."

"Mima," Bessie said, wagging her finger. "Bob would never have taken advantage of you like that."

"I know. It's just that he's been overseas for so long."

"He's fighting for all of us."

"I know. I just miss him."

The pair stood and set off around the circuit. Several laps later, Mima faced Bessie. "I'm going to get a soda. Want one?"

"Not yet. I'll be along in a moment. I want to hear the rest of this song."

Mima disappeared while Bessie listened to Ol' Blue Eyes. His soft and intimate voice caressed and serenaded her. The spell came to an abrupt end when she felt something brush across her palm. She tipped her head to see thick masculine fingers fiddling with her ring.

"Hey," she said, pulling her hand away. No way would she let this thief slip it off and pocket it. The ring was her mother's, and Bessie could wear it only on weekends.

"I didn't mean to frighten you," the handsome young man said. "The ring faced the wrong way. I thought I'd turn it right side up."

The ring always swung around. Bessie had large knuckles and skinny fingers. The setting often faced into her palm with the weight of it.

"It's all right," she said. "It won't stay, though. It's only a matter of time before it swings right around again."

"I can fix that," he said, swaggering on his skates.

"You can?"

"Sure." The young man laced his fingers through hers. "My name's Aldo. Since I'm the guy who's going to hold your hand for the rest of the night, you need to tell me yours."

Warmth infused her body, and she guessed she already turned at least eight different shades of red. She noticed his mischievous eyes and melted. "It's Bessie. Bessie McDougall."

"Well, Bessie McDougall," he said. He raised their joined hands and brushed soft lips across her knuckles. "There's more than one way to skin a cat."

Chapter 14

The phrase pulled her nose right out of the journal.

Instead of getting too hot to hold, the stone had gotten much cooler. Skye rubbed it between her hands to bring the warmth back.

While she worked on the stone, she thought about the clichéd words she'd heard uttered by Aldo and Jet.

There's more than one way to skin a cat.

Skye remembered everything about Captain Jet Dalry. Every time they touched, it felt like she'd been zapped by a live wire.

"Miss?"

Skye snapped out of her daze and realized a grumbling double-decker bus stood at the curb in front of her, the idling goliath's door held open by the driver who had paged her.

She climbed aboard the bus and made change for a day pass.

"It must be a pretty good book. You didn't even hear the bus pull to a stop," the driver said, motioning to the journal as he swung the door closed.

Skye nodded. "You have no idea," she said, sitting down in the first vacant seat.

Above the windows, Skye took note of the bus route. She had a dozen or more stops before she would arrive at the castle, so she opened the journal and continued.

Bessie and Aldo were inseparable. They spent every weekend together in Boston's downtown roller rink and dance halls.

He was dark and broodingly handsome. A smart dresser, he wore only the latest fashions: zoot suit with stovepipe pant legs and tight ankles, wide brimmed fedora, and black Italian leather shoes. A thick gold chain hung from his belt loop and swung down one leg with a money clip on the end stuffed inside his pants pocket. The outfit screamed antiestablishment, and Aldo wore it well.

On the weekends, they danced, skated, and went to the movies. Mostly, they talked.

Bessie didn't ask too many questions about Aldo's father's business because she got the impression it was less than reputable. Aldo worked for his father, down on the docks. His father obtained a special license for him so he wouldn't be shipped overseas to fight. Aldo didn't know how his father managed to obtain it, or even if it was legal, all he knew was that he hated it. All his friends were across the pond, dropping like clay pigeons. He thought of himself as a coward.

Aldo wanted to fight. He hated being left behind. He'd withdrawn and become resentful; his relationship with his father and mother had deteriorated to the point where they barely spoke.

Bessie tried to get him to open up, but every time she brought up the subject, he would sidestep. Quickly.

Bessie loved him. Ever the gentleman, Aldo brought her flowers, candy, even a ration of sugar to take home for her mother. But he refused to actually meet her family. And never once suggested he introduce her to his.

When he kissed her, she thought the pounding of her heart would crack her ribs. She'd already made up her mind. The next time she found herself in his car with soft music playing, she'd let him go all the way. Up until now, he'd always been the voice of reason and would stop before things went too far.

She trusted him.

She knew he would never hurt her, and everything would be okay because he said he felt the same way about her. Any day now he'd pop the question, and she didn't care about being a virgin on her wedding night. It really didn't matter when it happened, not in the whole scheme of things. And since they weren't too steady when he put a stop to their foreplay, it wouldn't take much to coax him to continue.

Dressed in a form-fitting kitten twin set, Bessie met Aldo on Saturday night at the Majestic Dance Hall. The orchestra played a wide variety of music, but their favorite was the big band sounds of Glen Miller.

Aldo held her all night. He didn't seem to want to sit down or let go of her. "Want to talk about it?" Bessie asked.

Aldo dipped her and pulled her close. "It's nothing," he said. "My father and I had another disagreement."

"That's not nothing."

He shook his head. "No, it's not. But I can't sit by and let him make decisions for me. I won't do what he wants me to do. I can't." He buried his head in her neck and inhaled. "You smell delicious."

"What does he want you to do?" Bessie asked. The raw need in Aldo's eyes nearly made her swoon. If he hadn't had such a grip on her, she would have slipped through his hands to the floor. "Maybe I could speak to him."

He stilled. "No, that wouldn't work."

"Why not?" Bessie placed her hands on his cheeks.

He encircled her wrists with his fingers. "Because he wants me to stop seeing you."

It took an instant for his words to register. Before she had a chance to respond, a commotion broke out at the entrance. She glanced over and noticed a couple of conservatively suited men had pushed past the hostess and were headed straight toward Aldo.

Aldo stepped around her pushing her safely behind him. "Did my father send you?"

"He's outside," the heavyset fellow said.

"He wants to have a word with you," the shorter man said, gesturing toward the door.

"Oh, yeah?" Aldo said. "I'd like to have a word with him too." He towed Bessie over to the table and sat her down. "Stay here. I'll be right back."

Then, he stormed outside, the two thugs in his wake.

Bessie had never seen Aldo so explosive. He'd always been sedate around her. She had a bad feeling. When male tempers flared, reason evaporated like puddles on a hot day. No way she was going to sit by and let her future be decided by others.

Gray clouds blacked out most of the stars and shrouded the night sky. Rain splattered the pavement. Bessie wrapped her arms around her waist to ward off the chill and searched the parking lot for Aldo. She spotted him in the back corner, shouting at a man she guessed was his father.

She hurried toward them and stopped. Aldo didn't know she stood behind him, but the older man did. He focused on her as he spoke. "Nothing will ever come of your relationship with this woman."

"You are not the one who gets to make that decision," Aldo said.

"Oh, but I am." The man reminded her of Aldo, only older.

"Nothing you say or do will change my mind," Aldo said, his hands at his side were balled into fists.

The older Aldo sighed and shrugged. "I hoped it wouldn't come to this, but you leave me no choice." He pulled a letter out of his breast pocket and tore it into little pieces. "As of this moment your service exemption is terminated. You, my boy, are going to war."

The man got into his car waiting beside him. The driver pulled ahead, and Aldo stepped aside to let it pass.

"Can he do that?" Bessie asked, her voice barely a whisper.

Aldo spun. "Bessie," he said. "What are you doing here?"

"I thought you might need help," she croaked. Her bottom lip quivered. "Your father would rather send you to war rather than see us together."

Aldo put his arms around her. "This has absolutely nothing to do with you. It has to do with the family."

She'd been so stunned by their confrontation she didn't notice the rain had strengthened. Her cashmere sweater was glued to her skin, and her teeth chattered like a cup and saucer in an earthquake.

"C'mon. You'll catch your death of cold." Aldo led her over to his Studebaker. He started the engine and switched on the heater. Then he rubbed her hands to get them warm. "I'm going to tell you something to help you to understand. My father's name is Don Vito."

"Don Vito...the mob boss?"

Aldo nodded. "My father's connections kept me out of the war."

"I don't understand." Bessie's eyes welled with tears. "Why does he hate me so much?"

"He has nothing against you personally. He's sending me a message. There's no room in our family for two decision makers. And..."

"What?"

"You're not Catholic."

Bessie confronted Aldo. "This can't be about religion."

"Not entirely." He leaned away from her. "It's about me being groomed for a position in the family hierarchy."

"Oh, I see," Bessie said. "Is that what you want? And what happens if he tells you to kill someone?"

Aldo sat perfectly still and deadly quiet.

"We've got to do something," Bessie said. "You'll have no more than a week or so to enlist. Maybe we should get married."

Aldo's head popped up. His eyes smoldered with sensual energy.

She didn't know who made the first move, but in the next moment they were in each other's arms—kissing, touching, feeling. Her chilled skin ignited. He explored her mouth with his tongue, and ever so gently his hands dropped from her face to her neck and even lower to her aching breasts.

All of a sudden, he pulled back and held out his hand. "I've been dying to touch you," he said, his breathing rapid and shallow.

She placed her hands over his and drew them toward her. When she felt his hands on her sensitive nipples, her eyes closed and her head fell back. With only a light camisole beneath her soaked sweater, he massaged her with his palm and her womb tightened.

Her breath caught.

Aldo stilled. "Am I hurting you?"

"Not yet. I think you might before the end of the night though. Mima said it only hurts for a second or two."

Aldo stopped touching her.

To let him know she wanted him, she placed her hands on his cheeks and leaned forward for a kiss. She took the lead and deepened it the way he had moments before. She let her hands trail downward. She never broke eye contact as she placed her hand on his erection.

Aldo grabbed her hand and brought it up to his mouth and kissed it. "As much as I want to make love to you, I can't let it happen."

Bessie didn't understand. "What does it matter if we make love tonight? I'll be your wife by week's end."

"Don't you see?" he said. "We can't be married."

"But why? We love each other." Bessie's tears flooded back.

"Let's say for a moment we got married and made love—a lot—because I don't think I'll be able to stop once I start. Say I got you pregnant. Do you know what would happen if I was killed overseas?"

Bessie shook her head. Tears spilled down her cheeks.

"My father would claim his grandchild."

"I would never stand between our child and your father. I'd want him to be part of our baby's life."

"No. You don't understand," Aldo said. "He'd claim his grandchild, whether you gave him permission or not. He would never acknowledge you."

"But he'd have to."

"No, he wouldn't."

"Are you saying he'd...kill me?"

He nodded.

She gulped. "What are we going to do?"

Aldo pulled her close and kissed her sweetly. "I'm going to war. God willing, I'll be back in a couple of years."

"What then?"

He hugged her. "Then we'll pick this up where we left off."

The brooch had gone stone cold in Skye's hand. The images in her head blurred, and the journal's flowing cursive writing changed back into the undecipherable archaic script.

When she checked their position on the bus route, she realized the castle was next.

For safekeeping, she shoved the brooch and journal inside a zippered compartment in her purse and waited until the bus came to a complete stop.

CHAPTER 15

The bus idled in the shadow of Edinburgh Castle.

Skye jumped off the bus, paid the fee for castle admission, and entered the turnstile.

She couldn't stop thinking about Bessie and Aldo. They loved each other and were never married. Skye's mind swirled with questions. What happened after the war? Why didn't they get married?

Bessie told Jason she'd had an affair with a married man. Did Aldo marry another woman? Was Aldo the married man she had the affair with?

These questions made her think about Jet. Why didn't he want Skye to touch him? Maybe he was married or about to be.

She gave herself a shake.

She noticed a guide gathering a group of tourists in the courtyard, so she fell into step with the other sightseers as they strolled into the first of many locations on the grounds.

"This is the Crown Room, it contains the crown, scepter, and sword of the State of Scotland," the guide, a little woman with thick-rimmed glasses, said. The crowd squeezed into the dark wooden-paneled strong room. The group took their time examining the contents of the cases. Many people asked questions of the guide, who really seemed to know her stuff. She filled in many details.

The castle grounds were very old, originally settled in 900 BC. The fortress was repeatedly battered and rebuilt over the centuries. Erected on an outcropping of volcanic rock, it proved itself to be both commanding and defendable, between the sea and the hills.

The group traveled the esplanade, taking the cobblestones through the Portcullis Gate and Foog's Gate to St. Margaret's Chapel—the oldest surviving roofed building in Edinburgh. Skye found all the sights interesting, but none stole her heart like the minute cemetery for officer's dogs on the chapel's semicircular grass terrace.

From there they moved to the Forewall and Halfmoon Batteries, the Crown Square, and the Royal Palace. Skye viewed the royal apartments; where Mary Queen of Scots gave birth to James VI. The Great Hall; where banquets and sessions of Parliament were held under ornate wooden ceilings. The vaults; used as a storeroom, barracks, bakery, and prison. She ran her hand along the cold cast iron of Mons Meg, a six-ton, fifteenth-century cannon.

"That concludes our tour," the tour guide said, coming to a halt where they began their walk about an hour earlier. "I hope you enjoyed it. Be sure to stop at the war museum on your way out; lots of memorabilia, weapons, and uniforms are on display."

Skye strolled into the Royal Scots Museum, where bagpipes were playing. She viewed the maze of galleries depicting the strategy, life, weapons, and conditions of the Scottish regiment.

Her throat went dry as she took stock of the various displays. She'd seen similar Royal Scots memorabilia when she cleared out Bessie's apartment. In one of Bessie's drawers, Skye found a strongbox containing medals, colors, and a large memorial medallion that belonged to William Patterson McDougall, Bessie's father. There were photos of him with his regiment, lying on his cot and laughing with his friends and mates.

When Skye's parents attended Bessie's service of remembrance, Skye's father suggested they be put to rest with Bessie in the family plot. But as Skye toured the museum, she had a much better idea. A warm feeling washed over her. She'd much rather donate them.

She approached a man in uniform standing at the information desk. "Excuse me," she said. "Is there any way I can speak with the person in charge of these exhibits? I have some memorabilia I'd like to donate."

"Is it Royal Scots memorabilia, miss?" The male clerk's eyes widened with interest.

"Yes, it is."

"Well, you've come to the right place. Everything here relates to the Royal Scots Regiment." He picked up the phone and dialed. In hushed tones he spoke to someone on the other end.

"You're very lucky, miss," he smiled as he hung up. "The bloke in charge happens to be on the premises today. If you'll follow me, I'll show you to his office."

Skye fell into step behind the private. They headed outside and into a peaked building immediately to the left of the museum; the sign read Home Headquarters—Royal Scots. A chain restricted entrance up the stone stairway. The man unhooked the links and waved her through. "It's up the stairs. First office on the left."

Skye thanked him and went inside. The narrow wooden door, painted high-gloss black, required a strong tug to open, probably due to its age. She knocked on the threshold of the opened office door.

She studied the man sitting at the desk, who seemed to be doing the very same thing. "I'll be damned," she said.

It was Captain Jet Dalry.

Jet couldn't believe his eyes.

He blinked to make sure his imagination hadn't conjured her. When she didn't disappear, his heart jumped in his chest.

What was it with this woman? Every time he thought he'd rid himself of her, she was right there.

Bad enough he'd relived their train ride about a thousand times in his head. Never before had a member of the opposite sex gotten under his skin so hard and fast. Skye was the last image he saw when he went to bed at night and the first when he awoke in the morning.

He'd been in a foul mood on the train, and he could barely contain himself right now. "Are you following me?"

Skye pulled back as if she'd been slapped. "I beg your pardon?"

Immediately he regretted his sharp tongue. He had the problem, not her.

"Don't you wish? I'm here on official business. And just out of curiosity, how many jobs do you have?"

Sometimes he asked himself the same question. He shrugged. These odd jobs were better than the alternative. "The regiment isn't really sure what to do with me. They believe I'm suited for administrative posts right now."

"And you don't?"

"I'm filling the cracks until I'm fit for active duty again." When he enlisted, he never thought he'd ever push a pencil.

"You say that like you've got something to prove."

"I do. My superiors are skeptical. They don't think I'll ever return to the field. I intend to prove them wrong."

"You're a man on a mission." She'd punched out each word.

"You could say that."

"In the meantime, you work for both the Commonwealth War Graves Commission and the regimental museum."

"That's right," he said, trying to keep the irritation out of his voice.

"Both jobs are kind of depressing. Everyone is...well, dead," Skye said, solemnly. She pulled the chair out from the wall and sat down.

Jet broke eye contact so she wouldn't see how his work affected him.

Skye stilled. "I know what it's like to lose someone."

Jet avoided eye contact and exhaled. John Smilie's request to oversee and grease the wheels in Kilmarnock came rushing back to him. She'd suffered a loss too. "On the phone, the private said you have some memorabilia you wanted to donate."

"Yes, I do. I have a saucer sized bronze medallion, regimental medals, and colors that belonged to my great uncle. Mustard gas killed him in the first World War."

"You have a Dead Man's Penny?" Jet raised his eyebrows.

"What?"

He shook his head. "It's the bronze medallion. We don't get many. Rank never appears on the coins because the value of each life lost is equal and constant."

"That must be it. The medallion is inscribed with his name only."

"May I see it?"

"I'm sorry, I didn't bring it with me. Initially, I planned to bury the medals with my aunt. I never thought about donating them until I toured the museum today."

"We'd be thrilled to acquire them."

"I have some old military photos too. There's one of him relaxing in his barracks on a cot."

"Smashing," Jet said, smiling. "Would you let us make copies?"

"You're welcome to the originals. The bloodline has run its course. Second and third cousins are all that's left."

"I'm sorry for your loss," he said, his smile dissolving.

"Thank you. My aunt lived a good long life. She was ninety when she died."

"I see." Not only did Jet hate small talk but also he sucked at it. He avoided it whenever possible. "Feel free to deliver the memorabilia at your earliest convenience."

"I'll deliver everything tomorrow."

"I'll be here until three if that suits you."

"I'll be here around two." Skye stood.

Jet mirrored her action, but the simple act of rising from his chair didn't always go smoothly. When he sat for any length of time, his traumatized leg muscles often fell asleep. He seemed to be the only one who knew he wasn't cut out for administration and sitting at a desk. Halfway to his feet he groaned. He planted his hands firmly on the desktop to pry himself from the chair the rest of the way.

Out of the corner of his eye, he saw her move, but he couldn't do anything to stop her from rushing to his aid. Before he knew it, she touched him again—she held on to his arm to steady him.

As soon as he found his balance, he slipped his arm free of her grasp and faced her. "Sometimes, I seize up. I'm fine now."

Skye blinked. Her eyes penetrated his soul.

In that instant, a thunderous crack shook the thick stone walls of the building.

Jet had grown accustomed to the boom of the one o'clock gun. Normally he checked his watch to see if it ran on time. But Skye, a tourist in Edinburgh, virtually rocketed into the air and into his arms.

She trembled.

It took barely a second for his standoffishness to dissipate. He wrapped his arms around her to make her feel safe. "It's all right," he crooned. "It's only the one o'clock gun letting everyone know the time."

Jet could feel her tenseness, so he pulled her even closer. He ran his hand over her silky hair and pressed his lips to the top of her head and trailed lower. She felt soft and warm. The curve of her body molded against his. She smelled like peaches and cream. He dipped his head and noticed her plump kissable lips.

"They shoot off a cannon?" Skye said. Her eyes still wild. "Haven't they heard of church chimes?"

CHAPTER 16

Skye molded to Jet's hard body and felt as if she'd come home, like she totally belonged there. The moment his lips touched the top of her head, her fear became complete and undeniable attraction—once again her heart rate spiked, her palms became slick, and she panted.

Desire. A full-fledged, ten-pin strike. It overcame her like nothing she'd ever experienced in her entire life—stronger than the rush of excitement from getting a good part or seeing a four-star review. This was a total knockdown.

She stood frozen, partly because the excitement stabbing her chest bordered on pain, and partly because she didn't want to budge in case he stopped. His lips moved below her ear to her neck and her cheek. She closed her eyes in anticipation of his lips on hers and startled when he pushed her away. When she resurfaced, she could only see the side of his reddening face. Obviously embarrassed, he couldn't even make eye contact.

He started talking as if nothing had happened. "I'll see you tomorrow then."

Skye shook off her trance. "Are you married?"

"What?" Jet faced her. "No."

She gritted her teeth and balled her hands into fists. What the hell was wrong then? She gathered her purse from the chair.

Jet grabbed his cane to steady himself and began squeezing her out of the room.

And she almost let him do it.

He was very attracted to her. She could see his desire smoldering like an ember. He'd pulled her so close he almost swallowed her. Her life was beginning to feel like a staged romantic comedy where the guy and gal took turns acting ridiculous. "What's up with you?" she asked. "Stop playing mind games with me and figure out if you're into me or not."

Jet's lips pulled into a grim line. "Not," he said succinctly.

He still hadn't had the decency to pay attention to her when he spoke. "Yeah," she said. "Better keep telling yourself that because your kisses say something altogether different."

Men.

She strode from his office, off the castle grounds, and down the street without breaking stride. Almost at Holyrood House, she stopped when she came upon a tiny shop called the Luckenbooth.

With her interest piqued, she faced the plate glass window of the quaint little shop. It seemed quite interesting, so she ventured inside.

The interior smelled of cedar and beeswax.

Skye leaned over the two display cases crammed full of different brooches. There were large ones, little ones, ornate ones, and plain ones. Some had stones and some didn't.

A kilt-clad elderly woman swished through the curtain at the back of the store. "May I help you?"

"I'm just browsing," Skye said.

"Please do," she said. A few moments later she asked, "Are you familiar with the Luckenbooth?"

"I have one, but in all honesty, I know nothing about it."

"If you have some time, I can share the history with you. I was just about to sit down for a cuppa."

A shrill whistle sounded from behind the curtain. "That would be lovely. My name is Skye, by the way."

"Pleased to meet you, Skye. I'm Lang." She held the curtain and waved her into the back room where a small kitchenette and table stood. "Have a seat."

Lang scooped two teaspoons of loose tea into the pot, filled it with boiling water, covered it with a cozy, and set it on the table. Then she placed two cups and saucers and sat down beside Skye.

"The word Luckenbooth means locked booths," Lang said.

"I'm not sure I understand."

"It has to do with Edinburgh's Royal Mile. The original Luckenbooth was built in the mid-fourteen hundreds and housed the city's first permanent shops—seven in a row were connected to the old tollbooth, parallel to St. Giles Church." She put a strainer in Skye's cup and poured.

"What does a string of stores have to do with the brooch?"

"The original shop tenants were goldsmiths and jewelers, until a little later. The list then expanded to bakers, hairdressers, milliners, *ane chymist*, and druggists." Lang placed the strainer in her cup and repeated the process.

"I know a milliner is a hat maker, but I'm not familiar with ane chymist."

"Ane chymist means one chemist. It is said he manipulated the components of precious metals and combined them with other minerals to obtain unusual properties."

"Huh," Skye said. "I guess the jewelers were responsible for designing the brooch."

"Aye, that's right. It's comprised of two overlapping hearts beneath a crown. Many have stones set in the teardrop overlap. You said you have one. May I see it?"

"Sure." Skye dug into her bag, pulled out the pin, and handed it to Lang.

Lang held it in the palm of her hand and raised both eyebrows. "This is a very early piece."

"How early?"

"One of the first."

"Really?"

Lang nodded. "The metal is hand tooled, mostly silver, and the stone is azurite."

"I didn't see any blue stones in any of the cases out front."

"There aren't any. Azurite is very rare in cut form. It is thought to have heavenly origins, not only because of the bright blue color, but because it's reputed to provide spiritual guidance."

Skye sat very quietly. "You seem to know an awful lot about a pin you say is extremely rare."

"That I do. You see, it was one of only two pins tooled by that ane chymist."

"There's another pin just like this one?"

Lang returned the Luckenbooth to Skye. She stood up and collected her purse from the far counter and brought it back to the table. She put her hand inside and pulled out another brooch. A near match to Skye's—Lang's stone and setting were fractionally larger.

Skye closed her hand around her brooch and it instantly warmed. She trailed her finger across the silver setting. "What's the significance of the joined hearts?"

"It means many different things. Most often lovers exchanged this pin. But it has a deeper meaning for a select few."

The door of the shop opened; a cool gust fluttered the curtain.

"Oh, my goodness, it's late," Lang said. "I've taken more than enough of your time." She cleared the cups from the table.

"Wait," Skye said. "Please tell me."

"They were used by oracles." Lang went through the curtain and into the shop. Skye grabbed her purse and followed.

"I'll be right with you," Lang said to the new customer.

Oracles? Stunned by Lang's words, Skye made her way to the door. "Lang is such an unusual name. I don't think I've ever heard it before."

"It's short for Languoreth."

"I've definitely never heard it."

"It's an old name, but then, so am I. I'll be celebrating my ninety-fifth birthday later this year." She shook her head and continued. "I was named after Queen Languoreth, who, like the ane chymist, was put to death."

"Whatever for?"

"For being a pagan prophet. For seeing the future."

That statement made Skye take pause. Lang and Bessie had sister pins. If Bessie could see the future, then it stood to reason that Lang could too. Not wanting to press Lang for more information, Skye let her tend to the customer. "I enjoyed talking to you," Skye said before she left the shop. As she strode toward Holyrood House, she thought about Lang. If Lang could see the future, she might have been expecting her this afternoon. Skye had been curious about the Luckenbooth, and it seemed that Lang had given her some context. If Skye hadn't been experiencing the powers of the pin firsthand, she would have deemed Lang's historical account interesting but impossible, and the bit about pagan prophets, total bunk. Throughout history, the unexplained had been considered the work of the devil. But Skye knew Bessie. There was nothing dark about her whatsoever.

Before Skye knew it, she stood in front of the official residence of the Queen, who happened to be in residence because all visiting hours had been cancelled.

Tired and still in a quandary, she hopped on the bus and rode it back through the tangle of city streets. She got off a block from Jason's loft, trudged up the back stairs, and when she went to put the key into the lock, the door swung open.

Never a good sign.

She poked her head inside and heard sobbing.

"Hello?" she called.

"In here," Jason said.

Skye dumped her coat and bag on the counter and headed into the living room where she found Tammy, inconsolable, sitting on the sofa.

Jason had his arm around her. "It's all right, Tam. You're okay, that's all that matters."

"No, it's not. Nothing will ever be okay ever again." Tammy hiccupped and blew her nose into a soggy tissue.

"What's wrong?" Skye mouthed to Jason.

"Poor Puddin'," Tammy cried. She pulled another two hankies from the box.

Jason rubbed her back. "When I went to take Tammy home tonight, her building was on fire."

"Oh my God," Skye exclaimed.

Tammy sniffed. "I jumped out and tried to get inside to get Puddin', but the fire brigade wouldn't let me. I told them where to find her, but they said that area was already engulfed in flames." Tammy dropped her head into her hands.

"Is Puddin' her cat?" Skye whispered to Jason.

Tammy nodded teary eyed. She took a big breath and straightened. "I guess I should make a few calls. I want to call my brother in London and let him know I'm all right. My insurance broker, maybe a hotel."

"You're not going anywhere. You're staying right here with me," Jason said. Then he glanced at Skye. "I mean us."

Skye nodded her agreement. This was a good thing. Not the fire, but Jason and Tammy living together. It would likely bring them together even quicker. All Skye had to do was get the hell out of their way.

Once she delivered Bessie's father's memorabilia tomorrow, she would pack up and go back to Kilmarnock to wait until the commission readied the plot and stone for interment. Only then could she put this whole trip behind her. She'd get back to the States and her acting.

At least that's what she hoped.

All she had to do was get her heart on board with it.

After seeing Captain Jet Dalry today, she wondered if being a career girl would ever, truly, be enough.

CHAPTER 17

Jason bunked on the sofa while Skye and Tammy shared the bed. Tammy was exhausted and fell right asleep, and Jason began snoring around the same time Tammy took to kicking. Wide awake, Skye couldn't stop thinking about Jet, so she grabbed Bessie's journal and the Luckenbooth brooch and shuffled into the kitchen. She fixed herself a cup of Sleepytime tea and palmed the pin. It seemed that both she and Bessie were destined to be in love with men who, for whatever reason, couldn't or wouldn't love them back. Maybe the journal would help her to understand the reasons why. She pulled the journal toward her and opened to the page where she left off.

Skye stood in the wings of the stage. Script held tightly in her hand, she read her lines and the stage directions for what seemed like the millionth time. She closed her eyes and imagined how she would handle the lead role of *Ruby Slippers*. She'd almost made it. Skye had three callbacks during auditions, and just when she thought the part was hers, Jessica Simpkin stole it from her.

Jessica. Who had no formal theatrical training?

Oh sure, she had a reputation and one hell of a body, but she couldn't act out charades let alone a Broadway production. It made everyone on the audition team wonder about the producer's credibility.

Not Skye.

She knew all about his thought process.

Jeremy Steel hadn't changed.

She remembered him all too well.

Jeremy was the producer that led her to the Big Apple after her graduation. He told her she'd be perfect for the lead in his next show. He didn't lie. She went to New York, auditioned, and landed the part. Until she realized the role required a little more than acting. Jeremy expected her to sleep with him too.

Skye quit when she figured it out. She stalked off the stage and purposely avoided his productions ever since. She'd gotten parts in five respectable Broadway productions. She'd honed her craft and made a good living—on her own terms, her determination, and talent, not because she had a vagina.

Until *Ruby Slippers*.

Jeremy Steel was the show's producer.

Immediately following her first audition, she requested a private word with Jeremy. She told him, quite emphatically, not to respond with a call back if his offer entailed anything other than acting. When she'd been called back three times, she assumed he'd accepted her terms and conditions.

But no.

He'd been waiting for something better to come along.

Jessica Simpkin had been on a television reality show, and her long blonde hair and curvy figure gave her an instant following. Jeremy decided to take her out for a spin. He gave her the lead and hired Skye as her understudy. If things didn't work out, he would yank Jessica and Skye would swoop in to save the show.

Skye cringed when Jessica stopped cold in the middle of the third act. She twisted toward the audience where the director, producer, and choreographer were sitting. "I don't understand Dorothy's motivation right now. Why is she in such a rush to get to Emerald City?"

Skye peeked out and saw the frustration on the director's face. He all but groaned out loud. He jumped to his feet and came toward the stage and waved Jessica over.

"What the hell is wrong with them?" Talbot came up and stood beside Skye in the wings. "You're hands down a better actor than she is. I don't know what all the fuss is about. I think you're way more beautiful than she is too."

Skye smiled. "Thanks, Talbot. I appreciate the vote of confidence."

The producer *was* the damn problem. But ever the professional, Skye kept her mouth shut. She wouldn't voice her frustration and certainly not to a member of the crew.

Moments later, Jessica threw her arms up in a daze.

"Okay, people," the director stood back and raised his voice. "The show opens tonight. Full dress rehearsal begins in one hour."

The crew scurried around and began making last minute adjustments. Jessica and all the other cast members rushed backstage to get into their costumes. The lighting and special effects team ran through their checklist.

Skye didn't have to change. She went and sat out in the seats and continued committing the script to memory. Jeremy was trying to calm the director down after his latest confrontation with Jessica. She wondered why the director put up with it. He had to know that Jeremy and Jessica were involved. It's not like it was a secret. They were sucking on each other's faces at the cast's favorite haunt a few nights ago.

Members of the orchestra filtered to their seats, and the chaotic sounds of musicians tuning their instruments rose from the pit. Very soon the lights dimmed, and the curtain rose.

They sailed through the first act and second act.

Skye's heart sank as Jessica got into character.

She recited the words as Jessica spoke them, analyzing her tones and inflictions. She wasn't half bad—for an actress with little to no formal training. She got her stage right and stage left mixed up when she left Professor Marvel's caravan, but she corrected herself and the mistake went relatively unnoticed.

The twister scene began.

A huge fan blew large streams of gauze-like fabric toward the front of the farmhouse. The fabric rippled and luffed and simulated gale force winds. Dorothy pressed toward the front of the house, clutching Toto in her arms as she struggled toward the storm cellar where moments earlier, Auntie Em, Uncle Henry, Hunk, Zeke, and Hickory had disappeared into the trap.

Jessica cuddled Toto and lifted her foot to stomp on the storm cellar door.

From where Skye stood on the stage, she noticed the storm cellar cap had moved about a foot backwards. In character, and screaming for Auntie Em and Uncle Henry, when she lifted her foot to stomp on the set one last time, she tipped like a teapot through the open trap.

Toto went flying and landed on the stage with a yelp. Skye heard a nasty thunk and a gut-wrenching scream geysered from the pit.

There was a good reason the space beneath the stage was called "hell."

Skye and other members of the crew hurried on stage and peered into the trap. Talbot screamed instructions to the people still on the communications bridge. "Call nine-one-one."

Two Munchkins backed away from the trap with hands covering their mouths. The weird spin of Jessica's leg made Skye's stomach churn too.

As soon as the paramedics arrived, Talbot led them beneath the stage where they stabilized Jessica's leg and gave her something for the pain. The paramedics secured her on the gurney and wheeled her from underneath the stage, loaded her inside the ambulance, and set off for the hospital.

Skye placed the lukewarm brooch on top of the journal and sat back on the stool in Jason's kitchen.

When Skye sat down, she expected to get the next installment of Bessie and Aldo's relationship. Instead, Bessie had shown an incident that happened before her latest production opened.

Everything had happened exactly as Skye remembered.

With more focus.

Skye sat in the kitchen and couldn't stop wondering why Bessie wanted Skye to revisit that particular incident? Why now?

Maybe Bessie was telling her she needed to get back to her career in the States. Or like before, maybe Bessie had been trying to get her to see something she'd missed before. But what?

She sipped her tea and thought back to that day.

A young and inexperienced stagehand had been blamed and ultimately fired for causing the accident. Jeremy and the producer spent a great deal of time examining the storm cellar set, and they came to the conclusion that the set's brakes had not been properly engaged.

The five actors who went through the trap door during rehearsal were responsible for closing the trap door after they dropped beneath the stage, but not one of them had remembered. Talbot had been on his way to shut and lock the door when Jessica fell.

Bad luck for Jessica. Good for Skye when she became Dorothy.

Ruby Slippers quickly became Skye's finest work.

Ticket sales skyrocketed, and the show's run had been extended twice.

Until Bessie took ill.

The entire remembrance not only made her homesick but also it reinforced her need to get her aunt properly laid to rest.

She loved her work. It was all she needed.

She didn't need a man adding to her troubles.

Her work provided her with more than enough drama.

Chapter 18

Skye grabbed a few hours' sleep and still managed to wake before either Tammy or Jason. She decided there was no time like the present to put her plan, "Operation Togetherness," into action. She organized her things by the front door and roused Jason sleeping on the couch.

"Wake up," she whispered. She grabbed his shoulder and gave him a shake.

He rolled, eyes blinking. "What's wrong?"

"Nothing's wrong with me, but Tammy's been crying most of the night. She's pretending to be asleep. I think you should go and talk to her. Maybe you can do something to help her get through this." Skye could just imagine his surprise when he realized Tammy wore only a bra and panties beneath that thin sheet.

He nodded and struggled into a sitting position. "Where are you going?"

"I've got an appointment this morning at the castle. I'm going to grab a coffee on my way." She collected her things at the door and left Jason and Tammy to their own devices.

At the coffee shop, she ordered a vanilla latte and sat down with her computer on one of the leather club chairs.

Her inbox contained fifty-three emails.

Skye scrolled through the list and opened them in order of priority. She'd gotten an email from her parents. Her dad was going to move his sister, Jane, Bart's wife—now in her eighties—out of her house and into an assisted living facility at the end of the month. Skye responded to their email and Moira's email and updated both on her progress. Then she deleted a dozen or more Big Willy emails and responded to five friends, actors from *Ruby Slippers*, who had already found work elsewhere.

All the other emails were casting calls. Oddly enough, she didn't bother opening them. Ordinarily, she would have opened them straight away. She loved setting her sights on new work. Often, she'd do research to get into a part. She'd get her hands on a script and begin the process of getting into character. Not today though. Perhaps she didn't want to make herself hungry for work when she was thirty-three hundred miles away. She didn't think so. She'd grown tired of the constant dog and pony show. Acting had always been enough up until now. It seemed there were other things she wanted to do with her life. Bessie got her thinking about family and finding her own Mr. Right.

She put her phone away and reached for Bessie's journal.

She couldn't seem to read fast enough. The book drew her. The more she saw the more she needed to see. She hoped there was some hidden message contained in Bessie's memories, some lesson or moral she could take away.

The stone in the brooch had changed. When Aldo first gave her the brooch, she could barely hold it in her hand because of the heat it generated. Now, as she dug it out of the zippered compartment of her purse, it was lukewarm at best. It made her wonder if she'd been draining the stone's energy with every use. She scanned the journal. She'd barely put a dent in the pages. Maybe she needed to give the pin more time between readings—a dilemma when she couldn't stop thinking about Bessie and Aldo and ached to know what happened next. Skye opened the journal and read.

Bessie took a three-month secretarial course and landed a job working at a doctor's office. Dr. Harrison Lamont's wife had been in charge for a few years, but the practice had outgrown her organizational skills. Bessie didn't have any medical training, but she knew how to interact with people. The patients loved her, the appointments ran on time, and she kept a cool head even in an emergency.

She never spoke of Aldo Genovese and safeguarded her feelings for him. Aldo told her it would be better that way. To that end, all his correspondence to her was sent to Dr. Lamont's office, and even then, there had only been a handful.

The letters were wonderfully romantic. Aldo spoke of getting married. War changed his mind about a lot of things. He didn't want to live his life by his father's rules. He asked her if she would move away with him, somewhere beyond his father's reach. Bessie would go wherever he asked, whenever he asked.

The war ended on the eighth of May, five years and eight months after it started. To celebrate, Dr. Lamont instructed Bessie to cancel all his appointments.

Crowds gathered in the streets and people paraded in cars, waving and celebrating victory. Bessie could barely contain herself. Aldo would return home and they would pick up where they left off, as promised.

August brought Hiroshima and Nagasaki.

Dr. Lamont told Bessie about the unseen effects of radiation; the invisible poison would slowly and painfully destroy a body's cells one by one. Bessie had been very young, but she remembered how her father suffered from mustard gas poisoning at the end of World War I. He lingered for months and died with shriveled lungs, a rack of bones.

Aldo wrote and told Bessie he would return to Boston sometime within the next few months but couldn't be certain exactly when. Every day Bessie held her breath with the mail delivery. And every day she left the office disappointed.

In late November, she found herself alone in the office. She had to cancel all Dr. Lamont's appointments because he'd been called away unexpectedly—summoned to pronounce a death down on the docks. A palette had fallen from a crane and crushed a man. She decided to stick around to finish some paperwork. Shortly after Dr. Lamont left, she heard someone enter the outer office.

"We're closed," she shouted. When no one responded, she went to investigate. She hurried into the waiting room and stopped dead. Barely one second later she'd been ensnared.

Aldo's lips were ravenous, and Bessie was willing prey. His hands wandered and caressed, held and felt. When she came up for air, she panted. "I've been so worried," she said. "I thought something happened to you."

"I should have contacted you earlier."

"When did you get back?" Bessie noticed his civies. If he'd just gotten home, he would have been wearing his military uniform. Instead, he wore one of the zoot suits he'd been famous for prior to going to war.

"I've been home for a couple of weeks," he said.

"A couple of weeks?" Bessie's world shattered. Her voice cracked. "Why are you only coming to see me now?"

Aldo held her at arm's length. "Things are worse than before I went to war. My father promised not to harm you or your mother if I stayed away from you."

Tears welled in her eyes. "Why would he do such a thing?"

"This has nothing to do with you. It's all about controlling me."

"Then why are you here now?"

"An accident happened down at the docks. I arranged for Dr. Lamont to make the pronouncement. In all the confusion, I slipped out without being followed. I needed to see you. I want to ask you something."

A million thoughts flooded her mind. Did he arrange to have a man killed so he could see her? Or had the opportunity simply presented itself? What was so important he placed her in danger? She'd become lost in his dark eyes. Were they the eyes of a loving man?

"Would you be willing to run away with me? You'd have to break all ties with your family and promise never to see them again." His eyes softened and became warm and pleading.

Ever since Aldo went to war, Bessie felt lost and alone. She'd been going through the motions, like a machine on automatic. She loved him. Her brother Bart would take care of mother, he'd have to.

"Yes." She nodded.

And he kissed her. He stretched it out and made it last. His lips were soft and gentle and full of promise. He ran his hand along her cheek and chin. "It won't be easy. We'll forever be fugitives. Always on the run."

"It doesn't matter. All that matters is being with you."

"That's my girl," he said. He reached into his breast pocket and pulled out a slip of paper. "Follow these to the letter. Don't say a word to anyone."

Then he kissed her one last time and, like an apparition, soundlessly slipped out of the office.

Aldo had written detailed instructions. A week Saturday, Bessie would meet him on the docks. She could take only one suitcase. He deliberately kept their destination a secret. The less she knew the better.

She packed her bag and hid it under her bed. Although she never said a word to Dr. Lamont about leaving, she made a checklist and placed it in her top drawer so her replacement would be able to master her routine quickly.

Bessie didn't want to desert her mother, but if the truth be told, her mother had beaten her to it years ago. Her mother deserted both Bessie and Bart the minute their father died. Not in the physical sense, but certainly from an emotional standpoint. In some strange way, Bessie had come to understand her mother's coldness, perhaps even forgave it. Bessie couldn't have been sure she wouldn't have acted the very same way if Aldo had been killed overseas.

On Saturday night, her mother was invited across town to Bart and Jane's for supper. When Bart came to pick her up, he asked Bessie if she wanted to tag along.

"No thanks," she said. "I've made other plans." Then she gave Bart a big hug and a kiss.

The simple display of affection flustered him. "What was that for?" he asked.

"Do I need a reason to hug my big brother?" Then she kissed her mother. "Have a good time."

Mother's stern expression didn't flinch. She fastened the top button of her coat, placed the strap of her handbag over her arm, and walked out the door.

Bessie watched them amble down the hall and into the elevator. A tear slid down her cheek and she wiped it away. "Good-bye," she whispered.

Aldo had told her not to say anything to anyone about leaving, and she hadn't. But she couldn't leave her family without telling them she was all right. She didn't want them to worry about whether or not she'd been abducted or taken against her will. So in a short note, she told them she'd fallen in love, and due to circumstances beyond her control, she'd left town.

She never mentioned they'd never see her again. What was the point? She placed the note on the table in the kitchen where her mother would find it in the morning and went to meet Aldo.

Bessie hated the idea of going down to the waterfront alone. The docks weren't the safest place for a young woman, but she knew Aldo wouldn't let anything happen to her. She glanced at the instructions to make sure the cabby had taken her to the right place because she didn't really know East Boston. Hesitantly, the taxi driver pulled away from the curb, but her confident wave made him press on. She stood in front of the East Boston Trading Company. Grain and coal silos loomed around her, and she could hear trains switching tracks in the distance.

Darkness draped the street.

A solitary light glowed above the Trading Company door, and a puddle glistened on the ground beneath her feet.

Great. The only puddle on the street and she had to step smack in the middle of it. When she glanced around, she spotted a figure standing in the shadows.

"Who's there?" Bessie called nervously.

A match strike illuminated a man's face sucking air through his cigar. It had been over a year, but she recognized the man as Aldo's father.

"You frightened me," she said.

He took a long drag. The tobacco's hot ember glowed red. "This is not a safe place for a young woman at night."

"I'm meeting someone," she said.

He surveyed the harbor. "It's nice to see the light again."

Bessie didn't understand. "I beg your pardon?"

"The three-mile light on Little Brewster Island. It was extinguished for the duration of the war. It throws 100,000 candles every thirty seconds," Vito said. He spun abruptly, and something sinister in his eyes took her breath away. "Who were you meeting?"

Bessie knew Aldo had told her not to tell anyone about their plans but making up some cockamamie story instead of the truth seemed like the wrong thing to do right now. "Aldo asked me to meet him here."

He nodded and took another long drag of his cigar. "I convinced Aldo he'd made a mistake." He examined his nails. "The captain of the vessel he'd booked passage with has met with an unfortunate accident."

Her stomach heaved.

"And once I told Aldo to do what was expected of him, he knew it would be in your best interest."

Bessie set her jaw. "And are you a man of your word?"

Vito nodded. "If Aldo keeps his end of the bargain, so will I."

She let out the breath she'd been holding and nearly collapsed in relief. Her hands began to shake uncontrollably. She wrapped her arms around her waist to still them, and when she turned toward him, Vito had evaporated into the mist. She dragged her suitcase to the main road and hailed the first cab passing by.

As she climbed into the back of the cab, she noticed a dark smudge across the toe of her brand-new white pumps. When she bent to clean it off, a coppery smell filled her nostrils. The smear was sticky. Since she began working at a doctor's office, the scent had become a familiar one.

It was blood.

She gawked at her red finger and shuddered. The captain.

The puddle.

For the next few days, she scanned the Herald's notice page for any news.

Nothing was ever reported.

She began worrying that maybe the blood had been Aldo's and not some phantom captain's.

One week later, as she read the *Boston Herald*'s newspaper headline it was made clear. She would never see or hear from Aldo, ever again.

"Two Prominent Mob Families Unite in Holy Matrimony."

"That rat bastard!" Skye slapped the journal shut and dropped the brooch on top of it.

Two people at the next table ogled her.

"Sorry," Skye said. Thank goodness the morning rush had already come and gone. She packed everything away in her bag along with the sleeve of medals she'd pulled out of her suitcase and went to the stop to wait for the next bus.

CHAPTER 19

V ito Genovese kept creeping into her thoughts as she waited. He was not a nice man and her aunt had learned a hard lesson. She could only imagine how heartbroken Bessie must have been when Aldo married another woman. The shock would have shaken the very beliefs Bessie lived by.

The simple fact that Aldo married someone else a few weeks after they were supposed to run away together meant he took his father's threat and promise seriously.

He must have loved Bessie very much.

Love.

It made her wonder if she would ever experience a love like that.

Immediately, she thought of Jet.

How could a brave man like Jet be such an emotional chicken?

The irony made her crazy.

It had been one of the reasons she decided to time her arrival at the castle after the sounding of the one o'clock gun.

Jet had obviously sustained a severe injury, one he was still recuperating from. But other than that, he was well put together, as far as she could tell.

He hovered around the six-foot mark. Her wandering hands told her he was a solid wall of muscle. The lines etched around his dark brooding eyes indicated he lived in constant pain.

Maybe the pain made it impossible for him to think clearly.

Over the years, Skye knew several actors with drug dependencies. Not that she thought Jet had a problem. His behavior may have been erratic, but he'd never appeared confused or disoriented, nor did he slur his speech or words. He made it perfectly clear he wanted her to leave him alone—which is exactly what she would do after she delivered William McDougall's medals.

Skye arrived at the gate, and the woman at the kiosk smiled and told her she could go straight through to the museum; the captain was expecting her. Well at least she didn't have to pay for another castle tour. He'd been thoughtful enough to put her on a list, yet another tick discounting the over-medicated theory.

When she arrived at his office, he was nowhere to be found, so Skye made herself comfortable in the chair across the desk. After a few idle moments, she stood up and placed her purse on the desk to dig out Bessie's journal, and in the process knocked a stack of files onto the floor. She bent down and collected the contents of a KIA folder.

She glanced at a photograph of a red-haired, freckle-faced soldier. Private Benjamin Graham, aka Busy□The twenty-four-year-old kid had been killed in action. She read the description. Private Benjamin Graham died as a result of his wounds. Deployed on Op Telic, the raid went deep into Basra, as part of the Black Watch Battle Group on assignment to locate and destroy Iraqi propaganda transmitters and militia headquarters. Upon mission completion, the squadron remained and Graham was severely injured when he uncovered an ammunition stash.

"Interesting reading?" Jet's voice boomed from the entrance to his office.

Skye startled and shoved the paperwork back into the jacket and put it back on top of the desk. "I was rooting around in my purse and knocked the file on the floor."

"Really? Cause it seemed like you were rooting around in my files, not your purse," Jet said, his arms crossed over his chest.

"When I saw his picture, I had to find out what happened. He was so young."

Jet's jaw could have been carved out of granite. "Busy was a member of my team. Hard worker, a little too eager." Jet's faraway demeanor sharpened. "They told me you were waiting in here. I thought you might like to see where we're going to display your great uncle's medals." He hurried away without waiting for her.

She put the file back on Jet's desk, grabbed her purse, and fell into step behind him. They ambled through the corridor and gift shop to the exhibits where the history of the regiment unfolded in chronological order with murals, maps, and dioramas.

Skye glanced at boards of pinned medals. "How large is the museum's collection?" she asked.

"Too large to be openly displayed. We rotate the artifacts. Only a small portion is out at any given time. The rest is housed in drawers that may be viewed on request. Your aunt's father was part of the S3-606 regiment, and I've made a spot for his medals alongside his mates."

Jet's consideration made Skye feel like she carried very precious cargo indeed. And she knew that Aunt Bessie would be smiling down on her for ensuring her father's sacrifice and memory would always be remembered in this place with his peers.

Jet opened a door on the far side of the room. Inside was a wall of drawers like safety deposit boxes in a bank. Each drawer represented a regiment.

"Here it is," Jet said. He slid it open. Gold buttons and medals gleamed. Protected from bright light, the ribbons suspending the medals were vibrant reds and greens.

"Would you like to place the medals beside William's name?" Jet asked.

Skye felt like she'd been given an honor. The drawer didn't just contain fabric and metal, it documented a fallen hero, a man who fought and gave his life so she could live a better one. Skye reached into her bag and removed the case Bessie stored them in. She opened the lid and placed each one inside the drawer. Finally, Skye removed the saucer-sized medallion with the personalized inscription.

"If you don't mind, I'd like that one to go on display," Jet said, "If you'll follow me, I'll show you where."

She strode along behind him.

Jet filled out his uniform indecently. He didn't wear strong cologne, but she thought she could smell fresh limes, a clean and invigorating scent. She studied him. He carried a cane, but he didn't depend on it very much. He seemed to have it just in case he lost his balance. She guessed he continually pushed himself. Pain etched deep grooves in his forehead, despite his efforts to conceal it.

"The exhibit is not open to the public yet, but it will be very soon."

Skye followed him into another room containing a diorama on chemical warfare.

"Your great uncle, being a victim of mustard gas, was of great interest to us."

The elaborately detailed exhibit explained the toxic agent in great detail. The horrific diorama nearly made her sick to her stomach. On the far wall, two hundred bronze saucer medallions surrounded a collage of black and white photos.

"I would like the medallion to be a part of the frame for our collage. Did you bring the photos with you?"

She dug into her purse again and pulled out an envelope. Inside were three photos, which she handed to Jet. One of William reclining on his barracks cot, one taken with a handful of his mates outside of the barracks, and one of Bessie's mother, Margaret. "I'd like to have these enlarged to add to the collage, if you don't mind."

"That would be great," Skye said.

Just then the door pushed open, and a uniformed man poked his head through the door. When he saw the captain, he saluted. "There's an urgent phone call for you in your office, Captain."

Jet nodded. "I've been expecting it. Private Muldowney, would you please entertain Ms. Andrews while I'm gone."

"Yes, Sir." The private came into the room and stood like a statue beside Skye after Jet left the room.

"At ease, soldier," Skye said, smiling.

The young private smiled back at her and did just that. "Old habits."

"Have you been stationed at the museum for a long time?" she asked.

"For the past two months," he said. "I came down with a case of the chicken pox the day before my deployment to CATT in Germany."

Skye mistook the private's blemishes for acne. Couldn't blame her, the young soldier couldn't be older than nineteen. "Chicken pox? How did you escape that childhood disease?"

"I never had any brothers or sisters. My mom homeschooled me. I guess you could say I led a very sheltered life up until I enlisted."

"You seem okay now."

"I am. But I was pretty sick for a while. I would have paid someone to shoot me. The pox went into my eyes, and I had to see an ophthalmologist. But I'm a hundred percent now. I haven't left to join the rest of my company in Germany because the captain insisted I stay for tonight's party."

"A party?"

"It's a Royal Scots reunion. Every few years, soldiers and family members get together to reminisce."

"Is it by invitation only?"

"No. In fact, you'd be quite welcome because you're here donating a loved one's badges and colors."

The door opened and the private jumped to attention. Light spilled into the room followed by Jet. "Thanks for your assistance, Muldowney. That will be all."

He nodded to Skye, saluted the captain, and left the room. Jet faced Skye. "I guess we're all finished here. If you have any questions or concerns regarding your great uncle's memorabilia, please don't hesitate to contact me."

Skye nodded and gathered her bag. "Come to think of it, I do have a question."

Jet gave her his undivided attention.

She became lost in his eyes and felt the attraction tugging at her. She appreciated his handsome face, and for a moment, she hoped he'd been receiving her obvious signals. Maybe the captain would actually relax his guard in a social atmosphere, perhaps even act on impulse.

"Not exactly a question. More like information."

"Okay, what would you like to know?"

"I'd like to know where the party is being held," Skye said. "And what time it starts."

CHAPTER 20

Skye could barely stop from laughing as Jet hemmed and hawed over telling her where they were holding the Royal Scots reunion. He tried to thwart her from coming by telling her the location was on the outskirts of Edinburgh and inaccessible by public transportation. When she told him she would get a ride, he all but groaned.

With the details for the party in hand, Skye left the castle. She began walking the Royal Mile, and before she knew it, she found herself in front of the Luckenbooth shop, again.

The bell above the door chimed as she entered. Lang appeared at the curtain. "I've been expecting you."

"I knew it! You're an oracle too," Skye said. "There's no way you could have known, because I didn't plan this visit, it just sort of happened."

Lang went over to the door and flipped the sign that said "Back in 10 minutes." "I think we should sit and have some tea while I answer all your questions."

All Skye could do was nod. She didn't even know she had questions to be answered until Lang mentioned it. Skye followed her into the back room of the shop and sat down at the table. Could Lang read her mind?

"No, dear, I can't read your mind," she said, pouring boiling water into the pot. "And before you ask, my knowledge has nothing to do with God, the devil, or religious affiliations either. To put it simply, there is a connection between our brooches. That's all. I'm not sure how I'll manage when my stone dies. It's been my constant companion my entire life."

"Your stone is dying?"

Lang nodded. "Yours too. Tell me, why don't you wear the Luckenbooth?"

Skye shrugged and folded her hands in her lap. "The pin isn't really mine to wear. Originally, it belonged to my Aunt Bessie, who passed away a month or so ago. She gifted it to a friend of hers, a man, and he asked me to lay it to rest with her. But even if the brooch was mine, I don't think I could wear it."

"Why not?"

"When I first got it, the stone stayed very hot. So hot I thought it might burn a hole in my jacket."

Lang laughed. "That's exactly why I've never worn mine. But mine won't burn much longer. The stone has cooled a great deal over the last little while. That's how I know it's at the end of its life. When it dies, the blue in the stone will...it will be as cold and clear as ice."

"My Luckenbooth has cooled too," Skye said. "Are you certain it's dying?"

"I am."

Lang sat down in the seat across from Skye. She poured two cups of tea. Her brow creased. "Your aunt must have been a very powerful Sibyl to give the brooch to another and still have the gift of sight. Was this friend of hers in danger?"

Skye's fingers and toes began to tingle. This woman seemed to have too much knowledge for Skye not to listen. "Yes." Skye opened her purse, dug out her aunt's journal, and handed it to Lang. "My aunt left this to me."

Lang placed her spectacles, suspended from a cord around her neck, on the end of her nose. She traced the pattern of the Luckenbooth hand-tooled on the leather cover and opened it. "I haven't seen this arcane script in well over eighty years."

Skye narrowed her eyes. "Can you read it?"

"No," Lang said, returning the book to her.

"Me neither. I couldn't decipher a word without the brooch." Skye's stomach lurched because she was nowhere near finishing the book. "How long do you think I have before the brooch dies?"

"Not long. It could be days or weeks. There is no way to be certain."

Maybe Skye should read the rest of the journal in one sitting.

Lang placed her hand on top of Skye's—she must have noticed her upset. "Your aunt saw all this. That's the reason she left you the journal. She's trying to tell you something. Or she's trying to keep you safe and out of harm's way."

Skye listened to Lang. The elderly woman's words had a formality to them. It took Skye a moment to interpret the meaning. "Am I in danger?"

"Only you can answer that question." Lang sipped her tea.

"I don't understand," Skye said staring at the unintelligible script on the pages. "If something bad is about to happen, why doesn't she just tell me about it?"

"Sibyls are bound by unwritten laws. Our magic doesn't work like that. Your aunt couldn't use her gift of sight to alter her own destiny. She could only see her future through the people around her. She couldn't tell you what would happen because the moment she did, it would no longer be a certainty. Knowledge makes the certain, uncertain. You must trust her. Her journal will show you exactly what you need to see."

Tears welled in Skye's eyes and a lump formed in her throat.

"What's wrong child?"

"She told me we had a connection, and she could see the future." Tears spilled. "I didn't believe her."

Lang reached over and gave Skye a squeeze. "At that time, you weren't supposed to. You know now, that's all that matters."

Skye finished her tea, and she said her good-byes. Skye had the oddest feeling their paths would never cross again.

She climbed onto the bus and headed back to Jason's loft.

A light drizzle misted the window beside her, and she could see her reflection.

Everything that had happened up to this point in her life, Bessie had seen. Skye needed to stay the path and pay close attention to everything Bessie showed her through the pages of the journal. Eventually it would become clear what it all meant.

Skye *had* changed since Bessie died.

In every way.

Skye had never been so bold. She'd been intent on pursuing Captain Jet Dalry since they first met. Why, when he'd told her he wasn't interested, did she keep making advances?

She'd never been attracted enough in someone to push herself on them. And yet, that's exactly what she intended to do tonight. She got off the bus and hoofed the three blocks to Jason's loft. She had the run of the place for another hour before Jason and Tammy got home from the Raverse.

It had been ages since she allowed herself the luxury of a bubble bath. The last time had been back when she lived in New York.

Right now, New York seemed like a lifetime ago.

She filled the tub with eucalyptus bath salts and sank into the soothing water with the journal and the brooch, eager to see how Bessie handled the heartbreak of Aldo's marriage.

It should have been one of the best Christmases of Bessie's entire life, considering the end of the war and the declaration of peace, but her heart had been skewered. She'd never been unhappier.

Heartsick, even her mother had detected her grief. Tears were never far from her eyes. Always lost in thought, she couldn't stop thinking about what her life would have been like if Aldo had been successful in eluding his father that fateful night.

She never heard a peep from Aldo. Not a letter, not a phone call, nothing. Not that it mattered anymore. Nothing he could say would change anything. He'd married another woman. He would never be hers. They would never be together.

Bessie tried to get on with her life. She threw herself into work. At the New Westminster Church, she enrolled in the choir, taught Sunday school, and ran a quilting bee every Tuesday night.

On Wednesdays, Dr. Lamont went to the hospital to check on patients. Bessie stayed at the office and answered the phone until three. She used the afternoon to catch up on her work and tidy the office.

She gathered her purse one Wednesday afternoon and was about to lock up the office for the day when Aldo paid her a surprise visit. The semblance of life she'd worked so hard to mend tore wide open at the seams.

She dropped her purse on the floor spilling the contents.

Aldo bent down beside her and helped her pick everything up. "I'm sorry," he said. "I know it's a shock to see me."

Bessie grabbed her compact and lipstick from his outstretched hand and placed them in her purse. "I'm happy to see you're okay. I saw the blood and I thought that..."

She must have been shaking because suddenly Aldo pulled her into his arms. "Shhh," he said. "I'm fine."

He comforted her. For the first time in months, she felt warm and safe. Before she knew it, he kissed her. And unlike all his previous kisses, this one lacked restraint. The onslaught of pent-up desire was raw. Obviously, he still wanted her. And unless she put a stop to his advances, he'd have her right across the desk.

With a tremendous effort, she broke free and pulled away. "No," she said. "We can't. You're married. You belong to another woman."

"I'm married, that's true enough. But my heart will always belong to you."

She felt her eyes well with tears. She covered her mouth with her hand. "Please don't say things like that."

"Why?" Aldo said. "I don't love her. It was an arranged marriage."

"You'll learn to love her."

"Perhaps."

"This is good-bye."

"It doesn't have to be," Aldo said.

"Yes, it does. I'm not as strong as you. I can't handle being your friend," Bessie said.

Aldo sat her down in the chair and knelt. "I have a proposition for you."

She saw the desire lurking in his eyes.

"I want to take care of you," Aldo said. "Get you your own place, buy you the best furniture and clothes, and take you to all the best shows. You won't have to work anymore."

"You're leaving her? Already?"

Aldo shook his head. "No. I can't do that."

"But…" Suddenly, she understood. She didn't want to believe it. "You want me to be your whore," she whispered.

"Those are your words, not mine. I love you. I'm just trying to fix this mess."

"And this is your solution? You want me to disassociate myself from my family and the church. Live in sin. See you whenever you get the urge?"

"Bessie, it wouldn't be like that."

"And what about your father? He threatened to kill my family and me. I'd always be afraid waiting for the worst."

"You and your family will be perfectly safe."

"How can you be so sure?" she asked.

"Because this was his idea."

Skye shook with anger. She closed the journal and tossed it onto the floor before she dropped it into the tub. She pulled the plug and let the water drain.

How could Aldo ask Bessie to be his mistress? How could he think Bessie would go along with such a ridiculous idea?

The slam of the flat door got her attention.

"Skye?" Jason's voice sounded on the other side of the bathroom door.

"I'm just getting out of the tub," she said. "Where's Tammy?"

"She's here. It's pouring outside. Both of us got soaked to the skin in a mad dash from the car. Can you pass us a couple of towels so we can dry off?"

"Sure. Hold on." Skye wrapped herself in her robe. She grabbed a couple from the shelf, opened the door, and passed them to Jason. "I'll be right out."

Skye ran a brush through her hair and smoothed some peach scented lotion over her skin. When she pressed into the hall, she nearly ran over Jason, who seemed to be hovering close to the door.

He put his finger up to his mouth. "I hoped you'd be home. Tammy's pretty down. I thought all of us could go out somewhere. Try to get her mind off the fire."

"Great idea because we've been invited to a party," Skye said. No one said she couldn't bring friends with her. The more the merrier, right? An evening out would help Jason make his move. Maybe all he needed was a push to take things to the next level.

Maybe that would be true for Jet too.

She prayed it would help him relax because she desperately wanted to feel his arms around her again.

"Tell Tammy to get dressed," Skye said. "We're supposed to be there by eight."

Chapter 21

The Dreghorn Barracks were located just beyond the roundabout, off Edinburgh's A720 bypass. The facility had been built on the estate of the demolished Dreghorn Castle when it fell into neglect and disrepair.

Jason drove onto the grounds, and signs led the partygoers to the community center with ample parking for over a hundred cars.

Inside the building, Skye, Jason, and Tammy were met by the same soldier who told Skye about the party earlier in the afternoon. "Ms. Andrews," he said. "Private Kevin Muldowney, at your service. I'm so glad you could make it."

"I wouldn't have missed it," Skye said.

Muldowney glanced over at Jason and Tammy.

"Oh," Skye said. "These are a couple friends of mine. Jason Hansome and Tammy Roundtree."

"Wonderful," he exclaimed.

"What was the name and rank of the Royal Scot you're representing?" Muldowney asked, grabbing three stickers.

"William Patterson McDougall. But I'm afraid I can't remember his regiment number," Skye said.

"53-606," Jet said from behind.

Skye's breath caught when she saw him in his uniform. She whispered thank you.

Muldowney wrote the information on each tag and handed them to Skye. "Just place them on your purse or on your shirt. Then introductions can be made from there."

Skye handed a sticker to Jason and Tammy. When she swiveled, Jet had vanished as quickly as he'd appeared.

"There's a cash bar in the north corner," Muldowney said. "Grab yourselves a table and enjoy."

Skye nodded. She tried not to let her disappointment show. Jet Dalry was the most confusing man she'd ever not gotten to know. Here, she thought she would have to actively pursue him all night. Then, out of the blue, he shows up, blows her plan into the stratosphere, and then vaporizes again. It would likely swing back and forth all night.

"There's a table right over there," Jason said.

He led the women through a maze of white-linen tables and mingling people. The hall pulled double duty as a gymnasium and theater, with twenty-five-foot ceilings. More than half of the guests were uniformed, but no kilts; the other half were outfitted in casual party-wear. Excitement and comradery shimmered in the partygoers and put Skye at ease right away. They found a seat, and Jason set off to purchase the first round.

"Has Jason made his move yet?" Skye asked.

"No. He's been the perfect gentleman, dammit. I don't know what I would have done without him in light of the fire and all, but sometimes I just want to grab him and kiss his face off."

"Why don't you?" Skye said.

"I'm afraid he won't kiss me back."

"At least you'd have an answer. Wouldn't that be better than this limbo?"

"Maybe."

Jason returned to the table carrying three drafts. "What did I miss?" he asked, setting the beers in front of Tammy and Skye.

"Nothing yet," Skye said, motioning toward the stage where a disc jockey worked to set up his equipment.

Skye winked at Tammy. "So how are things going at the Raverse? All the bugs worked out of the performance for opening night?"

Jason answered. "We've got a good show. I can see it running for a long time."

"What constitutes a long time?" Skye asked.

"Most of our projects are experimental, so six months is considered a long run."

"Six months is nothing in New York."

"Maybe so, but I prefer to always be working on new projects. Keeps everything fresh."

The disc jockey grabbed his microphone and tapped it, right before feedback from the equipment caused an ear-splitting squeal. "Testing, one, two, three," he said. Very soon he fixed the problem, and he began spinning songs.

While the music blared, Muldowney landed at the table. "My replacement just arrived, and I hoped I could sit with you?" He widened his big raccoon eyes and Skye guessed he wanted to hit on her. They were years apart, but his youth didn't seem to deter him in the least.

"Sure," Skye said, wondering how to let him down gently. "So Private Kevin Muldowney," Skye yelled above the pounding music. "Do you have a girlfriend at home, or did you simply break her heart when you left town?"

A smile spread across the young man's face. "My girlfriend's name is Gwen. We've been going out for about five years. I almost popped the question before I left. Then I came down with the chicken pox. You know the rest."

"Five years is a long time to stay with one person," Skye said. "You must love her a lot." And just like that, any idea he had entertained about coming on to her seemed to evaporate like early morning dew.

"I'm going to ask her to come and live with me on the base when I get back from Germany."

"Do all personnel live here on the base?" Skye asked.

The disc jockey announced his next song and Tammy groaned. 'In Your Eyes' by Peter Gabriel is my all-time favorite." She took a swig of beer and spoke to Jason. "Dance with me?"

Jason shrugged. "I'm not a fan of anything not choreographed, but I will if you insist." He got up and held Tammy's chair. The bass from the music caused the floor to vibrate. Skye gave her a *way-to-go* nod.

Kevin waited until Jason and Tammy left before he answered Skye's question. "Some people prefer living off base, but it can get pretty expensive."

"Does the captain live on the base?" she asked as conversationally as possible.

"No, he lives much closer to the castle. He moved there after he was released from the veteran's hospital. Actually, that's where I met him. We shared a room for a couple of days when they thought the pox were going to go into my eyes."

Skye nodded. "What happened to him?"

Kevin gave the hall a cursory glance.

"He doesn't really talk about it. I heard his company came across a buried ammunition store in Iraq. The stash had been booby-trapped. A younger member of his team didn't follow procedure. The captain tried to stop him, but it was too late. The private lost both legs and the captain sustained severe upper leg injuries."

Skye felt pummeled by the information. She knew Jet had been injured, but the fact that he sustained his injuries trying to save another man's life made her stomach roil.

"The private recently passed away from complications. The captain is attending the memorial service next weekend in Kilmarnock. I'll be giving him a lift to the train station."

Jason and Tammy came bounding back to the table. Tammy motioned toward Skye's half-finished beer. "Did you want another?"

"No," she said. "You go ahead."

"What about you, Kevin?"

"No, thank you. I told the captain that I'd be available to help him in case someone has too much to drink."

"I guess he's still on the clock then."

"I've never seen him off the clock. He's a machine. He's always working. This morning, before you arrived at the museum, we made room for your uncle's medals and colors in his unit's drawer."

Skye stilled. How interesting. Kilmarnock. William McDougall's regiment number. Why didn't she think of it before?

"Ms. Andrews? Is something wrong?"

"No," Skye said, snapping out of her trance. "I'd like to find the captain to thank him for all the trouble he went to. Do you have any idea where he might be?"

Kevin scanned the room. "The last time I saw him he was standing over at the door."

"I'll be right back," she said, smiling. Suddenly, she had a legitimate reason for seeking out the captain—something other than the magnetic attraction she felt every time they came into contact.

She meandered through the tables and nearly made it to the door when a burly uniformed man stood up and blocked her path. "Hey, gorgeous," he said. "How about a dance?"

Careful not to make eye contact, Skye moved left, then right to walk around the man who'd obviously had too much to drink.

"We could make beautiful music," he slurred. He reached out and clamped his hands around Skye's waist.

A familiar voice rang out. "Sergeant?" Jet tapped the bruiser on the shoulder. "Kindly take your hands off my date."

The sergeant stepped back and stumbled. Listing to the right, he saluted and nearly toppled a table in the process. Two of his buddies came to his rescue. "He doesn't want any trouble, Captain. He's had a little too much to drink. We'll make sure he gets home safely."

Jet nodded and grabbed Skye's hand. He pulled her along with him. Once they were out of the aisle, he faced her. "Are you all right?" he asked.

"I'm fine. Thank you," she said. "Your date? That's a good one. And here I thought it was a woman's prerogative to change her mind. You seem to be the only one flipping back and forth."

A grin wobbled on his face.

"Or have you reverted to not liking me, again?"

That question caused Jet to scowl. "Did you want something?" he asked.

"You don't waste any time with small talk, do you?" But two could play that game. She'd hit him with her suspicions to catch him off guard. "I wanted to know how you knew my great uncle's regiment number. I only casually mentioned his name in passing yesterday, a name you didn't write down or record."

Captain Jet Dalry didn't blink, nor did he appear to have an answer to her question.

"Let me tell you what I think," she said. "I think you already knew my information because you obtained it when you were at the Commonwealth War Graves Commission. I think John Smilie asked you to oversee the work in Kilmarnock to make sure everything gets done in a timely fashion because you'll be attending a memorial service there this coming weekend."

Jet couldn't stop staring at Skye's mouth and thinking about kissing her. Did she taste like peaches and cream—soft and sweet? He been fighting the urge to take her into his arms and kiss her properly.

He'd spotted her the moment she arrived.

Actually, he felt like he'd been riding a roller coaster from the very first moment they met. Damned carnival rides. Too bad his libido didn't seem to be aware of his new physical limitations.

He had to stop thinking about Skye Andrews and sex.

There were too many highs and lows. He was tired of being angry. Tired of lusting and being jealous of normal, unscarred people like Private Muldowney.

Every time he thought about what she'd said to him, he felt like a fish out of water—she could handle being friends if he could.

Being friends with a woman was something he'd never done before.

The explosion in Iraq had certainly changed the playing field. He had to learn how to defend this new position, learn how to accept his disfigurement. "You're absolutely right, but it's not what you think. I agreed to expedite the process for John Smilie because I was going to be there anyway. I wasn't supposed to see you every time I turned around. By the way, how did you know that I would be in Kilmarnock?"

"Kevin mentioned it," Skye said. "I connected the dots from there."

"I'm impressed," Jet said, raising his eyebrows. "I think I might have to start calling you Sherlock."

Skye became very quiet, deadly serious. "Really? Because I think I'm going to tag along with you when you go to Kilmarnock. The sooner everything gets done the sooner my aunt can be interred."

He swallowed. He understood the urgency. She wanted closure for her loved one.

"I leave Friday morning."

"If you give me the name of where you're staying, I'll make sure I'm there when Muldowney comes to collect you. Now c'mon," Skye said, grabbing his hand. "You've logged enough hours today. I'd like to introduce you to a couple of friends of mine."

Skye dragged him back to the table. When Muldowney saw Jet approaching, he jumped up and saluted.

"At ease," Jet said. "Let's dispense with the formalities at this table, shall we?"

Muldowney relaxed and promptly sat down. "Fine by me."

A man seated next to him stood up and stuck out his hand. "Jason Hansome," he said.

"Captain Jet Dalry."

Beside Jason sat a woman. "This is Tammy Roundtree," Jason said.

Jet nodded and sat down beside Skye. In no time, the conversation flowed.

Jet and Jason went to collect another round of drinks, and just when Jet was beginning to think he might actually be able to make a go of this *friends* thing, Skye went and threw a screw into the works.

She asked him to dance.

And she wouldn't take no for an answer.

Chapter 22

"I don't dance," Jet said.

"That's what all men say." Skye pulled him up from the chair and dragged him along behind her.

"Just because I didn't bring my cane this evening doesn't mean I'm any steadier on my feet."

"That's why I waited for a slow song. I can hold onto you and keep you balanced."

Great. Just what he didn't need—to hold Skye in his arms and feel her soft curves pressed against him. Out on the dance floor, she snuggled into his chest.

"I had to get you up here," Skye said. "Jason will never make a move on Tammy while we're hanging around."

"They're not together?"

"Oh, they're together all right, only Jason doesn't know it yet."

"Why the hell not? She's beautiful."

"Yes, inside and out," Skye said. "It's a long story. Jason's got a thing for her, but he's afraid of rejection."

"Hell. That's nothing new. It's called being a man." Jet had to keep talking. This had to be the longest rendition of "With or Without You" by U2 he'd ever heard. He concentrated on not stepping on her toes because the sway of Skye's hips had spiked more than his blood pressure.

How ironic. When he'd given her the brush off back at his office, he should have been more sympathetic, not so blunt. He'd go to flaming hell for telling such a blatant lie.

Finally, the song ended.

When Jet went to head back to the table, Skye stopped him. "We can't go back right now," she whispered into his ear. She leaned around his shoulder to see Jason and Tammy. "Tammy has got her arms around Jason's neck, and I think she's going to kiss him."

Jet couldn't handle Skye pressed against him for another dance, so he grabbed her hand and led her off the dance floor in the opposite direction. "How about a walk?"

He opened the rear exit of the hall, and they went outside.

The air was cool and crisp and fragrant with the smells of honeysuckle and boxwood. Skye's slinky thin black dress, which left nothing to his imagination, wouldn't keep her warm, so he shrugged out of his jacket and wrapped her in it. Her thin heels would aerate the soil and make her unsteady, so he held her hand. "C'mon. I want to show you something."

They trekked along a grassy path. The uneven ground might have been a huge problem for him if it hadn't been quite so light outside. "Do you know the history of the Dreghorn Barracks?" Jet asked.

"Jason mentioned something about there once being a castle on the premises."

"That's right. The castle was demolished in the fifties, but much of the rubble remains on the site. Only two of the original gatehouses survived. One in Dreghorn Loan and the other on Oxgangs Road."

The path narrowed and veered to the right.

"This here is the gatehouse of Dreghorn Loan."

In the moonlight, Skye could see the grand Tudor-Gothic gatehouse. He guided her around the front of the building where they could oversee the valley. "That's Redford Barracks down the hill. Here," he said, giving her a hand to step on top of the stone wall. A moment later he joined her. "I love coming here. You can see the whole valley—a rich patchwork of fields bordered by stone hedges. The way the gatehouse is situated, you'd almost think you're from a different century."

Skye faced him.

"What?" he said, finally.

"You never cease to amaze me. Just when I think I've figured you out, you go and do something that makes me think I've only scratched the surface."

If only he could tell her the truth.

"I've been thinking," he said. "You don't have to go to Kilmarnock if you don't want to. I can call you as soon as everything is ready for you if it's more convenient."

"No," Skye said. "It's time I moved out of Jason's loft. I've already worn out my welcome. Jason and I are just friends, but Tammy is another story. Her flat burned down, and Jason insisted she stay with him. I should have gotten a room somewhere right away, but he wouldn't hear of it. Believe me, going to Kilmarnock is a good idea all around."

Despite being a fair distance from the hall, the thump of the music filled the silence.

"Do you want to talk about the memorial service you're attending?" Skye whispered.

Another painful truth.

He didn't want to reopen that particular wound, but there was something about the way she asked. The intonation in her voice and the gentle squeeze of her hand loosened his tongue. "I thought Muldowney had already given you the scoop."

"He didn't mean any disrespect. He said you don't ever talk about what happened—all he's heard is scuttlebutt."

"Scuttlebutt? That doesn't sound good."

"He said one of your men got wounded by a booby-trapped cache of ammunition and weapons."

Jet's hands balled into tight fists. "He's the one you read about in my office—Private Benjamin Graham. The entire company called him Busy. He couldn't sit still. He was into everything. I should have known he would be the first to try to grab a gun and haul it out of that hole."

"It's not your fault," Skye said.

"All the men under my command were my responsibility."

"That's not what I meant."

"I know what you meant. But don't. I've heard enough psychobabble from shrinks in the last six months to float a boat." Jet looked away.

"Kevin said Private Graham lost both of his legs."

Jet's eyes teared. "Yes, he did." Quickly, he wiped them away.

"He said you tried to get to him, tried to stop him."

"I wasn't fast enough. When the smoke cleared, my lower extremities were chewed up, just as if they'd been put through a meat grinder."

Skye put her hand to her mouth. "I'm so sorry," she said.

"You know, Busy and I shared a hospital room for the longest time when we got back. We became really close. He said something to me before he died that still haunts me. He told me not to feel sorry for him. He told me to get mad." Jet tipped his head heavenward. "Busy chose the easy way out. Living seemed like too big a challenge. Unlike me. He said I was too stubborn a cuss to ever give up."

"I'm glad," Skye said.

Jet had been so engrossed in their conversation he hadn't noticed the music had stopped. "I guess we should get back. Sounds like things are winding down."

He eased himself off the wall and winced with the effort. It took a moment to catch his breath before he reached over and helped Skye. His hands nearly encircled her waist, and she placed her arms around his neck.

He waged an internal war to kiss her. He reached up to pull her arms free but stopped.

One kiss couldn't hurt.

As soon as her feet touched the ground, he set her aside. "After you." The beguiling sway of her hips taunted him. A short hike and they were back inside the hall.

"We were wondering where you two went?" Tammy said, spotting Skye's approach.

"For a walk," Skye said. She could feel the waves of intensity radiating from Jet standing right behind her. The man acted like a powder keg too. He needed to relax, enjoy life a little more.

"Are you ready to leave?" Tammy asked.

"You guys go ahead, I'll be there in a minute," Skye said.

"Would you like to be my guest this Thursday night at the opening of *The Other Woman*?" Skye faced Jet.

"I've never been to the theater," Jet said.

"Then you have to come," Skye said. She seemed to know he needed more convincing. "Please. For me?"

"Why not?" Jet said on a shrug.

"Terrific. Meet me outside of the Raverse at seven. Thanks for tonight," she said. Doing what he'd failed to do all night, she kissed him sweetly on the cheek. "I had a great time."

CHAPTER 23

Over the next few days, Skye went sightseeing and visited the Royal Botanic Gardens, the Grassmarket, and Greyfriars Kirk while Tammy and Jason were up to their chins with pre-show preparations.

Skye had been very angry with Aldo and had taken a brief hiatus from Bessie's journal. On Thursday, Skye didn't want to stray too far from the flat, so she flopped on Jason's couch, grabbed the journal and brooch, and dug in for the next installment.

Bessie said good-bye to Aldo.

Over the next few months, she lost twenty pounds and became a recluse. She took a leave of absence from the church choir, as she no longer felt like singing. She continued to teach Sunday school because she couldn't bear to disappoint the children. They were innocents. They didn't need to face upset so early on in their lives—it would find them soon enough.

She went through the motions of living and became fixated with the prisoners of war in Nazi Germany. Nazi Germany had become her morbid fascination—she lived to hear the Nuremberg trials.

The radio reports mesmerized her. She listened to snippets during work hours and immersed herself in the transcripts in the evenings. She desperately craved justice for the victims, and she dreamt about punishing the guilty parties. She listened to trial excerpts. Prisoners had been placed inside specially constructed boxes where the air pressure was removed and they tore their faces to shreds with their fingernails, but not before they went mad. After they died, their carcasses were tanned and made into purses for high-ranking officials' wives or driving gloves for SS officers. She listened to every last horrific detail. She fantasized about Vito being the next defendant on trial.

So much for daydreams.

All her friends and relations became concerned about her. Bart made a special trip to visit her one night. Both mother and Bart sat down and tried to get her to tell them what bothered her.

"I'm fine," she said.

"Something is wrong," Bart said. "You never go out with your friends anymore. How do you expect to find a man sitting inside listening to the radio?"

She didn't even have the energy to flinch. Her brother had no idea that she'd already gone down that road. She'd fallen in love and worried herself sick while he fought overseas. She'd given him her heart and soul, and no one—not her mother, brother, or even her best friend, Mima—had the least inkling anything had happened.

The following week it all came to a head when Dr. Lamont scheduled a complete physical exam for her.

"But I'm fine," she said, once again.

"You're not fine," Dr. Lamont said. "I think there's something else going on. I can't have my secretary passing along germs to my patients, now can I?"

She opened her mouth to protest.

"It's not a request, Bessie. If you feel more comfortable with another doctor, I can have Dr. Barry examine you."

She knew nothing she could say would make a difference. If she wanted to keep her job, she'd better relent. She went into the examination room and put on the green gown.

Dr. Lamont's patients told Bessie the good doctor was thorough. Now she knew why. He took his time. He asked questions and actually listened to her answers. He weighed and measured her, took a urine sample, listened to her heart and lungs, checked her ears and throat, and took swabs. His constant banter throughout the examination put her at total ease. He felt her left breast for lumps then switched to the right.

And suddenly he stopped talking.

She knew his routine. He pressed around the nipple in a circular pattern—but he must have forgotten because he stopped mid-exam and started over.

"Something wrong?" she asked.

Dr. Lamont retied my gown and helped me into a sitting position. "Why don't you put yourself back together," he said. "Then come into my office so we can chat."

Bessie got dressed and went into his office.

When she arrived, Dr. Lamont talked with someone on the telephone—an oddity because she hadn't heard it ring. He jotted something on a slip of paper and hung up.

"May I get back to work now?" she said, half-joking, half-serious.

"Bessie, sit down please." His usual smile and cheerful disposition disappeared. "I've taken the liberty of making an appointment with a specialist, actually he's the best in this field right now. He can see you tomorrow morning at nine."

"Hold on a minute. What's wrong? Why do you think I need to see a specialist?"

Dr. Lamont came around his desk and sat in the chair right beside her. "I found an anomaly while doing your breast examination."

"What kind of anomaly?"

"A few lumps. I want a second opinion."

If Bessie lived to be a hundred, she would never forget her appointment with Dr. Miskovic—he was the best in his field because he didn't pull any punches. Like Dr. Lamont, he'd told her to get dressed and come into his office after giving her a thorough examination.

"I concur with Dr. Lamont in his preliminary examination. There are a number of lumps in your breast," he said.

She felt battered. "How many do you mean when you say a number?"

"Four or five."

"Is it cancer?" Bessie felt like one of the prisoner's she'd heard about in the pressurized box—ready to implode.

"Based on the size and shape of these masses, I think so. We need to schedule a mastectomy as soon as possible. But not a radical Halsted mastectomy."

"There are different kinds?"

"There's been a new procedure developed by a Dr. Patey out of Middlesex Hospital in London. He's developed a procedure that's just as effective as Halsted's, only less debilitating. The breast and axillary lymph nodes are removed, but the chest muscle is left intact, so there are less complications and improved arm mobility."

Bessie tuned the doctor out. She felt numb. Who cared about salvaging the muscle underneath her breast? Her breast would still be gone.

"I want to stress the sooner you have surgery the better your odds of survival will be. We don't want the cancer to metastasize. If it has already, we'll run a course of radiation or use a chemotherapeutic agent to shrink the tumorous growths."

Bessie thought about all the mutations she'd read about in the aftermath of Hiroshima due to radiation exposure. Radiation? No thank you. "What's a chemotherapeutic agent?"

"Plant antibiotics and nitrogen mustard compounds."

That sounded somewhat better.

"I need to think about everything you've said." She laughed—a crazy, hysterical warble. Her options were death, Halsted radical mastectomy, or this new modified procedure. "I'll call your office in a few days."

"Leave a message with my secretary. Once you decide to go ahead, we'll need to run some tests. The earliest possible date will be mid-June."

Bessie thanked the doctor and took the Green T home. The surging movement rocked her. She felt like a stranger in her own body—an outsider watching from the sidelines. A homeless man sat on the other side of the boxcar. The surrounding passengers gave him a wide berth—as if he had a communicable disease they might catch if they sat too close. She'd seen the same thing happen in Dr. Lamont's office with influenza.

No.

She didn't want to be pitied or be ostracized, so she decided to keep her condition a secret. Dr. Lamont would be the only one to ever know.

Surgery was scheduled for the last week in July.

As the day approached, she began to have selfish thoughts. Regrets. Things she hadn't done and would likely never do.

Aldo plagued her thoughts.

She lay awake at night and wondered if he was happy. She'd wind the sheets around her, close her eyes and pretend they were Aldo's arms.

Her true love.

Aldo had awakened a passion within her. In the wee hours of the night, she burned for him.

Sometimes, she thought she could feel his hands on her breasts or other places, but when she awoke, she realized her mind was playing tricks on her.

Her confusion escalated. A religious woman having the kind of thoughts she was having made her faith fray around the edges. The hardships God presented her with were too much. Would it have hurt Him to dole out a crumb of hope in return?

The weekend before her surgery, Bart and Jane took mother to Albany to see a house they were thinking of buying. They picked her up Friday morning. They asked her to go, but Bessie wanted to be alone to mentally prepare for her upcoming surgery.

Bessie spent most of the day Friday itemizing a detailed list of her duties for her replacement while she recuperated. When the last patient of the day left, Dr. Lamont called her into his office.

"Are you ready for Monday's surgery?" he asked.

"I think so. Here's the list of duties for my replacement," she said, handing him the sheet in her hand.

He placed the paper on his desk. "I'll check in on you after your surgery. Make sure everything is okay. Then I'll visit on Wednesday to see how you're managing."

"How long do you think they'll keep me in the hospital?"

"Two weeks, maybe more."

"That long?"

Dr. Lamont nodded.

"How long will it be before I can come back to work?"

"That depends on you," Dr. Lamont said. "You'll need to take things day by day. I'd really like you to reconsider your decision to keep your condition a secret. No one is going to think less of you because you have cancer. You're going to need a friend to lean on."

"No. I'll be fine. I don't want anyone's pity."

Dr. Lamont gave up and went home.

The phone rang. She picked it up.

"It's me," Aldo said.

Bessie nearly swooned.

"Don't hang up. I need to see you," he said. "Please."

Bessie tried to still her racing heart. She concentrated on breathing in and out. "Is something wrong? You sound upset."

"Will you come?"

"Where are you?" She couldn't believe she asked that particular question.

"I'm at the Ritz Carlton, top floor, Presidential Suite."

"Did you leave your wife?"

"I can't talk right now," Aldo said in hushed tones. "Can you come at eight?"

Bessie couldn't say no.

She needed to see him as much as he needed to see her. Perhaps this was the crumb of divine intervention she'd pleaded for.

"I'll be there."

CHAPTER 24

The images faded. The stone in the Luckenbook had become cold so she placed it on top of the closed journal.

Skye's eyes welled with tears at the thought of her aunt going through something so traumatic on her own. Aldo had obviously caught her at a weak moment, the cancer no doubt.

Had Aldo left his wife?

Skye glanced at her watch.

Where had the day gone?

She didn't have the time to ponder anything right now. She had to get ready to meet Jet at the theater for opening night.

Skye dressed in a strapless dress—something simple and yet dramatic. She took a cab to the theater and arrived a half hour early. The sidewalk crowded with theatergoers, but she noticed Jet immediately. He was ruggedly handsome in his military dress—his chest gleamed with medals. Her mouth went completely dry. "I see you've left your cane at home again," she said, sidling up to him.

"For good, I hope. I didn't want to become dependent on it."

"Do you always push yourself to the nth degree?"

"Yes."

He didn't even take a moment to consider his answer. Skye shook her head and slipped her arm through his. "Are you ready to go inside?"

"In a minute." Jet reached under the jacket draped over his arm and pulled out a plastic container holding a simple but elegant corsage—a single orchid. "The woman at the shop assured me that it would go with anything." He glanced at her dress. "But there's nowhere to pin it. Your dress doesn't have any straps. Not that I'm complaining...you're gorgeous."

She felt warm inside. She had hoped for this kind of reaction from him. Just because he'd insisted they be friends didn't mean she had to be on board with those terms. Her dress had been a deliberate choice. The plunging back dipped low and kept undergarments to a minimum.

"The orchid is beautiful," Skye said, removing it from the container. She untwisted the elastic around the stem and placed the corsage on her wrist. "Thank you for being so thoughtful," she said. She stood on tiptoes and brushed a light kiss on his cheek.

The show was an engaging romp about love and misinterpreting your lover's signals—kind of like Jason and Tammy's real-life situation—except for the quirky dancing and the jovial singing. At intermission, Skye and Jet went into the lobby for Jet to stretch his legs.

"What do you think?" Skye asked.

Jet nodded. "It's better than I thought it would be. There's good chemistry between Jason and Tammy. Which brings me to my next question. Have those two gotten together yet?"

"I'm afraid not. I'm hoping things will heat up when I leave. I've been packed and ready since the first of the week."

A bell sounded and the show resumed.

Skye couldn't believe how comfortable she felt in Jet's company. Even the silent moments didn't feel awkward. He may have told her he just wanted to be friends, but his body language said something else entirely. He didn't want her to touch him, but he had no such rule for himself. While they'd been seated in the theater, she felt the periodic brush of his knee against her leg. And when they returned to their seats after intermission, his hand rested possessively on the small of her bare back.

After a standing ovation, roses were tossed on the stage and collected by the members of the cast as they came out one by one to take their bows. Skye invited Jet to the Backstage Pub for the private after-party. They sat at a table in the back and waited for the cast to arrive.

"Explain something to me," Jet said, sipping his ale. "How is it that Jason and Tammy aren't together? He spent the last ten minutes kissing her on stage."

Skye started to laugh. "It's hard to explain. But when you see an actor kissing in a scene, they're actually thinking about a whole bunch of unromantic stuff. The angle of their heads, where to place their hands, whether or not there is enough movement for the audience to feel the passion of the kiss."

"Is it that way even if they have the hots for each other?"

Skye stopped. "That I can't answer. I've never kissed someone on stage I've been attracted to."

"If I kissed someone the way Jason kissed Tammy and then had to pretend nothing passed between us, I'd be more than a little frustrated."

Jet's kisses in the castle office came to mind. She wanted to bring his attention to it but decided against it. "If that's the case, we'll know in an awful hurry," Skye said.

"How so?"

"Jason will be drinking scotch."

Over the next ten minutes, the bar began to buzz as members of the Raverse cast and crew filtered in. Brad Bradbury, a critic from the Edinburgh *Scotsman*, stood at the bar and began interviewing members of the cast as they arrived.

Through the din, compliments flew in every direction. It seemed the Raverse had a hit on their hands, and Hans Gruber was revered for his refreshing interpretation of the show.

Both Skye and Jet talked and mingled with the crew, waiting for Jason to work his way over to them.

Talbot sidled up to Skye. "It must be pretty crowded at Jason's loft with the three of you living there."

How did Talbot know everyone else's business?

"I don't know what you said to Tammy, but whatever it was worked," Talbot continued. "Her performance reminded me of you in the old days."

Skye didn't really do anything. She sat in on one rehearsal. Tammy was a talented actress. She smiled and put her hand on Jet's shoulder. "Jet this is Talbot James, the stage manager."

Jet shook Talbot's hand.

Jason waved and headed straight over. "What did you think of the show?" he asked.

Skye nodded. "Talbot said it reminded him of our school days."

Jason clapped Talbot on the back. "I thought so too, man. I mean there are a couple of things we need to work out, but all-in-all, I thought we rocked it." Jason flagged the barmaid and ordered another Glenlivet after downing the one in his hand.

Jet glanced back at her.

"Where's Tammy?" Skye asked. "I want to congratulate her."

"She's over there," Jason said, pointing toward the bar. "Talking with Hans."

"I'll be right back," she said.

Skye left Jason, Jet, and Talbot and went to speak with Tammy. When she caught up with her, she pulled her aside. "Terrific performance," she said. Then she leaned in to give her a hug and whispered in her ear. "Jason's drinking scotch again."

Tammy scanned the crowd. "Bugger, with Bradbury here? We've got to get him out of here before he commits professional suicide."

Skye spotted the exit in the rear. "You say your good-byes and Jet and I will take him out the back door."

Jet watched Skye weave her way over to Tammy.

"How do you know Skye?" Talbot asked.

Skye and Tammy huddled. They appeared to be discussing Jason who, a moment ago, slung his arm around the waitress. Both Skye and Tammy put their empty glasses on the bar. Tammy headed toward the front door and Skye went to rescue the waitress.

Jason staggered. He'd knock Skye over if he put his full weight on her. "Can't talk right now," Jet said, squeezing Talbot's shoulder. Jet strode over to Jason and put his arm around his neck. Skye led them out the back door of the pub and into the alley.

"Tell me why we're kidnapping a grown man?" Jet asked. He guided Jason down the narrow alleyway.

"The last thing Jason needs right now is a review from Brad Bradbury describing him as a drunken sot."

"Where the hell are we going?" Jason whined.

"Home," Skye said.

"Why?" Jason slurred. "The party is just starting."

"Yes, but you've already had enough to drink," Skye said. "And you and Tammy have to figure a few things out."

"Tammy?" Jason got a silly grin on his face. "She's great, isn't she?"

"The best."

At that moment, Jason's Mini pulled up in front of the alley. "Hop in," Tammy yelled.

Jet folded Jason into the back seat and got in beside him. Skye climbed in the front seat and Tammy sped away.

"Is he as bad as the last time?" Tammy asked.

"Last time?" Jet adjusted Jason in his seat when his head drooped on Jet's shoulder. "He's done this before? Does he have a drinking problem?"

"He has a problem all right. He doesn't handle liquor very well. He generally drinks beer." Skye eyed Tammy. "You've got to put a stop to this. You've got to tell him how you feel."

"I know. I know," Tammy said. "I will. First thing tomorrow."

"Tonight," Skye said.

Jet dragged Jason up the loft stairs and sat him in the kitchen. Tammy put on a pot of coffee.

While Skye tried to keep Jason upright on the stool, Jet went into the living room to make a phone call. Skye patted Jason's face and shook him, but nothing seemed to work. His head slipped to the surface of the table.

"Well, so much for talking this out tonight," Tammy said. "The only way I'd get his attention is if I tied him to the back of the chair."

Jet returned to the kitchen and hauled Jason out of the seat. "Where's the bathroom?" he asked.

Both Skye and Tammy stood back while Jet tossed Jason, fully clothed, into the shower. Then he switched on the cold water.

Jason sputtered and screamed for mercy.

"Leave him under the water until he sobers up enough to pour some coffee down his throat," Jet said to Tammy.

Then Jet herded Skye out of the bathroom. "Get your bag," he said, above the commotion.

"Why?" Skye asked.

"Because Tammy and Jason need some time to sort this out by themselves, and a cab will be here any minute. You're coming with me."

CHAPTER 25

Skye had already packed her suitcase for her jaunt to Kilmarnock the next day, so she zipped it up and followed Jet outside. By the time they got to the street, a cab rolled to a stop, and they climbed inside and rode to the Thrift Hotel.

She sat on the edge of her seat wondering what kind of arrangements Jet had made for her—if she'd be sharing a room with him or if he'd gotten another room for her? They stepped up to reception and Jet requested an early wake up call. Then the young attendant with spiked blue hair passed Skye her key card.

Damn.

She gave him her credit card information and she and Jet rode the elevator to the third floor where she discovered their rooms were side by side.

Jet put out his hand for her key and he opened and held the door. "I had a very interesting evening."

"You mean bizarre, don't you?" Skye stopped in front of him. "I'm sorry about tonight."

"Don't apologize."

He limped as he moved aside.

"Are you all right?" she asked. "Did you hurt yourself?"

"Between hauling Jason's ass out of the bar and up those stairs, I've had one hell of a workout. I'm just tired." Jet rolled her bag toward her. "It's not the Ritz," he said, "but the rooms are clean."

Instead of stepping around him, she stepped forward. "Goodnight." She rose up on her toes and kissed him.

Electricity danced between them.

He didn't reach out to hold her, but he definitely kissed her back. The kiss was full of promise and way too much politeness. When she pulled away, she found herself yearning for so much more.

Unfortunately, he backed off and disappeared into the next room.

She wheeled her bag inside her room and got ready for bed. At least he hadn't thrown up any more roadblocks. She didn't have a clue why he held himself in check. All she knew was she'd worn down his resistance. He may not have been jumping up and down, but he wasn't kicking or screaming anymore either.

At least not with her.

The walls were thin, and he sounded like he might be fighting a battle with himself in the next room. She heard him slamming doors and drawers before he climbed into bed.

His restlessness made her chuckle. It seemed he wasn't as unaffected as he led her to believe.

She heard him toss and turn. Eventually he gave up and he switched on the television.

Skye flipped on the light and reached for Bessie's journal and brooch.

The journal fell open to where she'd left off. She fanned the remaining pages—there were dozens left. Unfortunately, the stone in her brooch appeared to be a paler shade of blue and felt much cooler to the touch. She blew hot breath on it and rubbed it against her pajamas. Over and over, she repeated the process. She was just about to give up when the color of the stone brightened and its temperature spiked.

Bessie sank into a tub of lavender scented bubbles and began to question her decision to meet with Aldo. This was not the time to make life-altering decisions. The cancer might have already spread, and she could very well be dead by year-end.

Talk about a selfish decision.

She tried to rationalize it. She remembered what Dr. Lamont had said—she needed someone to lean on. If she lived and agreed to be his mistress, how long would it last? She would be a seductress with one breast. She might as well run off and join the circus.

Bessie dressed in the brand-new white kitten set she purchased as part of her trousseau. The skirt and sweater combination had fit her perfectly back then. It clung to her curves and accentuated her womanly shape. She studied her reflection in the mirror. It still fit, though the angora draped in spots.

This would be the last time she'd ever wear such a plunging neckline. She popped her lipstick inside her purse and hailed a cab to the Ritz Carlton.

The landmark hotel's foyer contained richly appointed golden hues. She strode up the stairs to the elevator where an operator held the door.

"What floor?" he asked.

"The Presidential Suite," she said.

She rode the car to the top and exited. The attendant pointed as he held the door. "It's down the hall to your left."

Bessie put one foot in front of the other and stopped partway down the hall in an alcove. She placed her purse on the small table and straightened her hair in the mirror.

Last chance to reconsider.

She checked her reflection. Either way, her life would forever be changed. She took a deep breath and continued down the hall.

A brass nameplate scrolled across the door of the Presidential Suite. She knocked, quietly at first, then again louder.

A moment later, the door swung open. Aldo, decked out in his trademark suit, took her hand and pressed it to his lips. With a look that could melt ice, he pulled her inside. "I'm so glad you came. For a moment, I thought you might change your mind."

Beautiful original oil paintings donned the walls. Brocade and tufted upholstery sat upon polished wood floors. The furnishings were fit for a queen, let alone a president.

Bessie's entire apartment would fit inside this room. There were two sofas, clusters of chairs and occasional tables, and a Louis XIVth desk. On the center table, a fruit tray overflowed with exotic berries. Beside it, a silver tureen of caviar sat on top of an assortment of cheeses and flatbreads.

"Are you expecting company?" she asked.

Aldo shook his head. "I had this sent up in case you were hungry."

"Wow." She had to give him points for thoughtfulness, but soon the gesture's true meaning came into focus. "All this to seduce me? What's wrong with your wife?"

The second the spiteful remark crossed her lips, she regretted saying it. Anger burned. How dare he think she could be wined and dined into spreading her legs? "I thought you were in some kind of trouble. I'm the worst kind of fool." She fled. Two steps from the door, she felt a hand on her arm.

"I don't blame you for being angry. I didn't hold out a lot of hope after last time."

"What part of no didn't you understand?" she asked.

"I wanted to apologize for being so selfish. I didn't invite you here for any other reason. My intentions are honorable."

Bessie stopped but didn't turn around.

"I was way out of line last time. Hell, I damn near raped you across your desk." Aldo plunked himself on the sofa. "I felt like a sinking ship, and the only way I could keep my head above water was to latch onto you. In the process, I pulled you under."

The defeat in his voice made her heart slam. Aldo sat on the edge of the cushion; his shoulders slumped with his head in his hands.

"Being a mistress goes against everything I believe in. It's too big a sacrifice. I'd never be able to face my family or the church, and for what? I still wouldn't have you. You will always belong to another woman."

Aldo lifted his head and they faced each other. "You don't have to explain. I fell in love with you because of your strong moral values. I had no right to ask you to compromise them."

"Why did you?"

"Because I couldn't sleep or eat. I missed you like crazy. You were always on my mind." He shrugged. "You still are."

Her eyes welled with tears.

Aldo pulled his handkerchief out of his breast pocket and held it out for her. "Don't worry. As long as I stick to my end of the bargain, you and your family are perfectly safe. I would never do anything to hurt you. Ever."

More tears fell.

"Bes, I'm so sorry," he said, jumping up. "C'mon. Are you hungry? Want something to drink?"

She sobbed.

Aldo folded her into his embrace.

He stroked her hair and whispered assurances until her hiccups abated. Only then did she let his warmth affect her. She heard the steady cadence of his beating heart—smelled the citrus undertones of his cologne. She felt safe and protected. And that said something, in view of her cancer. She didn't realize how much she craved these feelings. It made her wonder how something so honest and true could be so wrong.

Then her mind switched gears. This couldn't be wrong. They were in love, and for reasons beyond their control, they couldn't spend their lives together.

All they had was now.

He needed her as much as she needed him. And she wanted to make love to him, even if it meant she'd have to spend the rest of her life begging God's forgiveness.

Her entire life would change after her operation. She would likely never be in love or be loved ever again. She could very well be dead in a matter of months.

"Neither of us can seem to get the other out of their head," Bessie said. "In my experience, wanting something so badly can drive a person mad."

"I'm a raving lunatic." He pulled his hair.

"Perhaps having a taste is the cure to this madness."

Aldo's eyes widened and he reached for her.

Bessie put up her hand. "This weekend can be ours on one condition. This is an all-or-nothing proposition. You must promise that after this weekend, you will never again contact me to be your mistress. And because neither of us is capable of just being friends, it'll be good-bye."

Aldo stood back unblinking.

"Say something," she said.

"Given the choice of never loving you, or loving you for only a short while, I chose the short while. And I'll consider myself very lucky. Some people never experience a love like ours."

They came together and Aldo kissed her. Tenderly. He nipped at her lips. "We're going to take this very slowly. You will be the one to tell me when you're ready. I want to savor every moment and accumulate enough memories to last a lifetime."

Then he deepened the kiss.

Bessie sagged against him. She opened her mind and body to the sensations washing over her. He kissed and suckled her lips and plundered her mouth with his tongue. A hot wire burned within her. It seemed like a coiled spring connected her nipples to her womb. Every time his tongue tangled with hers the wire wound tighter.

He stopped and pulled back. "Open your eyes."

She did. She saw the tortured and yet rapturous expression on his face as he worked the pearl buttons of her angora sweater. His fingertips brushed her skin, and although his light touch merely feathered her skin, she felt singed by the contact.

"I've done this a thousand times in my dreams, but now it's actually happening, my hands are trembling like an old man." He leaned forward and trailed kisses down a line from beneath her ear to the tip of her shoulder. Somehow, he unhooked her bra and continued his descent.

Would he feel the lumps in her breast?

She held her breath as he skimmed kisses around her areola. When he didn't notice any anomaly, she felt dizzy—hot and cold at the same time. She closed her eyes and groaned.

Aldo reversed and ascended until he reached her lips and he kissed her once again. Then he whispered in her ear. "Undo my shirt the way I undid yours."

She pulled back and reached for him. She shoved his jacket over his shoulders and let it fall. With trembling fingers, she loosened his tie and slid it out from the collar. She took each hand in hers to remove the cuff links, then ever so slowly she unfastened each button. When her fingers brushed against the leather of his belt, she pulled the shirttails from his waistband and slid the cotton to the floor.

Her hands trailed the ridge of his collarbone and down his muscular arms. He was steel and she was satin. She marveled at their differences. She had pale translucent skin and he had tanned and swarthy—her frame was willowy and his was sturdy.

She'd fantasized about what making love would be like, but as it happened, she found herself shaking with the enormity of her emotions. She'd been in love with Aldo for some time, and she didn't expect her heart to feel so enlarged or full to bursting before the consummation.

In the blink of an eye, everything tilted on its axis. Tucked safely in Aldo's arms, he carried her into the bedroom. He set her on her feet and dimmed the lights.

She eyed the king-sized bed. Its billowing linens made it float like a cloud in the room. She'd never seen a more beautifully appointed room. The perfection would make their time together even more special.

"You take my breath away." Aldo had come up behind her and whispered in her ear. "I'd like to leave the light on, but if it'll make you feel uncomfortable, I'll switch it off."

"Leave it on," she said. She wanted to commit every detail to memory.

Aldo nuzzled her ear and undid the zipper of her skirt. He pushed the fabric over her hips and spun her around. Then he discarded his pants and ushered her to the bed. In a flurry of hands and tongues they toppled to the surface.

He worked his magic so effectively their underclothes seemed to evaporate into thin air, and a chill washed over her, making her shiver.

All at once, Aldo stopped kissing and caressing her. "Are you okay?" he asked. "Did you want me to slow down?"

She appreciated him in all his glory. "I'm feeling overwhelmed," she said.

"Are you frightened?" he asked.

He knew her well. She nodded. "Don't be. We're going to fit together perfectly."

"Are we?" She'd stolen a few glances at Aldo's erection and wondered.

"Trust me," he said. "By the time you're ready, you'll be crazy to have me inside you."

And so he began. He kissed and suckled almost every square inch of her body, and just like he promised, an incredible pressure started to build. The yearning made her feel as if she'd outgrown her skin. When he reclined, she took the initiative. She trailed kisses along his strong sinewy muscles—watched them flex and twitch in response to her light touch. The control she wielded over him empowered her. It gave her the confidence to do things she'd never dreamed of doing. When her fingers brushed his thick erection, his breath caught. She gripped him and he groaned like a tormented animal.

"Your touch feels almost too good," he said between clenched teeth.

"I wish I knew what to do."

He wrapped his hand around hers and guided her fist up and down. She fell into a quick and steady rhythm until he sprang forward and stilled her hands.

"Did I do something wrong?"

He shook his head amidst ragged breaths. "It's my turn." He laid her on her back and shimmied to the foot of the bed. He started with her toes and worked his way up her legs—running his tongue along the sensitive skin of her inner thigh. She bit her lip wondering what his intensions were. The tingling in her extremities had become out and out trembling.

"Relax," he said. "This won't hurt."

Before she knew it, his tongue lapped at her intimate folds. The fire spread rapidly through her abdomen. Her nipples shriveled and hardened. Every swipe of his tongue ignited more flames.

She wanted to laugh and cry at the same time. Her quickness of breath and restlessness must have tipped off Aldo, because in the next moment he climbed on top of her, the slick head of his penis poised for penetration.

"I promise, it will only sting for a second," he said, and he drove himself inside.

She didn't have a moment to brace before pain speared through her. True to his word, the pain disappeared quickly with Aldo raining kisses along her neck and shoulders. When she opened her eyes, she noticed his mask of concentration and sweat beaded on his brow. "From the expression on your face," she said. "That hurt you more than it hurt me."

"You're so tight I have to focus to keep myself from going too far."

"You mean there's more? I thought it was all over?"

"Darling," he said. "We've just begun." And with those words he withdrew on a slow glide and reseated himself with another thrust. Each stroke added more oxygen to smoldering embers, and before she knew it, the backdraft made her implode. He continued fanning the fire, until he, too, burst into flame.

When the spasms abated, he rolled beside her.

"What was that?" she asked, catching her breath.

He put his arm behind his head. "That, my love, was an orgasm."

"Oh my." She gulped. "Does it happen every time?"

"If I'm doing everything right it will."

"Was it okay for you?"

"Better than okay."

She became quiet for a moment. "Do you think we can do it again?"

He chuckled. "You'll have to give me a minute or two. I think I might have to fill a plate with some food to boost my energy. This is going to be a very long night."

She rolled to her side to face him. "Well? What are you waiting for?"

They made love all weekend long, on nearly every horizontal, even some vertical, surfaces of the suite—each time as perfect as the first.

Late Sunday evening, Aldo's mood changed.

He became somber. She could see him wrestling with wanting more.

Unfortunately, she'd given him all there was to give.

While he showered, she threw on her clothes and dug her brooch out of her bag. Bessie rarely used its magic. She could see certain things with or without it. The pin would channel the gift of sight to whoever possessed it. She scratched a note on the hotel's embossed stationary.

Dearest Aldo,

Covet this Luckenbooth. No harm will befall you if it is kept close. Please respect my wishes and don't try to contact me.

All my love,
Bessie

She straightened the bed and kissed the Luckenbooth. She set it and the note on the coverlet.

Then she went out into the night, alone.

CHAPTER 26

The telephone rang at seven the next morning, jerking Skye out of a fitful sleep.

Once she witnessed Bessie's romantic liaison with Aldo, the Luckenbooth ran out of juice and the images faded. But that didn't stop her mind from imagining what it would be like making love with Jet. As a result, she'd only gotten an hour or two at the very most.

Damn frustrated is what she was. In her dream, Jet brought her to full arousal repeatedly, and just as she was about to find release, she'd wake with a start, making him more curse than enigma right now.

She showered, dressed, and closed her bag when she heard a knock at the door. "It's open," she shouted.

Jet pushed through the door and placed a coffee on the dresser for Skye. "Pretty risky leaving the door unlocked."

"Why? If I screamed, you'd have come to my rescue." She could have told him that she'd only flipped the deadbolt mere moments before, but she wanted to see his reaction.

"Why would you take that kind of chance?"

"You were up all night," Skye said. "I heard you pacing the floor into the wee hours. The walls are pretty thin."

"Obviously, you were up all night too." Jet dug a creamer and sugar packet out of his pocket. "Either that or you're not a morning person."

Skye closed her eyes. She was downright grumpy. "I haven't slept well since I arrived in the UK. I guess it's finally caught up to me."

Jet looked out the window while she fixed her coffee. "Kevin will be here any moment to drive us to the train station."

Skye zipped her bag and extended the handle. "I'm ready anytime you are."

"Let's go, then."

She grabbed her coffee and wheeled her bag to the door. Jet collected his rucksack from his room, and they rode the elevator downstairs. When the doors opened, they found Kevin pacing the lobby.

"Ms. Andrews? What are you doing here?" Kevin asked, right before he saw Jet with his hand on the small of her back. "Ah, never mind."

Kevin took Skye's bag and picked up the captain's duffel. "After you," he said to Skye.

She smiled to herself as she climbed into the back seat of Kevin's car. Jet said he only wanted to be friends, but he didn't mind letting another man think they were together.

On the way to the train station, Jet rhymed off a list of instructions—things Kevin had to do at the museum during his absence. As she and Jet stood in line for tickets, Skye casually mentioned her observation. "Why didn't you tell Kevin we slept in separate rooms?"

When she faced Jet, her breath caught. His eyes smoldered with a strange mix of sadness and desire. His vulnerability caused Skye to backpedal. "Is something wrong? Do you want to talk about it?"

"Something's definitely wrong, but no, I don't want to talk about it."

She didn't push. They moved to the head of the line. Jet punched the information into the machine, and it spit out two tickets. They boarded the train, stowed their luggage in the overhead compartment, and settled in.

Skye hungered to know more about him—something that would give her a clue why he kept her at arm's length. She had many questions that needed answers. "What's the Army like?" she asked.

Jet straightened. "It's disciplined. When you enlist, you're an individual. By the time you're sent to a hot spot, you're a cog in a well-oiled machine."

"Sounds clichéd," Skye said.

"It is, but it's true." Jet sat back in his seat.

Skye shook her head. She wanted him talking, not brooding. Soon the color leached out of his cheeks.

"Every team is made up of a varied cross-section. There's infantry, cavalry, engineers, aviation jockeys, and medical and logistical support."

"A winning combination."

"In war, there are no winners, just losers," Jet said. "Every candidate must endure painful anthrax immunizations, jungle training in Belize, and winter training in Norway, but it all falls short. A mission, like Operation Telic, strips you naked."

"Operation Telic?"

"The codename for all British operations during the invasion of Iraq."

Skye saw Jet's pupils widen. She listened to him and knew talking about it had sent him right back into the fray.

Hundreds of vehicles and equipment snaked toward the Emden docks to board ships destined for Kuwait. Not to mention men. The taskforce was one of the largest deployed since the Falklands War.

Jet got his orders and worried his men weren't ready. They were pretty young—many as green as new grass. But command didn't ask for his opinion.

They landed in the Persian Gulf, then traveled north by Warrior truck to their desert home base. Jet sat upfront beside the driver. A hot oppressive breeze wafted through the open window. Sweat dripped off his brow and streamed down his face. He could only imagine his men riding in the back—baking inside the thick walls of armor plating.

The desert base was nothing like Jet had ever seen. There were thousands of tents—white canvas sails bobbing on a sand sea. Jet opened the vehicles' plated doors and his men spilled out, soaked, as if they'd been swimming in the Gulf.

Within a few days they were shoved into battle.

During their trek to Basra, they showered an outlying town with howitzer shells. Busy, the ears—or communications expert—of the assault, screamed information at Jet during the pounding of the gun. "There's enemy activity between the squadron and the brigade," he said. "Command wants us to attack those fronts and work our way toward the city."

Jet followed those orders. They moved forward in their Challenger tanks, slowly, closing the distance. After several hours of combat, more troops joined them in their effort to destroy as many T-55 battle tanks as possible.

The raids continued into Basra.

Prisoners were taken and party extremists were driven off. Slowly, the city surrendered its outer suburbs. Jet's men seized the ancient Gateway to the city and it fell.

Warfare became welfare overnight.

Basra's water and electrical services were in a total state of disrepair, and engineers were recruited to begin the arduous task of repairing the city's neglected infrastructure. Jet's battalion patrolled the streets to offer assistance and try to restore order.

It seemed the mornings were the best time to make rounds, as the temperatures were merely double-digit, unlike the afternoons when heat radiated from the clay buildings like waves from a potter's kiln.

Jet rode in the first of two jeeps. Rubble edged the road as the vehicle surged through the inner-city streets. Eight men, four in each jeep, wormed their way through the dilapidated buildings. Heavy mortar fire had made most of the structures unstable, and no matter how many times Jet tried, he couldn't convince the residents their homes were unsafe. Every day they encountered something new—abandoned stores of live explosives and ammunitions, and the severed limbs of the children who found them.

Jet lifted his arm and his jeep slid to an abrupt halt in the road.

Busy, in the second jeep, pulled alongside him. "What's up?" he asked, holding tight to his rifle.

With his hand still in the air, Jet motioned ahead to the side of the road where two small children lay, stiff and unmoving. Jet studied the surrounding area. He didn't want to miss any detail that might wind up getting them killed. Something was off. There was no blood. The children appeared posed. They were dirty, but then, all children living in this rubble heap were.

"Doc and Busy, come with me. Cover us," Jet said to the remaining men. Doc was the brigade medic and Busy knew the language. As the trio approached the two small bodies, Jet kept thinking about the Fedayeen hardliners they'd encountered a few days ago. They'd used children, just like this pair, to get them to let their guard down. Then they attacked and seriously injured one of Jet's men. Fool me once, shame on me. Twice would never happen.

The trio approached the children with the utmost care. The older child's chest rose and fell, and the younger one appeared gray enough to be dead.

His rifle remained in firing position. All three men scanned the area through their rifle sights.

Nothing.

"Hey," Jet shouted.

Neither child stirred.

The men inched even closer.

Finally, the eldest child blinked. He stretched and sat up.

Had he really been asleep? The boy jumped to his feet and began making wild hand gestures and rambling in Arabic.

Busy translated. "Last night mortar blasts caused their house to crumble. His brother was crushed. He says it took over an hour to dig him out."

Jet noticed the boy's raw hands.

"He carried his brother here because he knew there were patrols in the area."

Jet motioned for Doc to examine the younger boy.

Doc sat down beside him and pulled his kit out of his knapsack. He stuck his stethoscope inside his shirt and listened. Then he felt all his extremities.

He faced Jet. "He's unconscious. A couple of broken ribs—one may have pierced his lung. He needs medical attention ASAP."

Jet signaled all clear. "Busy, tell the brother what's happening. Doc, can he be transported in one of the jeeps?"

"I don't think we have any choice at this point."

Jet bent down and lifted the boy who weighed a mere fraction of his battle gear. Jet's heart ached with the injustice. Gently, he placed the boy on Doc's lap in the backseat of the second jeep and issued instructions to the driver. "Get them to the Army hospital and meet us at the school."

Doc took out the supplies he needed and tossed the remnants of his medical kit to Monk. "Just in case."

The jeep sped away and the temperature continued climbing.

"Let's move out," Jet said. He and Busy, Monk, and Spider climbed into the other jeep and headed for the school—next on the list, in quadrant D.

The school seemed to be in pretty good shape—an oddity because very few buildings in this vicinity were still intact. Children sat at their desks in the classroom working on their lessons. When Jet's men arrived, the teacher sent them outside to play in the adjacent field.

Jet split them into two teams so every closet and cupboard could be inspected. Spider and Monk worked together as did Busy and Jet. When there was only a couple of classrooms left to investigate, Spider shouted for assistance. He and Busy ran to help.

Spider stood beside the window, like a statue, and Monk crouched beneath it. Spider motioned for them to get down and move toward him. The men crawled over to the outside wall. Spider stole another glance through the window. "Check it out."

On the other side of a massive rubble pile was a clearing where the children were playing a game of football.

"What's the problem?" Jet asked, giving the field a cursory glance.

"Zoom in on the ball," Spider said.

Jet did just that. "Shit." He strode over to the door where the teacher hovered. All four military men herded the teacher outside into the courtyard. Jet told Busy to translate. "Tell the children to stop what they're doing. Recess is over. It's time to come inside."

The teacher shouted instructions at the children who stopped playing their game and began heading back toward the school. All but one little boy, who intended to give the football one last kick.

Finger on the trigger, Jet lifted his rifle and fired into the air. The kid ducked and his foot missed the mark. The boy shot like a bullet back into the schoolyard.

All of Jet's men issued a collective sigh. As soon as the boy joined the others in the courtyard, Jet faced Spider, the munitions expert. "Go and check it out," he ordered.

Busy and Monk kept the children together while they waited for Spider to inspect the children's plaything in the empty field. Moments later he rushed back. "It's an unexploded anti-personnel mine."

Monk raised his brow. "Jesus. How the hell did they get their hands on one of those?"

"They found it," Busy said.

Jet wanted to scream. Since he'd arrived, he'd seen bucket-loads of limbless children. He needed to do something to make a lasting impression—make these kids think twice about sifting through the rubble for treasures. He had an idea. A little demonstration might do the trick. He took careful aim at the mine sitting in the open field and fired.

Kaboom.

The explosion sent sand, shrapnel, and smoke rocketing into the air. When the dust cleared, a gaping hole tore into the ground.

The little boy who'd been about to kick the mine soiled himself and took off running from the schoolyard and out of sight. Jet hoped he'd been the only one who saw the boy's pants dampen. He felt bad for him, but the lesson he'd learned had been a valuable one.

While the teacher tried to calm the students, Jet and his men resumed their search of the two remaining classrooms. He and Busy took one and Spider and Monk searched the other. He was about to call it a wrap when he noticed a trap door in the floor beneath one of the student's desks.

Inside the cellar, he and Busy discovered a huge store of weapons and ammunition.

Logistically, the cache presented a problem. Jet would have to bring in a truck to remove the weapons—roping or cordoning off the area wouldn't work unless he posted guards. Without guards, only half of this stockpile would be intact by the following morning.

Jet called command to requisition a truck.

Out of the corner of his eye, he saw Busy as he reached for a rifle and pulled it upwards. A trip wire strung through the finger cage removed the pin from a carefully positioned grenade.

One Mississippi. Two Mississippi.

Jet dove toward Busy, knocking him over. He dragged him as far away from the pit as he could.

Three Mississippi. Four.

Light strobed and a series of deafening explosions staccatoed.

Blood splattered everywhere.

The last thing Jet remembered was Monk's face and the sweet rush of morphine right before everything faded to black.

Chapter 27

Skye sat perfectly still and waited for Jet to stop talking. He'd been kneading the muscles in his legs like they were clumps of sourdough. "How badly were you injured?"

"Not as bad as Busy. Both of his legs were blown off. He never really recovered."

"I'm sorry," she said. She quickly swiped the tears from her eyes and hoped like hell he hadn't seen her. "What time is the service tomorrow?"

"The graveside service is at eleven. Afterward, there's a get-together at his parents' house."

The train slowed and pulled into Glasgow station. Though they didn't have to change trains, they had a twenty-minute layover. This time, when they got on their way, Jet asked the questions.

"How famous are you?"

Skye had to laugh. "Not very. Though I did get rave reviews in my last New York Broadway production."

"What was it called? Would I know it?"

"Not likely. It's a remake of *The Wizard of Oz.*"

"Sounds interesting. Are you going back to New York when you finish your business here?"

For the first time in her life, she didn't have a direction. The indecision scared her. She'd always been driven. Always working towards the next big part. Bessie's death and her journal made her realize everyone was on the clock. "I really like New York, but I think it's time I went home to spend some time with my family."

"Where do they live?"

"Little Brook, New York. And, before you ask, the town is every bit as quaint as the name." Skye pictured the mature trees that tunneled her street in the summer.

"What does your father do?"

"Not a lot of anything anymore. He's retired from the county's hydroelectric plant."

"And your mother?"

"She's always been a stay-at-home mom."

"That's the best kind." He watched Skye and his brow arched. "I'm not a male chauvinist, I just think if a family can afford it, the kids are better off."

"Relax. I happen to agree." Skye smiled. "Did your mom stay at home to raise you?"

"I wish." Jet snorted. "I grew up in Haywood Boy's Academy. An orphanage and school run by the order of St. Agnes nuns in Aberdeen."

Skye felt like an idiot. "I'm sorry. I didn't know."

"How could you? It wasn't all bad. Sister Mary Catherine took me under her wing. At sixteen, I'd had enough and enlisted with the intention of becoming a career soldier. Now, because of this, the service doesn't really know what to do with me."

"When will you get back to active duty?"

"My question exactly. They're telling me I might not ever be ready. Which is a real problem because I'm not cut out to be an administrator. I can't sit for too long without getting really stiff."

"Ah, that's why you were rubbing your legs," Skye said. "I just thought you didn't like talking about your past."

"I don't. I try not to dwell on the past. I focus on the future."

"And what do you see?"

"Nothing definitive yet. I've been thinking about becoming an instructor at one of the bases in Germany or Holland once I get the all-clear from my doctors."

The train slowed and pulled into the Kilmarnock station.

It had been an insightful trip, not a pleasant one. But it did give Skye an inside look into Captain Jet Dalry's often confusing behavior. The man was an orphan. No wonder he had difficulty forming interpersonal relationships. He had every right to want to go slowly.

Jet stood, donned his jacket, and gathered both of their bags. After several minutes, he sat back down.

They waited. And waited.

Something had to be wrong because the disembarking line hadn't budged. When Skye peered out the window, she understood why. The station, not overly large, was jammed. People were oozing from two other trains on different platforms. When they finally got outside, there were various stands in the terminal selling Killie colors.

"What's going on?" Jet asked a balding street vendor.

"Everyone's gearing up for tomorrow's big game."

"What game?"

The man rubbed his smooth head. "Where have you been? It's the FA cup semifinals. Killie versus the Celtics tomorrow at Rugby Park."

"That's tomorrow?" Jet asked.

"Are you hard of hearing too? The game starts at three, but the celebration begins tonight. Where are you staying?"

Jet eyed Skye and then the vendor. "We don't know yet."

The vendor started to laugh. "Well good luck then. You're going to need it."

Skye led Jet outside to a quiet alcove. She pulled out her phone and searched for all the hotels in the area. Then she proceeded to plow through the list. The Howard Park Hotel and the Kilmarnock Travelodge were booked solid. Not a vacancy to be had anywhere.

On John Finnie Street, they asked a passerby if there were any other hotels in town they could try. "The Portman Hotel is down the way," a woman carrying a sac full of groceries said. Then, "Or you could always pitch a tent."

They tried the Portman Hotel. No vacancies.

They were considering the notion of camping when Skye decided they had nothing to lose trying the Killy Inn. She'd stayed at the inn a few weeks ago on her first visit to Kilmarnock. The owner's wife made Skye feel like a harlot because she was an actress and a single woman traveling alone.

The quaint little B&B stood on the outskirts of town. Once an old country manor, the owners Joan and Bob had been refurbishing it room by room. Skye and Jet decided to go in person, thinking it would be more difficult to turn repeat business away.

With Jet's legs already bothering him, they hailed a cab.

Joan recognized Skye as soon as she came through the door.

"Ms. Andrews," she said. "Have you come to see the game?"

"Afraid not, Joan. We weren't aware there was a tournament this weekend."

Joan's expression became apprehensive when she noticed Jet. "We need a place to stay and I'm really hoping you have a room." Skye had noticed the No Vacancy sign on the desk as soon as they came through the door.

"You're out of luck," Joan said. "We've been booked solid for weeks."

"Are you sure there's nothing? We've been all over town. I don't know what we'll do."

Joan watched Jet who had busied himself with a copy of the local paper. She leaned toward Skye and whispered. "There is one room. Bill just put the last coat of paint on the walls yesterday. It's the Honeymoon suite."

"We'll take it," Skye said.

Joan glanced down at Skye's hand, specifically her ring finger.

Oh gawd. Really? "The captain and I are engaged."

Careful not to pay any attention to Jet, Skye could feel the hairs on the nape of her neck being singed by his overt attention.

She opened her wallet. "Here's my card," she said, but before she could hand it to Joan, Jet reached over her with his. "Put that away, darling. You know how I feel about you paying."

Joan took the card from Jet and blushed. "It's so nice to see a man with old-school values. Have you two set a date yet?"

Jet continued to glare at Skye. She knew the exact moment he decided to dish up a dose of the same medicine. "No, but we intend to discuss it with the reverend tomorrow, don't we sweetheart?"

She had no intention of letting him have the last word. "Maybe we should reconsider our stay, honey. I forgot about all the stairs. They might present too much of a challenge with your injury and all." She spoke softly to Joan. "He was wounded in Iraq." Skye figured steam would come out of Jet's ears any second now.

"I think I can manage," he said.

Joan handed Jet the key and told him to go to the top of the stairs and down the hall. Then Jet swung his duffel over his shoulder, picked up Skye's bag, and headed up the stairs.

At the landing, Skye tried to reclaim her bag, but Jet wouldn't part with it. He'd dug in and she figured he'd make it to the top of the stairs carrying the two, even if it killed him.

He became quiet.

Dangerously so.

When she studied him, she realized the toll the stairs were taking on him.

"Jet, please. I'm sorry. I took things too far. I didn't think Joan would give us the room unless we were a couple. You have nothing to prove to me."

At the top of the stairs, he stopped to catch his breath before inching his way down the hall. Skye hurried ahead and opened the door. Jet strode into the room, dropped the bags on the floor, and sat down in the closest chair. He closed his eyes and held onto the armrests so tightly his knuckles were white.

Jet focused on his deep breathing.

He'd used this technique when he'd pushed himself too far on the weight machine. He squeezed his eyes shut and hoped the dizziness and nausea would pass.

He couldn't believe that he'd gone along with Skye's harebrained scheme.

Engaged? That would have been in a perfect world.

The more time Jet spent with Skye, the more he wanted to. She was interesting, fun to be with, unpredictable, and so sexy he nearly groaned out loud.

What was he thinking? Spending the night with her and not being able to touch her was going to be torture. He had no clue how he would ever get through the night.

He hoped to hell she didn't sleep in one of those slinky little numbers.

Flannel. He could probably handle flannel.

Slowly, his breathing and heart rate approached normal levels. His legs tingled and rubbing hadn't worked. Massaging his legs had become second nature to him; sometimes, he was totally unaware of his kneading hands.

But when he opened his eyes, he wasn't.

Skye was.

She'd knelt down in front of him and was massaging his thighs. He grabbed her hands. Her brow creased. "I'm so sorry," she said. "Are you in a lot of pain?"

And as much as Jet wanted to yell at her, he knew he couldn't be mean to her anymore. She didn't deserve any of this. He held her hands. "This is not your fault." He strained to stand. The aroma of fresh paint tickled his nose, and for the first time since they'd arrived, he surveyed the room.

Golden oak floors gleamed beneath the enormous king-sized bed. A white feather duvet floated on top of the mattress. The armoire housed a modest sized television. Beside the secretarial stood a chair and a loveseat in the window alcove.

Skye hurried to the window and pressed her forehead to the old pane. "From this dormer I can see all the way down the lane. I can even make out the rooftops in Kilmarnock. Do you want to lie down and rest?" She must have seen him staring at the bed.

"No," he said. He assessed the loveseat and knew he couldn't sleep very well on it tonight. "That would be the worst thing I could do. I need to keep moving. Keep the muscles limber."

"In that case, how about we head back into town. There's a nice little pub called the Bull and Finch where we can get a sandwich and a beer."

Jet braced his hands on the arms of the chair and stood up. "Sounds like a plan."

Chapter 28

Jet opened the door of the Bull and Finch and the crowd, crammed wall-to-wall, nearly spilled outside. He grabbed hold of Skye's hand and forged his way through the throng to a table in the back.

Killie would do battle for the Scottish Cup, and according to the pregame forecasts, they were the wild card. The bar patrons made their wagers, and very soon Jet found it hard to hear Skye over the slurring, opinionated, red-headed bruiser sitting at the next table.

"Can you explain how you forgot about the semifinals this weekend?" she asked, sipping on her lager and lime.

Jet narrowed his eyes at her. He knew exactly what caused the lapse. It was about the only thing that could divert a Scotsman's attention from the game.

A woman.

And not just any woman.

Skye.

"Are you going to answer me?" she repeated.

"No," he said, finally.

"What's the big deal? It's only a game."

"Are you serious?"

"Seems kind of silly. A bunch of grown men running around a field kicking a ball."

"Have you ever been to a game?" Jet asked.

"No."

"That's your problem," he said. "You have to go to one to fully appreciate the sport."

Jet glanced over Skye's shoulder to the belligerent bruiser who'd picked a fight with a bloke standing at the bar. The two squared off like a couple of heavyweights. The guy at the bar pushed the loudmouth and he fell against Skye's chair, nearly knocking her over.

Jet jumped up and steadied her in her seat. Then he marched over to run interference. "I think you two need to take this outside so you don't hurt anyone," he said as politely as he could muster.

"Who asked you?" The redhead pulled back and threw a punch.

Jet ducked out of the way and grabbed his fist on the follow through and wrenched his arm around his back. "Like I said." Jet spoke firmly and evenly into his ear, "Take this outside so no one gets hurt."

The owner of the bar and the bouncer interceded. "Time for you to go home, Sandy. You've had enough." The owner clapped Jet on the back. "Thanks. We'll take it from here."

"No problem," Jet said. He passed Sandy over to the bouncer and went back to the table and sat down.

Skye had her arms folded across her chest. "Aren't you afraid of anything?"

Jet was afraid of a lot; a normal relationship made him break out in a cold sweat—a problem since he didn't want to spend his life alone. He nodded. "I'm afraid of Busy's service tomorrow."

Skye leaned forward in her chair and put her hand on his. "Would you like some company?"

Tears hit the back of Jet's eyelids. Over the past year, he'd been no stranger to pain, but not once had he shed a tear. Skye's simple act of kindness, her caring and concern, touched him like nothing else had in his life. "I don't know what to say."

"You don't have to say anything. Just nod."

Jet put his other hand over hers and did just that.

They ate dinner and talked into the evening and returned to the Killy Inn after ten. They climbed the stairs in complete silence and entered the room. Skye collected her nightclothes and toiletry bag and headed down the hall to the loo.

Jet stripped down to his boxers and pulled on sweats to cover the criss-crossing scars on his legs. Since he couldn't face an intimate situation with Skye, he grabbed a blanket from the closet, dimmed the lights and covered himself on top of the sheets. When he heard the door open, he closed his eyes and pretended to be asleep.

Skye entered the room, Jet seemingly oblivious to the noise she made. She snapped the latches of her suitcase and thumped her toiletry bag on the counter. Hell, she even sidled up to him on the bed.

"Jet? Are you asleep?" she whispered in his ear.

He didn't flinch.

He focused on deep breathing, drawing oxygen into the deep recesses of his lungs and completely expelling it. It took all his concentration to keep his eyes tightly closed.

In his mind, he held her in his arms. Pictured her wearing a silky teddy. Her peaches and cream scent filled his nostrils, and he thought he might go crazy wanting her.

How could Jet have fallen asleep?

He'd been so attentive all night. She thought they'd finally made a connection. She bathed and brushed her teeth and had only been gone for ten minutes.

She wanted him.

She twisted in front of the bathroom mirror, wishing she had something sexier than her normal sleeping attire—a tank top and boxer shorts. She'd never put much stock in sexy underwear or silk teddies and generally thought they were overrated, until tonight.

Not that any of her fretting mattered at this particular moment.

He'd been so excited to be with her he'd fallen asleep. Sheesh. What the hell was his problem?

A little voice in her head told her to make the first move. She lifted his blanket and snuggled against him. She ran her hands down his back.

The loud snore he grunted pissed her off.

She jumped out of bed and stomped over to her bag. She grabbed Bessie's journal and brooch, switched on the light, and plunked down on the sofa.

The stone in the Luckenbooth had become an even paler blue than the last time. It seemed that each foray into the journal drained it further. So far, she couldn't make sense of Bessie's journal accounts. If there was a lesson or a message, Skye only hoped it would become clear before the stone died.

She set to work rubbing and blowing on it. She would work on it all night if she had to. There was no way Skye would let Jet make love to her now, even if he got down on his hands and knees.

This time, it took much longer to ignite the stone. Once she found success, journal pages flipped as if they themselves knew time was running out.

Bessie was determined not to let cancer get the better of her. If she survived, she'd spend the rest of her life trying to atone for her sins. But first, she had to convince Him to spare her life for breaking the seventh commandment.

While she recuperated, she spent her waking hours reading and studying passages from the Bible. She prayed endlessly and asked for mercy and forgiveness. It didn't get more straightforward than Leviticus 20:10—the adulterer and the adulteress would be put to death. She slept with another woman's husband, and as a result, she would die.

Bessie didn't have any visitors at the hospital, not even her mother. Bessie told her not to visit. Her mother would be busy soon enough, taking care of her when she came home.

She divided the Bible into sections and focused on those verses where sinners were saved. During the mornings she would read Psalms, afternoons were Romans, and evenings Corinthians. Dr. Lamont came by midweek to check on her progress. "It appears that everything went very well," he said, glancing at her chart. "Dr. Miskovic briefed me on your surgery. He said he got all the cancer and it hadn't had a chance to spread to your lymph glands. He's very optimistic for a full recovery."

She hadn't yet worked up the nerve to examine Dr. Miskovic's handy work. The nurses were very considerate of her wishes. They changed her dressings and checked the drainage tube with very little hoopla. She didn't need to rush to view the carnage—she'd have the rest of her life to adjust to her new shape.

"Dr. Miskovic sent the diseased tissue for analysis," Dr. Lamont said.

"Why?" she asked.

"Because there is so much to be learned from cases like yours. The more we know about this condition, the easier it will be to diagnose and treat. Just think, if Dr. Miskovic hadn't kept up with the current studies, your surgery would have been far more invasive."

"You're right," she said, shrugging. "And I'm grateful. I'm just tired."

"And you will be for quite a while. You've just had major surgery. It'll take time for your body to recover. You can't rush your recovery. You need to take time to adjust."

Her eyes felt heavy.

"Dr. Miskovic gave me the name of a woman who makes custom brassieres. In a few weeks, she'll call to set up an appointment with you to fit you with a prosthesis."

"That's fine," she said adrift in her own world.

Her chest throbbed—damned phantom pain. How could *nothing* hurt so much?

Every day she grew stronger.

Dr. Miskovic discharged her a week or so after the procedure. At her two-week post-op appointment, he expressed some concern about her mental state. He told her she needed to grieve for her lost breast.

She didn't want to mourn the loss of a breast if her life still hung in the balance. Until she obtained forgiveness for her sins, she didn't know if she had a life to lead. While she waited, she tried to return to normalcy.

The seamstress furnished her with a couple of bras. Three weeks into August, Bessie resumed work part-time at Dr. Lamont's office. She went back despite the doctor's protests about it being too soon.

She needed to keep busy.

At the end of her first week back, late Friday afternoon, the phone rang.

It was Aldo.

She figured it was God testing her.

"I can't stop thinking about you," Aldo said.

A million memories flooded her mind.

"I know you told me not to call, but I thought you might need to tell me something."

"What would I have to say that hasn't already been said?" Bessie fingered the phone's rotary dial.

"I called to find out if you were pregnant."

Her stomach bottomed. Aldo made love to her tirelessly for an entire weekend without using any protection. Had he purposely tried to impregnate her?

When she didn't answer he made the incorrect assumption. "I knew it. It's okay. Don't worry. I'll take care of you and the baby. I'll get you an apartment. The baby might even bring my father around."

Bessie could hear the excitement in his voice. She pictured him smiling as he made plans.

"I'm not pregnant, Aldo." As Bessie spoke the words, her womb ached.

"You're lying," he said.

"I would never lie to you about something so important."

"Bessie, I love you," he said, his voice breaking.

"I know you do," she said. Sometimes love isn't enough.

"I don't love my wife."

"It doesn't matter. You and I were never meant to be together. Not in this life." The phantom pain struck with a vengeance. "Please don't call me again." Bessie hung up. It had been the hardest thing she'd ever done, and she put her head down on top of her desk and cried.

When Dr. Lamont came bounding out of his office he came to an abrupt halt. "Oh, Bessie," he said. He squatted beside her and placed a comforting hand on her shoulder. "Emotional highs and lows are to be expected after what you've been through."

She didn't bother to tell Dr. Lamont the real reason for her melancholy.

He sat back on his heels. Then he said, "Your biopsy reports arrived today. I've got good news." He went into his office, grabbed a large envelope, and returned to her desk.

The day of reckoning had arrived. She'd passed God's test and now he would pass judgment.

He pulled out the papers and read the analysis. "It's over. According to the pathology report, you're cancer free. It's time to get on with your life."

The phone rang.

She answered. It was for the doctor. She handed him the phone.

"I'll be there as soon as I can," Dr. Lamont said. He dropped the receiver, removed his white coat, and put on his jacket. "I'm needed for a death pronouncement. Go home and celebrate, Bessie. I'll see you tomorrow." And with that he left.

She didn't know how long she sat at her desk. She grabbed the envelope that contained her biopsy results and stood to put it inside her patient file in the cabinet, but something stopped her. She pulled out the paperwork and sat back down at her desk.

Her eyes skittered back and forth over the pages, each pass wilder than the one before. That's when she saw it—the word *benign*. The tumors were consistent with cancerous lesions, but all the tests were in fact normal.

Dr. Miskovic had lopped off a perfectly healthy breast.

Suddenly, she began to laugh. The hysterical giggle bubbled up through her chest, making her feel quite insane.

She'd passed.

God had forgiven her indiscretion.

But He didn't want her to ever forget what she'd done, so He made sure she'd have a constant reminder.

CHAPTER 29

Jet always enjoyed the first few minutes of wakefulness, before the fog of sleep cleared and the pain kicked in. Since the accident, he woke with stiffness in his lower joints and muscles, and this morning, things were no different. Gone were the days when he awoke comfortable and loose as a wiggly tooth.

But there was something very different this morning. Something very warm and soft nestled beside him.

Skye.

Sometime during the night, she must have crawled beneath his blanket and snuggled next to him. Her warmth acted like a heating pad on his aching muscles. Tendrils of silky hair tickled his chin and her small hand rested on his abdomen. His plan to sleep on top of the covers hadn't worked at all. Skye had simply lifted his blanket and pressed against him. He glanced beneath the blanket and his mouth went dry. She wore a tube top and boxers that hugged her curves like a second layer of skin. Her long legs wound around his legs like vines.

He balled his hand into a fist and itched to hit something.

His palms were sweaty, and his heart raced. Thank goodness he'd donned his sweatpants. If she ever caught a glimpse of the flesh on his legs, she would have run away screaming. Hell, he could barely stand the sight of them.

Last week he'd gone back to the specialist to talk about his options. He kept telling Jet that he'd done the very best he could do. He'd successfully reattached all the nerves, but he'd pretty much exhausted his options. Skin from his back and buttocks had been grafted to the front of his thighs, but the amount of damage didn't make for a really pretty job.

His disfigurement became even more painful to endure once he met Skye. Most men took making love for granted. Lately, he found himself wondering if he would ever make love again. He remembered seeing the nurse's face when she changed his bandages. A nurse, a medical professional who'd supposedly seen it all, could barely stand the sight of them.

His scars would be a big turn-off for any woman.

He wanted to pull away from Skye, but he couldn't seem to do it. He indulged himself. As long as she slept, he didn't have to explain or apologize for anything. He closed his eyes and imagined kissing every inch of her silky body. He thought about gliding in and out of her until the thread of his control broke.

When he couldn't take any more sweet torture, he untangled her legs from his and extricated himself from the bed.

He stood with difficulty. His muscles were stiff from inactivity during the night. He grabbed his toiletries and clothes and hobbled down the hall to shower.

On a scale from one to ten, Jet knew the day would be a minus three. He let the water beat down on him. The only upside was that he didn't have to say good-bye to his friend alone. Skye would be by his side.

He'd gotten to know Benjamin's parents during his stay in the hospital. The last time they'd spoken, he'd offered his condolences. They had been so very British about their son's death. They'd been dry-eyed when they asked him to attend the memorial service.

The time had come to heal on so many levels.

Jet shaved and got dressed, then went back to the room and woke Skye when he walked inside.

"You gave me heck for leaving the door open at the hotel in Edinburgh and yet you did the very same thing here," she said, still half asleep.

"I didn't want to disturb you if you weren't awake." Jet couldn't help but stare at her. Her cotton boxers and tank top might as well have been see-through for all the coverage they provided. He'd always had a pretty good imagination, but the picture of her body in his head didn't even come close to the real thing. Her toned thighs suggested she spent a fair bit of time at the gym too.

"Is there something wrong?" Skye asked. "You're staring."

Jet snapped out of it. "No, nothing." He limped past her and tucked his sweats into his bag. "I thought I'd go downstairs and get us some coffee."

Skye jumped out of bed and grabbed a pair of dark slacks and top from her bag. "Why don't you wait? I won't be very long." She breezed past him with her clothes and toiletry bag. "Try to stay awake this time."

Jet got the message.

Although she'd been nice enough, she'd let him know in no uncertain terms that he wouldn't get away with falling asleep on her ever again.

He'd been such a coward last night.

She deserved the truth, and he intended to tell her the truth later—the reason why they couldn't be together. He thought about running away. But that was almost as bad as faking sleep. She'd been too much of a lady to throw herself at him, but he knew she wanted him to make love to her last night.

A battle raged within him.

He knew Skye wanted to be kissed.

And he desperately wanted to kiss her.

But then what?

Jet put on his jacket and sat down on the sofa and picked up the book Skye had been reading last night. He ran a finger along the interesting leather tooling on the binding and flipped it open.

Handwritten, the flowing cursive writing was in a language totally foreign to him. Only the name written on the inside cover made any sense. Bessie Ferguson McDougall, Skye's late aunt.

He shut the book and squeezed it in his hands. He'd promised John Smilie he'd be the voice of the CWGC in Kilmarnock—he'd make some calls to help expedite the committal process so Skye could lay her aunt to rest and return to the States. A job he'd come to regret with each passing day.

Skye opened the door to the room and found Jet sitting on the sofa with Bessie's journal in his hands.

"Are you ready to go downstairs for a spot of breakfast?" she asked.

He placed the journal on the table and stood. "I'm right behind you."

They sat in the dining room and Joan filled their coffee cups. "How did you two lovebirds sleep?" she asked.

"Very well," Skye said. "The room is very comfortable."

"I'm glad," Joan said. She faced Jet. "What time's your meeting with Reverend Taylor?"

"Eleven o'clock," he said.

Skye did a double take. She hadn't known the good reverend was officiating over Busy's memorial service. Then again, there likely wasn't another reverend in a small town like this.

Joan handed Jet and Skye a menu of this morning's specials. "I hope you don't think I'm being too forward, but I thought I'd mention that we, the Killie Inn, have wedding packages. We can accommodate twenty-five couples inside and, if the weather permits, double outside with a tent and tables in the courtyard."

"Good to know," Jet said. "We'll keep you in mind. We haven't made a decision whether we're going to put our money into the reception or the honeymoon." He gave Skye a discrete wink.

Skye got the idea he was having a good time messing with Joan.

"I understand," Joan said. "When you decide, don't hesitate to call."

Jet and Skye ordered their breakfast, and Joan went to put in the order. "You're really getting into this, aren't you?"

"Excuse me?" Jet folded his arms across his chest. "This is all your doing."

"I know," Skye said. "But you don't have to enjoy it so much."

Chapter 30

Skye thought the day was quite fitting for a graveside memorial service—gray and dismal. Jet helped her climb out of the back seat of a cab at the Kilmarnock Cemetery, and he opened a large umbrella to shield her from the pelting rain.

Since Busy's service didn't start for another half hour, Jet suggested they go to see if Bessie's father's headstone had been removed so the new inscription could be added.

"The lair is in Section K," Skye said.

"I know," he said.

Skye nodded mutely.

Of course, he had all the details.

As they trudged along, the wet ground sucked on their shoes and the pungent odor of black loam perfumed the air. Skye tugged her sweater closed, but her chill had absolutely nothing to do with the inclement weather.

She knew Jet would be distracted today, but she hadn't expected the systematic shut down of all emotion since they left the Killie Inn. This man had seemingly become very adept at insulating himself from people.

Skye assumed he'd mastered the defense mechanism early in his life. A survival tactic he'd learned to endure his tenure at the orphanage.

Jet held the umbrella for Skye at arm's length. He didn't seem to care about getting soaked. He could have snuggled underneath, but then he'd have to encroach on her personal space.

Skye had a feeling he'd drown before he let that happen.

One way or another, Jet knew their visit to the cemetery would be the beginning of the end of his time with Skye. Whether another inscription had been added to the stone or not, she'd be on her way back to the States very soon.

End of story.

Jet trekked through aisles of headstones feeling like a dead man walking. He'd been trying to brace himself. As much as he knew they could never be together, he couldn't help wanting her.

They passed Section J.

The rain made Jet's bones ache and his feet seem lead-filled. Water trickled off the umbrella. He could smell the grass and earth. Skye's feet were soaked in her open-toed sandals, and she struggled to keep up. She took two strides to every one of his.

He slowed his pace only when he reached their destination.

They stood in front of the stone reading the inscription. *Private W.P. McDougall, Royal Scots, 30*

October 1918, age 37. A Celtic cross was etched in the center of the stone—years of weather had dulled and eroded the granite. Beneath the cross was the next inscription. *His wife Margaret, 2 October 1980, age 96.*

Another six inches lay empty between Margaret's information and the ground. "I guess the stonemason needs a nudge to get started on another inscription."

Skye closed her eyes and sighed. "It appears so."

Both he and Skye grew quiet. Like they'd run out of things to say.

"It's ironic really," Skye said. "Nearly a hundred years has passed, and nothing has changed. Soldiers are still fighting wars and still being killed. My uncle was in his thirties. How old was Busy?"

"Twenty-four and my responsibility. I let him down."

Skye reached around and placed her hands on Jet's face. "Listen to me," she said. "You did everything you could to try to save him."

"It wasn't enough."

Skye held fast. "I think you feel guilty because you're still here. That's why you avoid doing things that make you feel alive."

"Is that what you think?" Jet's eyes searched hers.

Without breaking eye contact, she rose up on tiptoes to kiss him. Her velvety lips brushed his so sweetly he thought his knees would buckle.

And he couldn't restrain himself any longer.

The umbrella slipped out of his fingers and fell to the ground. He wrapped his arms around her and deepened the kiss.

She clung to him, and suddenly, he felt whole again.

She wound her arms around his neck and threaded fingers through his hair.

Seconds became minutes. Then, without warning, the sky opened up. Rain pelted them, soaking them to the skin. He bent down and whipped the umbrella back over their heads. "I think we should go. Busy's service is in the newer section over the knoll."

In the distance, he could see a cluster of people.

Black umbrellas formed a dark cloud over the gathering. As they got closer, he could hear the voice of the good reverend.

"Benjamin's inquisitiveness got him into trouble on more than one occasion. I remember him, as a young lad, lifting my robes to discover what I wore underneath."

The crowd chuckled.

"The day Mrs. Appleby fainted in church, he thought he'd killed the poor woman. He didn't know she'd been diagnosed with low blood pressure. You see, he'd let his pet mouse loose in church, hoping the ruckus would cut the service short. When I asked him why he did it, he said he wanted enough time to get home to change before he went to the game with his father." The reverend smiled fondly. "Benjamin loved his football."

Busy's mom must not have known about her son's prank because she covered her mouth and shook her head.

"The day he enlisted, he came to my office in the rectory and told me he wanted to make a difference in this world."

Jet watched Skye. Tears lined her cheeks. He dug a handkerchief out of his breast pocket and handed it to her. "Are you okay? Do you want to leave?"

Skye shook her head and dabbed her eyes. "No, I'm fine. I always cry at weddings and funerals."

"Does anyone else have any stories about Benjamin they'd like to share?" Reverend Taylor asked.

"I do," Jet said.

All heads turned.

"One of the most difficult tasks we were faced with in the Persian Gulf was winning the trust of the Iraqi civilians. The Americans had stern rules about forcing protection on the civilians. We didn't use such strong-arm tactics. We replaced our metal helmets with cloth berets. The fabric headgear created a less threatening appearance and instilled a measure of trust in the locals."

Jet rubbed his chin and shrugged.

"Busy thought we could do more. He organized a football tournament between the Iraqi Cadets from a nearby Military Academy and the Baghdad Support Unit."

"Who won?" Busy's father asked.

"Busy's team. Who else?"

A tear slid down Busy's dad's cheek and he put his arm around his wife.

Reverend Colin Taylor said, "Let us bow our heads. The Lord is my shepherd..."

The Grahams consoled one another. And in that second, Jet saw Busy reaching down to grab one of the booby-trapped rifles.

Skye squeezed his hand.

He leaned his head toward her.

"Shall we pay our final respects?" she said.

A line had formed in front of the Grahams. Beside the couple stood the good reverend. They stepped into the queue.

"Thank you for coming, Captain Dalry," Mrs. Graham said.

Mr. Graham stuck out his hand and shook Jet's. "We appreciate your kind words."

Jet nodded. "Busy was a good friend."

Skye stepped forward and shook Busy's parents' hands. "I'm so sorry for your loss."

When Skye came to Reverend Colin Taylor he stepped forward. "I thought I recognized you," he said.

May Graham interrupted. "I hope you'll join us back at the house for tea and a light lunch."

Finally, it stopped raining.

Skye and Jet hitched a ride to the Graham's modest home from one of their neighbors. The Women's Auxiliary from the Grange Manse had set chairs out in the living room and prepared food for the guests. Jet joined Mr. Graham out in the garden, and Mrs. Graham showed Skye around the tidy house. The floors gleamed and the counters were polished. Skye leaned inside Busy's tiny bedroom. The coverlet pulled across the pillow and mattress without a wrinkle. Skye noticed Busy's football helmet perched on a shelf above the headboard—likely set there for easy access if an impromptu scrimmage on the pitch arose.

Mrs. Graham acted like a zombie as they paced through the rooms. When they walked into the living room, Skye figured she'd run out of things to say. Her only child had died and, with him, all her hopes and dreams. There would be no fruitful old age. No daughter-in-law, no grandchildren, and no one to visit when she became infirmed.

Jet met Skye in the dining room. They sat by themselves until the luncheon was almost over.

Mr. Graham sat down beside Jet and gave him an envelope. "I bought them a few months ago. I thought they might help Benjamin get his fighting spirit back. I'd like you to have them."

A large woman from the ladies' auxiliary leaned into the room. "Mr. Graham? Mrs. Graham would like you to come and say good-bye to your guests."

Jet jammed the envelope inside his pocket and he and Skye got up and made their way to the door.

They were a half a block away when Jet reached in and opened the envelope. For the first time all day he cracked a wide smile.

"What is it?" Skye asked.

Jet pulled out two stubs. "Tickets to this afternoon's game.

CHAPTER 31

Rugby Park Stadium was filled to capacity.

The crowd sang and cheered as Skye and Jet wormed their way through the gates. Their seats were located at the end of an aisle, specifically designed for wheelchair access.

Busy's dad had obviously thought of everything.

Skye couldn't help but get caught up in the excitement. Instantly, she became a fan, though she didn't know much about the game. The teams ran out on the pitch and the crowd went wild. The commentator announced each of the player's names as they sprinted toward the bench.

At the other end of the field, three kilted spectators stole onto the pitch. Before they could be escorted from the field, all three bent over and tossed up their kilts. Each man had two letters scrawled on each cheek of their buttocks. KI, LL, IE. The crowd chanted the name over and over and went wild as security removed the three blokes.

Once the game started, Skye sat back and watched Jet. It didn't take long before he got into it. Every so often, he'd lean toward Skye and give her the lowdown on one of the players or explain what happened and what the team would likely do next.

For the first time since they met, she felt optimistic. Perhaps the memorial service today had allowed him to put the past where it belonged.

She still savored the slow burn from this morning's kiss at the cemetery. She had no doubt he was attracted to her, and he couldn't continue to deny his feelings for her. She daydreamed about what might happen later. Jet's intense personality made her nervous about being intimate with him. She wasn't a virgin, but she wasn't experienced either. She'd never been in love before.

Is that what this was?

At times like this, she wished that there was some sort of foolproof checklist she could refer to.

She'd certainly become fixated on Jet. The easiest thing would be to walk away from him and never give him another thought. She'd never had to work this hard to be noticed before. It had been a total role reversal for her.

Maybe it was God getting even with her.

She stilled.

Who thought such things? Aunt Bessie did. But then, after reading her last journal entry, Skye believed Aunt Bessie had been somewhat fanatical when it came to her beliefs.

It stunned Skye that Bessie chose to live her life alone.

God didn't get even with anyone.

Bessie's own insecurities kept her alone.

And Skye would not let her insecurity win.

Suddenly, everything coalesced. Everything she'd been feeling since the moment she'd met Jet.

She loved him.

There. She admitted it. Why else would she be pursuing a relationship with a man when she'd be halfway around the world in a couple of weeks?

They'd figure something out.

"Skye?" Jet said. "Are you okay?"

Skye snapped out of her thoughts. "Fine," she said. "What happened?" she asked, suddenly hearing the roar of the crowd.

"Killie just scored."

She glanced up and the board. "Woohoo."

An excited fan sitting beside Skye pushed her and she pressed against Jet. The close proximity made them lunge for each other.

The kiss exploded.

Both free-fell into the abyss. Tongues danced and hands explored. In their own little world, they didn't notice the game had resumed until the man seated beside Skye, the same one that shoved her against Jet, started snickering. "You two best get a room," he said.

Jet and Skye broke apart, just as Killie stole the ball, and thankfully, their heavy petting was forgotten.

Killie won against the Celtics six to five.

The crowd filtered out of the park, and the after-party had begun.

"Do you want to go to the Bull and Finch to celebrate?" Jet asked.

"I'd rather we had our own party." Her sultry suggestion could not be misinterpreted.

They went straight back to the inn.

Upstairs, as Jet put the skeleton key in the lock, Skye placed her hand on his. "I'm nervous," she said.

"Skye," Jet said, opening the door. "We need to talk."

Skye didn't like his tone. Talk?

Unusual didn't begin to describe this man. Most men would want to make love first and talk later. He held the door for her, and she went inside. He tugged her over to the couch where they both sat down.

"I don't think we should do this," Jet said. "Why start something that has to end in a couple of weeks?"

"Why does it have to end?"

"Are you going to stay in Britain?"

Skye didn't answer immediately.

"My point exactly."

"Is that why you've been keeping me at arm's length—because there's no future in it? Surely your accident has taught you the importance of seizing the moment."

Jet picked up her hands and kissed them. "There are certain things you don't want to know."

"You're wrong. I really do. It's the only way I can make sense of it."

Jet stood and paced. "My legs are horribly disfigured. They're not pretty."

"And you think 'nice legs' are what I want in a man?" Skye got up and blocked his path. "You're doing great! You're walking without a cane. When I first met you, you were quite unsteady on your feet. I don't care about a few scars. I'm in awe of you."

"Don't be. You don't know the half of it."

Skye sat on the sofa. "Then tell me."

Jet couldn't seem to look at her. "My legs weren't the only things disfigured in the blast. I only have one testicle."

Realization dawned on Skye.

"That likely means my fertility is in question. Surely, you'll want to have children someday. Kids aren't something I can guarantee."

"Neither can I. Who's to say that I don't have fertility issues? No one knows whether or not they can conceive a child until they're actively trying."

"Why get involved with damaged goods when you can avoid the heartache?"

"That's not your call. It's mine. And if you think I'm not going to get involved with you because there's a chance we'll have to work at getting pregnant, you don't know me very well. Besides, aren't you putting the cart before the horse? We haven't even slept together and you're talking about getting pregnant."

Jet moved her aside and sat down on the sofa. "It won't work."

Skye had heard enough. Tired of reasoning, she knew actions spoke louder than words. She straddled him, held his face, and kissed him.

Initially, he didn't kiss her back, but the moment her tongue gained entry into his mouth, he relented. The kiss became carnal, but that's all.

He never so much as touched her breasts. And right now her breasts ached to be touched. Gentlemanly ways, be damned. She picked up his hand and placed it on her breast.

The groan that tore from his lips was like that of a wounded animal. "No," he said. "I can't do it. I want you so badly I'm shaking."

"So am I."

All at once he lifted her off his lap and stood up.

"Did I do something wrong?"

"You didn't do anything wrong," Jet said. "I'm impotent."

Chapter 32

Skye opened her mouth to say something, but she couldn't think of an appropriate response.

Jet jammed things into his bag and swung it over his shoulder. He reached for the door.

"That's it then?" The words burst from Skye's mouth.

He didn't respond.

"What do your doctors say?"

He didn't turn around, but his back shot up. "You deserve more than half a man." He marched out the door and disappeared down the hall.

Suddenly Skye had the strongest feeling of déjà vu. Bessie wrote a note to Aldo and fled their hotel room. Now, Jet had done the very same thing.

She closed the door and sat down.

The relationship similarities were spot on. Bessie had one breast and Jet had one testicle. Right now, Skye could really use some of the advice her aunt used to dole out. What did this all mean? Was Skye supposed to fight for Jet or accept that their relationship was over?

She needed a sign.

She grabbed the journal and the brooch, and based on the color and temperature of the stone, she knew time had nearly run out. In a matter of days Skye would lay Bessie to rest, and she needed to be finished reading the journal so she could place the Luckenbooth in the lair. Skye knew she didn't have a moment to waste. With a little luck she'd finish the journal by the morning.

Last time it took quite a while to manually warm up the brooch and make it hot enough to work. She had a better idea. She dug through her suitcase and pulled out her blow-dryer.

Bessie truly believed the loss of her breast was penance for fornicating with Aldo. And as one of God's servants, she had to be held accountable for her actions.

It had been a hard lesson to learn, but she learned it. The void held her prisoner. She told the children in her Sunday school class to always consider the consequences of their actions, or they would have to atone later.

She tried not to have second thoughts.

Bessie didn't blame Dr. Lamont or Dr. Miskovic for removing a perfectly healthy breast. Both doctors were innocent pawns in her blasphemy. If He could part the Red Sea, He could certainly make a diseased breast healthy again.

He'd shown her mercy. And for that concession, she promised never to commit adultery again. Of course, there were safeguards to make sure her course didn't waver. The scars were angry. She'd become a poor excuse for a woman. A freak. A circus act. No man, not even Aldo, would find her physically attractive ever again.

Adultery problem forever solved.

Too bad her traitorous heart never got with the program. Every night she dreamed of Aldo—touching and making love to her.

Dr. Lamont scheduled an appointment for her to talk with a psychiatrist. "I'm worried about you," Dr. Lamont said. "You've lost so much weight you remind me of an Auschwitz survivor. It's time you talked to someone to help you come to terms with what happened."

"You make it sound like I'm half dead."

"In some ways I think you are. You're a totally different person today than before your surgery. You were outgoing and personable, and now you only talk when spoken to."

"Are you unhappy with my work?"

"No," Dr. Lamont said. "Your work is commendable. This has nothing to do with your job. You used to be very active, go out regularly on a social basis."

"And because I prefer to stay in to care for my elderly mother you think I should see a psychiatrist?"

Dr. Lamont sighed.

"There's nothing wrong with my head. As for my breast, it's gone, and nothing is going to bring it back."

"That's not exactly true. I've been doing some research on reconstructive surgery and injections."

"Surgery and injections?"

"There are some new surgeries, rotating the muscle from the chest wall or silicone injections."

Bessie had enough.

Those fixes would go against God's plan. "Pass," she said, wiping a tear from her eye. "No more unnecessary surgeries."

The scene in Skye's head began to flicker. The brooch had already begun to cool.

No. This couldn't be happening. She needed more time. She glanced at the journal. There were many pages still unread.

She grabbed the blow-dryer again. As she reheated the stone she flipped ahead in the journal. She didn't know if jumping ahead would even work, but she was out of options.

Aldo sat in the library of his prestigious Chestnut Hill home, a wedding gift from Vito. Built at the turn of the century, the Georgian style estate sat on three acres of prime real estate in the town of Newton, less than ten miles from downtown Boston.

Angelina, Aldo's wife, knocked and opened the polished maple door. Maple bookcases flanked the marble fireplace and a large desk sat in front of French doors leading out onto a tiled patio above the grounds. "Daddy's here," Angelina said. "He'd like to talk to you."

Aldo's attention flipped to his wife. He took off his glasses and sat back in his chair. "Send him in."

Angelina was a beauty. She knew how to throw a dinner party and how to disappear when the men talked business. Vito thought he'd arranged a profitable union in joining the two families. A mistake. Rudolph "Blues" Massimo had no business sense. After Blues last scheme, Aldo knew Angelina's father couldn't manage a successful bowel movement without help.

The door opened once again, and Blues sauntered inside. He wore a fedora, wing tips, and a pinstripe suit. If nothing else, he dressed smartly.

Aldo stood up and shook his father-in-law's hand before turning to the sideboard. "How goes it?" He held up the cut glass bottle of whiskey in a silent offering.

Blues nodded. "Can't complain." He unbuttoned his jacket and sat down in one of the leather chairs facing the desk.

Aldo placed the glasses on the edge of his desk and splashed whiskey into one, then the other. He passed Blues his glass and sat down across from him. "What can I do for you?"

"I'm here to make you rich beyond your wildest dreams."

Aldo took a sip of his whiskey. He surveyed the room. "Do you think I need money?"

"Anthony Pino's been casing a joint for months. I'm telling you, it's a slam dunk. It's all planned down to the last detail." Blues drained his glass.

Aldo poured him another. "Then what do you need me for?"

"We need some strong-arm support. There ain't none better than my son-in-law."

Aldo supposed he should be flattered. The hairs on the back of his neck bristled. "Anthony Pino's a pretty good case-man." That's when Aldo felt it—the searing heat in his pants pocket. He stood up so the Luckenbooth brooch wouldn't press against his groin and burn him. The last time the brooch became this hot, he was having a meeting at Trattoria Giulliana's. When he went to the bathroom to remove it from his pocket, the restaurant was hit. Three of his men were slain. He eyed Blues. "I'll pass," Aldo said. "I'm short-handed right now."

"Sure," Blues said. He acted like he understood, even if he didn't. "Would you be willing to hide my cut? I mean until the heat's off?"

Aldo fingered the brooch that had already begun to cool.

"Sure," he said. "I can do that."

Crap.

Once again, the images from the past flickered.

It seemed that both Bessie and Aldo lived separate lives in the years that followed her surgery.

Skye wasn't surprised.

The only certainty now was the brooch, the chemically treated azurite, had nearly run its course, and Skye still didn't have a clue what message Bessie was trying to send her.

Skye switched on the blow-dryer, a final attempt to reenergize it. This time she flipped about a dozen pages from the end of the journal.

Skye stopped at Java Joes to pick up a double non-fat latte on her way back to her Greenwich Village townhouse. She'd spent all day at a casting call for the leading role in an upcoming new production called *Dogs*. She'd been home for a couple of weeks and had fallen into a routine. Her audition today had gotten her a second call back.

She missed Jet. The pain dulled each day. If she kept busy, she'd be over him in no time. She buzzed herself into her building and unlocked her apartment.

The cell phone in her purse chimed. She dug it out and answered. "Hello." Skye heard sniffing on the other end. "Is anybody there?"

"Skye? It's mom." Mary Andrews's voice shook.

"What's wrong?" Skye asked.

"I told your father not to move Aunt Jane by himself, but he wouldn't listen."

Skye remembered responding to her mother's email while she was in the UK.

"Aunt Jane got an apartment in this new retirement village called Rolling Meadows. Her house had too many stairs and too many rooms for an eighty-seven-year-old."

"You told me," Skye said cutting off her rambling. "What happened to dad?"

"You know your father, always acting like a twenty-year-old. He started having chest pains."

"Is he all right?"

Mary's breath caught on a whimper.

"Mom! Is dad all right?"

"No," Mary said, breaking down. "He's gone."

Just as Skye catapulted back to the present, the azurite stone in the Luckenbooth brooch died, leaving behind a crystal-clear stone, as cold as a chunk of ice.

Chapter 33

The Luckenbooth slipped from Skye's fingers along with Bessie's journal. Tears filled her eyes, and she could barely think straight. Her dad? Dead? In what, a few short weeks?

Skye jumped to her feet and paced.

She had to get home. She needed to lay Bessie to rest and go and spend time with her dad, however little he had left.

She gathered her clothes and placed them in her bag. She tossed the journal into her purse, and she picked up the Luckenbooth.

Lang had been right. The azurite stone was crystal clear and cold to the touch. When Skye held it in her hand, she felt nothing. She caressed the pin, thumb running over the stone. Lang told Skye that Bessie could never reveal the future because it would no longer be a certainty—knowing the outcome would change it. If Lang was right, Skye might have a chance to alter certain events.

She glanced at her watch and did the time conversion. Her mom and dad would just be getting up and having their coffee. She flipped open her cell and dialed.

It rang about five times.

"Hello?" Mary, Skye's mother, said.

"Mom, it's me."

"Skye? Is everything all right?"

Skye didn't want to alarm her mother. "Everything's fine. Is dad there? I need to talk with him."

"Hold on, I'll get him."

"Hi, honey. What's up?" Ross, Skye's dad, asked.

Skye took a deep breath and relaxed just hearing his voice. "I want you to listen to me very carefully," she said. "You need to hire someone to move Aunt Jane into the retirement home at the end of the month."

"Not you too." Ross groaned. "You and your mother are in cahoots."

"Dad. It's not like that. Do you remember our conversation right after Bessie died? I told you Bessie said she could see into the future."

"I remember."

"You told me about how Bessie had called you one day, right out of the blue, and told you to take the scenic route home after you finished work, rather than the highway."

"That's right, and there was a forty-car pileup that killed over twenty people the same day." Ross paused. "Wait a minute. What are you saying?"

A magical Luckenbooth brooch would be too difficult to explain, so Skye thought fast. "I had the journal Bessie left me translated. You need to hire someone to move Aunt Jane, and you need to make an appointment to see your doctor straight away."

There was silence on the other end.

"Dad? Are you still there?"

"I'm here." Ross spoke in low tones. "I'll call and make arrangements to do both this morning."

"Good. And I want you to take it easy. I'll be home as soon as I get Aunt Bessie laid to rest. A week at the outside." Skye hung up and sat back down on the sofa. She grabbed a piece of inn stationery and began making a list of things to do.

She went downstairs and ate her breakfast at eight, and shortly after nine she called John Smilie at the Commonwealth War Graves Commission. "The stone mason hasn't added the new inscription yet," she said after salutations.

"I know," John said. "Jet texted me last night."

"Do you have the name and address so I can expedite things?"

"Hold on and I'll get them for you." Skye could hear John shuffling papers on his desk. "Here it is, Moffat Monuments and Memorials." John rhymed off the address and phone number. "You'll have to visit the town council too, to take care of the fees."

"It's on my list of things to do. Thanks for all your help, John."

"No problem, Skye. It's a really nice thing you're doing—getting things settled for your aunt."

Skye hung up and dialed the Grange Manse Church. Reverend Taylor was not available, so she spoke to Ruth, his assistant. "I'm hoping Reverend Taylor is available to officiate the committal of my late aunt this Saturday."

"If you can hold a sec, I'll get the reverend's calendar."

Skye heard her put the phone down and she heard footsteps click on the hardwood floor. "I'm afraid he's busy this Saturday with a wedding."

"What about Sunday after church?"

"No, that won't work either. He's got a christening party."

"I see."

"He's free on Friday," Ruth said.

"Okay, we'll shoot for Friday afternoon then. Say two o'clock. Pencil it in for me and I'll get to work making the arrangements. I'll call and reschedule if I run into any snags."

The spring day called to Skye, so she decided to hoof it into town to clear her head. The fresh air invigorated her, full of the scents of heather. The beds of daffodils were eye candy. She had to make sure everything came together for Friday so she could make her travel arrangements to get home. When she reached Dickie Street, she went inside the Town Centre and up to the front desk. "I'm here to settle interment fees for my late aunt."

"I'll get Mr. Craig. Committals are his department," a stout woman said before she disappeared down the hall. Moments later she returned. "Is your name Skye Andrews?"

"Yes, it is."

"He's expecting you." The woman lifted the counter for Skye. "His office is the third door on your left."

Skye thanked the woman and headed down the hall. A bald man with a jiggling midsection stood and shook Skye's hand.

"I'm Michael Craig. Captain Jet Dalry called first thing this morning and told me to expect you."

"That was very nice of him," she said. Michael reached into his drawer and pulled out a pamphlet and handed it to her. "These are the current burial fees. If you could just tell me what type of service you require, I'll help you fill out the form."

Skye perused the list. "An interment of a cask of ashes."

"Do you have a bill of sale for the lair?"

"Yes, I do." Skye dug through her purse and pulled out the original paperwork from 1918.

Michael wrote down the pertinent information. "When would you like to hold the service?"

"This Friday afternoon, if possible?"

"I'll call the grounds keeper to make the arrangements for you." He picked up the phone and dialed. Moments later he hung up. "It's all set. Is there anything else I can help you with?"

"There is one more thing. You could tell me how to get to Moffat Memorials."

Michael drew her a map. Skye left the Town Hall and headed there directly.

The showroom was located a couple of blocks from the cemetery. Skye opened the door of the showroom brimming with multi-colored granite and marble—sharp edged stones gleaming with mirror-like finishes.

"May I help you?" The deep gravelly voice startled her. The voice belonged to a man who'd come through a door on the far side of the showroom.

"I'm trying to locate James Moffat," Skye said.

"That's me."

Skye stuck her hand out to shake his. "My name is Skye Andrews."

"Oh, yes," James said. "Captain Jet Dalry called this morning and gave me the location of the stone. According to my paperwork, I did the previous inscription in the late eighties. I understand this inscription is for Private McDougall's daughter."

"That's right."

"How many lines do you think you'll need?"

"No more than two. Her name, her date of birth, and when she died."

James recorded all the pertinent information and figured out the appropriate wording. "When is the service?"

"Can you have it done for Friday?"

He checked his schedule. "It'll be tight, but I'll make it happen."

Skye paid for the inscription and headed back to the inn.

She sat down in the lounge with a pot of tea and called Moira. Skye expected to leave a message, but oddly enough, Moira answered.

"Have you set the date yet?" she asked.

"As a matter of fact, everything is in line for this Friday afternoon. Sorry for the short notice, but I really have to get back to the States. Are you still interested in attending?"

"Let me check my calendar." Moira put the phone down and moments later picked it back up. "I've only got a couple of things slated. I should be able to rearrange them. I'll try to get there on Thursday, so I can spend some time with you before you turn around and head home."

It had taken the better part of the day, but Skye had done it, with a little help from Jet. It seemed he'd do everything he could to get her out of his life as quickly as possible.

She'd book her return flight in another day or two.

Joan freshened her pot with boiling water.

Skye's cell phone buzzed.

Maybe Moira couldn't get away after all.

"Hello?"

"What are you doing one week from today?"

"Jason? Is that you?"

"Of course it's me," he said. "You sound a little disappointed. Is everything all right?"

Skye's heart skipped a beat when she heard the male voice. She'd hoped Jet had finally come to his senses. "I'm tired. I've spent all day making arrangements for Bessie's committal this Friday."

"Oh, shit, Skye. I don't think I can make it. All our shows are sold out for the next three months."

"Don't worry. That's okay. I didn't expect you to be here." Skye put her cell to her other ear. "What's happening Monday?"

"Tammy and I are getting married."

CHAPTER 34

"It's about time," Skye said. She glanced up and noticed Joan hovering close by. "But why Monday?"

"Our weekends are shot because of the show. If we tie the knot on Monday, we can take a couple of days together before we have to get back to work."

"Monday doesn't leave you a lot of time to get the paperwork in place." Skye hated herself for being so pragmatic. She should be happy for Jason, instead of wishing it was her and Jet tying the knot.

"I have a friend at the registrar's office. The certificate and license will be issued by the end of the week."

"That's great then."

"You don't sound very happy."

"I am, really. I'm just tired."

"I'd like you to come. You're my best friend and I'd really like you by my side."

How could she refuse? "I can catch the train back to Edinburgh late Friday or early Saturday, depending on when Moira leaves."

"Smashing," Jason said. "Oh, bugger. I almost forgot. My cell died. And I'll be too busy to get a new one this week, so call the Raverse to let me know when I can pick you up."

"If you think I'm staying with you two at the loft you can think again. I'll come to your wedding, but I'll find my own hotel room somewhere." She didn't have a clue where yet, but she'd figure it out. "I'm going to make arrangements to fly home after the wedding."

"You're leaving?"

"I've done what I came here to do. Besides, I need to get home. My dad's not well."

"What?" Jason said. "When did that happen?"

"Recently."

"I'm sorry." So was she. She'd begun to think the purpose of Bessie's journal was to save her father's life.

"What about Jet?"

"What about him?"

"Nothing," Jason said. "I thought you two had a thing going."

"Yeah, well, so did I." Once again Skye noticed Joan flitting around. "Where are you holding the ceremony?"

"At the Raverse. We're going to use the wedding set from the show. Can you believe it?"

It couldn't be more perfect. "What time does the curtain go up?"

"Very funny," Jason said. "It's going to be an afternoon service, so come around three. The Backstage Pub is hosting the reception."

"I'll be there," Skye said, and hung up the phone.

Joan hurried over to Skye. "Another friend of yours is getting married?" No wonder Joan lingered. The woman thought she might score another wedding. "I'm sorry about eavesdropping, but I've been concerned about you since the captain left last night."

"The captain and I have split up." Who was she kidding? They never were together.

"Nonsense," Joan said. "I've seen the way you two act together. You were meant for each other." She sat down on the sofa beside Skye and squeezed her hand. "Bill and I used to fight a lot before we were married." She reached into the pocket of her apron and pulled out a folder and handed it to Skye.

"What's this?" Skye asked.

"I've worked out three different menus and pricing schemes for your wedding, and I've broken it down by cost per guest."

Skye had taken this little charade way too far. She wanted it to be true, longed for it, but Jet obviously didn't suffer the same angst. Tears hit the back of her eyes. "Joan, I appreciate all of your hard work, but Jet and I haven't made any decisions yet."

"I know," Joan said. "And I don't want you to feel pressured. This has always been my plan to offer this type of service for my guests. You simply got my motor running."

Great. At least someone's motor was running. Skye thanked her and escaped to her room so she didn't embarrass herself by dissolving into tears. She pushed inside her room and sprawled on top of the bed and fell fast asleep.

For the first time since she arrived in the UK, she fell into a deep sleep. She slept right through supper and awoke at eight the following morning. It took her several moments to clear her head because she'd been right out of it. After washing up, she went down to grab a coffee and toast. She didn't dawdle because she didn't want Joan to corner her again. After breakfast, she booted up her computer in the room.

It took her only a few minutes to figure out she had to fly into Albany and rent a car to get to River Glen, New York. There were two available flights on Tuesday—one at nine in the morning and the other at noon. She booked the noon flight so she could enjoy herself at the wedding. Then she opened a new page, and before she knew it, she'd Googled impotence.

The whim wound into hours of research.

She scanned site after site on erectile dysfunction. The term "impotence" referred to a failure to achieve or maintain a firm erection—a very common problem. One out of every ten men suffered from it.

According to the articles she read, most forms of ED had a physical cause—only ten percent had a psychological cause. Diabetes and prostate cancer were at the top of the culprit lists because treatments reduced or prevented blood flow and nerve impulses. Other causes were the use of drugs or pelvic injury.

Skye quickly discounted drugs.

In the time she knew Jet, she'd never seen him take any pain medication. She jotted notes as she sifted through the data. She began with the least invasive procedure and worked her way to the most.

The first treatment involved drug therapy—tadalafil, sildenafil, and vardenafil—the least invasive and it allowed for more spontaneity. These drugs would only work when a man was sexually stimulated.

Unfortunately, thirty to forty percent of men who tried oral drug therapy failed. So, the next option became injection or suppositories. These treatments were more successful because they were more direct, but the idea of injecting or shoving a small applicator into the urethra sent shivers up Skye's spine. She could only imagine how a man might react.

The vacuum device sucked. Literally. The cumbersome apparatus could cause bruising, painful tingling and impair a climax.

The most invasive procedure, the penile implant, had some merit. Insertion required a two-day hospital stay, but the benefits seemed to outweigh the detriments. Gently squeezing the concealed pump in the scrotum resulted in an erection. Depressing the deflation site would end the erection. Simple and immediate.

Issue handled.

She checked her watch.

Where did the day go? It would be suppertime in an hour. What was wrong with her? She'd just spent the entire day researching a condition for a man who didn't want anything to do with her. She shut down her computer and shoved it into her suitcase.

Then she reached for the velvet bag that contained Bessie's bronze urn and set it out on the coffee table beside the journal and Luckenbooth. Skye grabbed the brooch and squeezed it. The azurite was devoid of any color or warmth.

She thought about Aldo Genovese. His cold, sad eyes.

She'd only met the man once, but his eyes still haunted her. Those eyes brimmed with pain and longing. Despite a lifetime of being apart, he still loved Bessie.

Is that what would become of her and Jet?

Skye didn't know if Bessie saw Aldo ever again. She doubted it, but she'd never know for sure. The last journal pages would forever be shrouded in mystery. If the azurite in the Luckenbooth hadn't died and things had taken their normal course, her father would have died. He might still, but at least she'd get to spend some time with him before it came to pass.

For that, Skye would be eternally grateful.

Skye picked up the brooch and kissed it.

She slid the urn out of the velvet casing and unscrewed the lid. She dropped the Luckenbooth into her aunt's ashes, and as she resealed it, she said a silent prayer of thanks for the glimpse into the past, present, and the future.

Chapter 35

Skye didn't know what was wrong with her—Wednesday she couldn't stop crying. She should have been relieved her responsibilities with her aunt were almost at an end. But no. She couldn't stop thinking about all of Bessie's sacrifices.

Skye's emotions were in a state of total upheaval.

With everything she learned about Bessie's life, she no longer felt the stabbing grief over losing her. Skye would have liked to strangle her aunt for being such a zealot—believing in something to the end of all else.

A little part of her was awestruck at believing in something so strongly. She'd always thought she and her aunt had a lot in common. Bessie thought so too. Or at least that's what her aunt had said. Skye sat back and wondered how her aunt survived the loss of Aldo and her breast, one right after the other. And what about regrets—did Bessie have any? Her sacrifices were astounding.

If Bessie had been bitter, she never showed it.

Or maybe after a while, the bitterness faded.

Skye would never really know.

Soon she found herself comparing Bessie and Jet.

These two loved ones were hauntingly alike. Both had lost body parts that forced them to question their sexuality. Bessie cut Aldo out of her life, and Jet had tried to pull the same shit on her.

Certainly, Bessie had her beliefs, but somewhere they'd run amuck. God wasn't punishing or letting her live. What kind of a God would dole out such harsh penance? Skye had a less strict view. In her opinion, God should have been a lifeline, not an anchor.

Bessie had options. Jet had them too.

Options Skye investigated yesterday. She skimmed through the pages of options she'd copied. Today, she knew she'd wasted her time. Like Bessie, Jet would rather push her away than work things out.

Skye dropped her research in the trash. Then she lay down on the bed and cried herself into a deep sleep.

Early Thursday afternoon, Skye met Moira at the Kilmarnock train station. The train arrived five minutes late, but Skye spotted Moira right away with her salt and pepper hair bobbing above the crowd. She couldn't believe how close she felt to Moira for only knowing her a short while—this would be the second time they'd met. It seemed they shared a connection.

Bessie.

Moira and Bessie had communicated often, though Skye doubted Bessie had shared any of the details of her love life with Aldo, the notorious mobster, or her mastectomy.

"Did you have a good trip?" Skye asked, grabbing one of her bags.

"Feels like I've been around the world, twice. The train pulled out of Southampton Central just after five this morning, and I had two connections."

Skye checked her watch. "You must be exhausted. You've been on the move nearly eight hours."

"I know. But I made the most of it. Caught up on some notes and read some studies on some new techniques in the industry, so it's all good."

"I'm glad you're here," Skye said, giving Moira a hug.

When Skye pulled back, concern marred Moira's face. She held Skye at arm's length. "Are you okay?"

"I've been better." Skye really needed some advice right about now. "I've got a cab waiting outside. How about we get you settled, and I fill you in on what's happened."

They headed back to the inn, and Joan greeted them upon their arrival. "This must be cousin Moira," she said. Skye made formal introductions, and Joan processed the paperwork by running Moira's credit card. When she was finished, she passed Moira a key. "You'll be staying in the yellow room, one floor up, and three doors down on the right."

Skye grabbed Moira's bag. "I'll help you upstairs first. Then we'll meet down here in a half hour."

"Sounds great." Moira faced Joan. "Is there any chance we could get a cup of tea and some scones?"

"I'll put together a tray. It'll be in the dining room for you," Joan said.

Skye dropped Moira at her room.

"I'll be down in a flash," Moira said. "I just want to freshen up a little.

Skye waited. Joan delivered the tea, biscuits, and clotted cream and had been grilling Skye about Jason's wedding this weekend.

"It's odd getting married in a theater," Joan said.

"Not for Jason and Tammy," Skye said. "The theater is their home."

Just then, Moira came bounding in the room.

"I'll give you two some privacy," Joan said, disappearing into the kitchen.

"Did I hear right?" Moira asked. "Is the infamous Jason Hansome getting married?" Moira sat down beside Skye.

"Hard to believe, isn't it?" Skye poured her a cup of tea.

"Kind of." Moira dropped a cube in her cup and stirred. "I thought he was in love with you?"

Skye's gaze flipped to her face, and she shot her a questioning glare.

"Bessie might have mentioned it in one of her letters. I think she said he came to Britain to try to forget you."

Skye really had been the only one out of the loop. "That might have been true once upon a time, but that ship sank long ago." A lump formed in her throat and Skye swallowed hard. Suddenly, just like the other night, her eyes filled with tears.

Moira put her cup and saucer on the table and reached for Skye. "Oh my God. Bessie told me you jilted him. Are you still in love with him?"

"No." Skye mustered a laugh in between the sniffles. "Bessie wasn't wrong. I'm in love with a totally different man who I met a few weeks ago. His name is Captain Jet Dalry, and I'm frustrated because, this time, I got jilted."

"Okay. Back up. Tell me everything," Moira said.

And Skye did—minus the bits about the Luckenbooth and the journal.

Moira waited patiently until Skye brought her up to speed. "For what it's worth, I don't think you should go back to the States without having another conversation with him. You need to tell him you're in love with him."

"I'm not sure it would do any good. And what's the point? I've got to get back to the States. My dad has some medical issues." Issues, Skye prayed, were presently being identified and worked out.

"Then you need to go and say good-bye so you'll have closure. If you don't, you'll never put him behind you. You'll always be wondering 'what if?'"

"I'll think about it," Skye said. "Want to go with me to the flower shop? I'd like to order some flowers for the service tomorrow."

"Sure," Moira said.

"If there's time, I wouldn't mind having a peek in a little dress shop I spotted the other day. I could really use a new dress for Jason's wedding."

"Sounds like fun."

Skye carried three dresses into the change room and had already modeled the first two. She'd saved her favorite pick until last. She slipped into the form-fitting indigo cocktail dress. Her eyes shimmered like blue topaz. The silky fabric cascaded off her shoulders and across her breasts. She opened the door to the fitting room and stepped in front of the full-length mirror. "What do you think?"

Moira, who'd been glancing at another rack, spun to face Skye. "Wow. That's my favorite. Just the right amount of elegance and enough cleavage to be considered sexy."

Skye checked both left and right. "I agree." She went back into the fitting room and changed. "What time is it?"

"Nearly six."

"Why don't we grab a snack at the Bull and Finch?"

"Heck of an idea."

Skye carried the dress over to the cashier and paid. They stopped at the train station and made arrangements for their return trips on Saturday. Their respective trains, Skye's to Edinburgh and Moira's to Southampton Central, would depart within a half hour of each other, so they could ride to the station together.

At the Bull and Finch, they drank some lager and ate bangers and mash. It was only nine when they returned to the inn, but both women were exhausted and retired to their respective rooms.

On the way to the Kilmarnock Cemetery, Skye and Moira stopped to pick up the floral arrangement—a beautiful spray of flowers filled with heather, Bessie's favorite.

The cabby dropped them graveside.

Steel-gray clouds threatened rain.

The grave had been excavated to accommodate a cask of ashes. A green carpet edged the small square plot, and the headstone had been freshly etched with Bessie's information. Skye set the flowers at the base of the stone and placed the urn on the carpet.

In short order, Reverend Colin Taylor arrived, and Skye made introductions.

"Shall we begin?" he asked. "I took the liberty of contacting Bessie's long-time minister from the New Westminster Church in Boston. She helped me with some of the details to make this a more personalized committal."

The reverend spoke for about ten minutes.

He asked Skye to place the cask of ashes in the ground and it was all over. She thanked him and said good-bye.

Once the reverend left, Skye and Moira stood in front of the plot for a while. Skye found her voice first. "It's finally done," she said. "Thanks for coming. I'm sure Bessie's smiling knowing you're here."

The two women hugged and strolled along the row of stones and out through the gate. They continued along the road and very soon found themselves in the center of town.

"What do you want to do now?" Skye asked. "Our trains don't pull out of the station until first thing tomorrow morning."

"Let's find a pair of killer shoes to go with your dress."

CHAPTER 36

S kye and Moira sat on the bend at the train station while they waited for their trains to arrive.

"I'll be flying home Tuesday," Skye said.

"To New York?"

"No. I'll head to Albany, then I'll rent a car and drive to visit my parents in River Glen."

"Are your dad's health issues that serious?"

It would be fatal in a few weeks, if Skye didn't get home to waylay Mother Nature. "I'm afraid so."

A train lumbered into the station.

"That's mine," Moira said. The two women sat and waited for all the passengers to disembark. When the flood of people slowed, Moira hugged Skye. "I'm going to miss you."

Skye put her arms around Moira. "Me too."

Moira pulled a tissue out of her purse and dabbed her eyes. "Don't be a stranger. Keep in touch."

The two women hugged, and Moira stood and climbed aboard the train.

A half hour later, Skye boarded her train set for Edinburgh via Glasgow. By lunchtime, she arrived at Haymarket Station and hailed a cab. She collapsed the handle of her suitcase and the driver hefted it into the boot. "Where to?" he asked.

"The Thrift Hotel," Skye said. Moira's words of advice had made enough of an impact, and she decided the time had come to tempt fate. If Skye and Jet ran into each other at the hotel, she'd speak her piece. If not, then it wasn't meant to be.

The cabby sped through the streets and dropped her in front of the main entrance. The hotel wasn't much, but Jet had been right, the rooms were clean. Jet probably chose this particular hotel because he could walk to the castle and exercise his leg every morning and evening. She grabbed her bag and stepped up to the main desk to check in. The same male attendant with spiked blue hair greeted her. "Would you like a room?"

"Three nights, please." Skye fished out her credit card and handed it to the young man. "The last time I stayed here I had the room adjacent to Captain Jet Dalry. Is that one still available?"

The lad faced Skye. "I thought I remembered you. Let me check." He inputted some information into his computer. "It's free. Would you like me to reserve it for you?"

"Yes, please."

Ten minutes later, Skye found herself walking down the hall. She stopped in front of Jet's room. The maid's cart was down at the far end of the hall, unattended, so she pressed her ear to his door.

Nothing.

No surprise really. Why would he be in his room at one o'clock in the afternoon? She grabbed her bag, opened her door, and went inside. She unpacked the bare necessities—her dress and shoes for the wedding went into the closet, and her toiletries went into the bathroom. She washed her face and hands and brushed her hair. Then she picked up the phone and called the Raverse.

"Is Jason there?" she asked.

"He's on stage smoothing some bumps out of a scene."

Skye recognized the voice. "Talbot? Is that you?"

"Skye? I'm *so* glad you're back."

"Can you let Jason know I'm staying at the Thrift Hotel? Just in case he needs to get in touch with me."

"Sure. No problem. Are you coming to the wedding tomorrow?"

"I wouldn't miss it." Skye said good-bye and hung up. Stomach growling, she grabbed her purse and left to get some sustenance.

The dull morning sky had burned away leaving an empty clear blue sky. As she walked, she removed the jacket that she'd needed earlier and tied it around her waist. She didn't have any particular direction in mind, but very soon she found herself on the Royal Mile. She stopped at a coffee house and grabbed a sandwich and latte. Afterward, she headed towards the Luckenbooth shop. She thought she'd say good-bye to Lang, maybe even purchase a keepsake for her mom.

Skye took her time and window-shopped along the way. She would miss being in the UK and the people—Jason and Tammy, Moira, and most of all, Jet. As she approached the Luckenbooth shop she could see a sign on the door that read, "Closed Until Further Notice."

Lang never mentioned she was going away. Not that it was any of Skye's business.

She cupped her hands and peered through the front window. A light glowed in the back room, but all was quiet out front. The display cases were pulled apart. Maybe she'd gone to a jewelry show somewhere?

Just then, a young woman came through the back curtain carrying a box. The twenty-something gal had short brilliant red hair and a diamond piercing through her nose. She waved, set the box on the counter, and unlocked the door. "May I help you?" she said.

Skye motioned toward the sign. "I'm here to see Lang. I wanted to say good-bye and pick up a few things."

"What's your name?"

"It's Skye."

"I've been expecting you. Come on in." The woman stepped aside. "I'm Ariadne, by the way."

Sheesh. Why was Skye surprised? Lang always seemed to know about her comings and goings. Skye entered the shop. "Is Lang away? It seems like more than half of her inventory is missing."

"She isn't away. I'm afraid there's no easy way to tell you this. She passed away last Tuesday."

Skye wobbled on her feet. "Oh." She sucked in deep breaths and held onto the counter.

"Are you okay? Would you like a glass of water?" Ariadne put her hand on hers, disappeared through the curtain, and came back with a chilled bottle. Skye cracked the seal and took a sip. "What happened? Lang didn't appear to be unwell the last time I visited."

"She passed away in her sleep. Doctor said it was her heart, most likely."

"Are you a relative?" Skye asked.

"No. She didn't have any. Only me. We were good friends. I met her about five years ago when I came into the shop to see if she wanted to sell. She refused me flat. Said I knew nothing about upholding the tradition of the Luckenbooth. Ha. She was right."

"You work here?"

"I've been working here part-time ever since."

"Are you closing the shop?"

"No. Lang had papers drawn up last week. She signed the store over to me on Monday. Made me promise to continue selling the Luckenbooth."

Skye glanced at the cases.

Ariadne cleaned the glass on the top of the cases. "It's not what you think. I'm having new velvet liners made for the cases, so I thought I'd do inventory. All the Luckenbooths will be put back on display alongside some of my own custom-made jewelry."

Skye released the breath she'd been holding. She faced Ariadne. "You make jewelry?"

"Yes, would you like to see some?"

"I'd love to."

Ariadne reached beneath the counter and unrolled a velvet sleeve on the counter.

Skye regarded all the hand-tooled pieces. Rings, necklaces, bracelets, and brooches—all made out of silver and precious gemstones. She chose a ring with an amethyst stone for her mother and a money clip with a tiger's eye for her father.

"I'm not officially open, so I don't have a float, but you can pay by check, debit, or credit card."

Skye handed Ariadne her card. As Ariadne figured out the bill, Skye thought back to when she first arrived. "When you opened the door, you said you were expecting me."

"Oh, I almost forgot." She reached beneath the counter and pulled out a brown bag. "Lang asked me to give this to you. She said you'd be in on Saturday to collect it."

Skye opened the brown paper bag and pulled out a small cardboard box with one of Lang's business cards taped to the top. Two words, "Use Wisely," were scrawled across it.

Skye wiggled off the lid. Nestled inside on a cushion of cotton was Lang's Luckenbooth brooch.

CHAPTER 37

Skye signed the chit for her purchases and thanked Ariadne. She left the shop in a daze, mulling things over in her mind.

Lang, like Bessie, couldn't use the brooch to see her own destiny. Therefore, she saw her death through her connection with Skye. Both Lang and Bessie saw the end of their days through her. She felt like the grim reaper of Sibyls.

She pressed the bag containing the Luckenbooth to her heart and thanked Lang for such a noble gesture—sharing the brooch with her. Based on the pale color of the stone, Skye knew she had no choice but to use it wisely—there would only be one or two last forays into Bessie's journal.

As Skye meandered through the streets on her way back to the hotel, she stumbled across a hairdressers called A Cut Above. A sign in the window said "Walk-Ins Welcome," so Skye did just that.

Trixie, the owner, sat her down at her station and spun her around.

"What's it going to be? Do you want a makeover or a trim?"

"A trim," Skye said. "I'm going to a wedding tomorrow."

"How about some layers and highlights? It'll give you more volume and shine."

"You talked me into it," Skye said.

By the time Skye finished, it was after seven. She immediately went to her room and removed her shirt to wash away the hair that had fallen during the cut.

While she rubbed her back with a towel there was a knock at the door.

Crap. "Just a minute," she said. She shook out her shirt, put it back on and did up the buttons. It had to be Jet. She checked her reflection in the mirror and ran to open the door.

No one was there. She took a step further and noticed Jet walking toward the elevator.

"Jet? You know, you give up way too easily," she muttered.

He seemed taken aback.

"Didn't you just knock at my door?"

He shook his head.

Metal scraped. Skye noticed a man pushing through the emergency exit at the end of the hall.

"Oh, nevermind," Skye said.

"Are you here to see me?" Jet asked.

She shook her head. "I'm staying here for a few nights."

One of his eyebrows shot up.

"It's not what you think," she said. "I'm not stalking you."

"I wasn't thinking anything," Jet said. "I was just on my way out to eat. Want to join me?"

"Sure." She collected her coat and purse and joined him in the hall. They headed to the elevator and pushed the button.

"What do you feel like?" he asked. "For dinner." He added the two words almost as an afterthought.

In her mind she'd been wondering what he'd do if she backed him against the wall and kissed him. She squashed the image and tried to act indifferent. "I don't care. I'm easy."

Crap. Tell him something he didn't already know. What was wrong with her? She'd never been this nervous with a man before. Probably because she'd never had to work so hard at getting a man before.

The elevator dinged and the doors slid open.

Both Skye and Jet climbed aboard. They rode the elevator to the main floor and left the hotel.

"I know a quiet little place not too far away." Jet grabbed her hand and led the way.

The second he touched her, she felt the spark again. Her hand in his felt right. She wished he would never let go.

At the end of the block, they veered right. Halfway down the side street they came upon a deli called Etcetera. Jet opened the door and held it for Skye. "They have a little bit of everything in here."

Skye went inside and her mouth started to water. "It smells like freshly baked bread."

The honey oak floorboards were worn beneath her feet, and they creaked as she moved past the deli and cheese counter.

"There's some tables in the back," Jet said.

Skye stopped in front of the pastry counter. "May I start with dessert?"

"You can if you'd like." He chuckled.

They sat down at a table and Jet passed her a sandwich menu. She noticed he didn't bother to take one for himself.

"Aren't you eating?" she asked.

"I'm having my usual. The Ploughman."

The server arrived at the table to take their order.

"I'll have what he's having," Skye said.

Jet ordered two of the specials and a couple of soft drinks. When the waitress left, he faced Skye. "How was your aunt's service?"

"Reverend Taylor said some very nice things. Thank you for making some calls and introducing me to the townsfolk."

"It was the least I could do."

"My cousin came up from Southampton. Bessie would have been pleased."

"How nice."

Skye eyed Jet. She could spend hours in the depths of his chocolatey eyes. Soon her focus dipped to his lips. She remembered all too well the way they felt against hers.

"Skye," he said, his voice breaking. "I'm sorry I left the Killy Inn the way I did. I don't usually run away from my problems, but this one kind of got the better of me."

"Is that what you think I am? A problem?"

"What?" Jet reached over and put his hand on hers. "No. I'm the one with the problem."

Skye didn't move for fear he'd stop touching her. "After you left, I did some research on the internet. There are a lot of things you can do to...well, you know, to help or even fix the problem."

"You sound like one of my doctors." He scowled at her and then caught himself. "I'm sorry. Believe me, I'm doing everything I can to make things right."

"You are?" Skye hoped she didn't sound too eager. "I mean that's terrific."

He leaned close and lowered his voice. "If you don't mind, I'd like to stop talking about it now."

"Sure. Whatever." Skye sat back in her chair and noticed the waitress was headed back to the table carrying their plates.

They sat and ate the selection of boiled eggs, ham and cheese, and bread and chutney. Skye didn't realize how hungry she was until she dove into the assorted tapas.

Jet could barely taste the food he shoveled into his mouth.

He didn't dare make eye contact with Skye.

She'd been staring at him earlier, and it took all his strength not to drag her across the table and kiss her.

He found everything about this woman exciting—it was much more than her beauty; it was her attitude, her obstinacy, and her fearlessness.

He finished eating, and when he hazarded a glance, he discovered she had been watching him.

"What?" he asked.

"Are you mad at me?"

If only he were. That would make things so much easier. "No, I'm not mad."

"Good," she said. "Because there's something I want to ask you."

"Oh, yeah?"

"Are you busy tomorrow?"

"Mondays are slow days at the castle. There's nothing pressing. Why?"

"Feel like playing hooky?" His wrinkled brow told her he didn't understand.

"Hooky is slang for skipping school."

"What did you want to do?"

"I was hoping you'd be able to be my escort. Jason and Tammy are getting married tomorrow at three o'clock at the Raverse. The reception is afterward at the Backstage Pub."

"Why the rush to get married?"

"There's no rush," Skye said. Eyes wide, she dabbed her mouth with her napkin. "Why put off the inevitable?"

Damn.

A direct hit.

This woman knew how to push all the right buttons to get him going. "Are you finished?" he asked. "Your food, that is."

Skye nodded.

Jet stood up. He dug some bills out of his pocket and tossed them down on the table. Then he grabbed her hand and hauled her outside. He set a grueling pace back to the hotel. She had to take two steps to his one.

"What's wrong? Why are you so upset?"

Jet stomped inside the hotel and punched the elevator call button. Skye panted beside him. He'd had about all he could take. The doors opened and he pulled Skye inside.

"I'm sorry, okay?" Skye said.

The doors closed and Jet couldn't wait one second longer. He pulled her into his arms and kissed her.

She tasted so damn good, both sweet and tart, like raspberries and pomegranates. She melted against him, and he deepened the kiss.

The elevator pinged and slid to a stop. Jet stuck out his foot to stop the door from closing, and he set Skye at arm's length. She wobbled and her eyes fluttered open.

"After you," he said.

She straightened and hurried down the hall.

A man with an ice bucket tucked under his arm came out of the alcove and strode ahead of them. At her door, they stopped and noticed the man continuing down the hall. Skye rooted around in her purse for her key.

"I guess this means you're going to take me to the wedding," Skye said. She slid the key card into the door at the same time Jet lifted the hair from the nape of her neck and nuzzled it. The key card slipped out of her fingers and fell to the floor.

"Oh, gawd." She wrapped her arms around his neck. "Two days won't ever be enough." She went to kiss him, and he pulled back.

"What do you mean two days?"

Her hands fell to his chest. She seemed to be waging an internal battle. "I'm flying home on Tuesday."

"Oh," he said. He faced the wall. Two days? What the hell was the point? Why go through the agony of even trying to make love? Especially since he had the worst kind of performance anxiety—not only was he worried about getting it up but he didn't know if he could keep it up. By the time these thoughts swirled in his head, he'd completely switched off. No way. He wouldn't put himself through it. He was dead in the water before he'd swum a single stroke. "What the hell are we doing? We live on different continents. This is never going to work."

"Lots of people have long distance relationships."

"Not me." Jet bent down and handed her the card key. He dug his own key out of his pocket and leaned away. "If you still want to go to the wedding as friends, I'll knock on your door tomorrow at two."

Chapter 38

S kye didn't sleep well. Shortly after three in the morning, she got on her cell and called home to see how her dad's appointment went.***

"Hey, kiddo," he said. "You'll be happy to know my blood work came back completely normal, and I've got a stress test booked for this afternoon."

"That's terrific, Dad. Did you make arrangements to have someone move Jane?"

"Mort's Movers are handling it."

Whew. Skye breathed a sigh of relief. She'd be home well before he was supposed to have his heart attack, and with a little luck, these subtle changes would alter his fate. "Jason and Tammy are tying the knot tomorrow at three. I'll be flying home the day after. I can't wait to see you guys."

"Are you sure you don't want me to pick you up at the airport on Tuesday?"

"Nah. You never know with these international flights. I'll grab a rental when I land. Make sure you leave the door open."

"Your mother will be up waiting. She'll never be able to sleep knowing you're on your way."

He was probably right. "Okay, I better go," Skye said. "It's the middle of the night here and the walls in this hotel are paper thin—I've probably woken everyone up already. Love you."

For the next couple of hours, she soaked in the tub and painted her fingernails and toenails. She ran over last night's details a hundred times or more. Jet was one of the most private people she'd ever known, and she didn't think she'd ever figure him out. Earlier in the evening, he seemed to want her as much as she wanted him. Hell, he dragged her all the way back to the hotel so he didn't make a public spectacle kissing her.

The man could kiss.

He didn't hold anything back. She felt the raw need pulsing inside him.

But the moment they were alone, he froze.

Right after she told him she was leaving.

Damn her timing.

Maybe it was better this way. She got the impression he would have run away even if she'd been naked beneath him. She remembered how he felt as she pressed up against him.

Or did she?

Come to think of it, she didn't *feel* anything.

She'd been close enough to hear his heart pounding in his chest, but she didn't *feel* him hard and pressing against her.

Maybe her comment about leaving had given him a way out from an embarrassing situation.

Jet knocked at her door at exactly two the next afternoon. Military men were nothing if not punctual.

She opened the door and she nearly swooned. He was a delicious sight in his stone jacket, pants, and tie. His collar and pocket were striped with red colors.

"How many different suits do you have?" Skye asked.

"A few. This one is called number four dress. It can be worn on formal occasions that are not service related."

"I like it."

Jet appreciated her. Her silky indigo dress plunged and curved like waves on the Mediterranean. She could tell by the glint in his eye he liked what he saw. He handed her a corsage.

"How lovely." She opened the box and passed the orchid back to him. "Would you help me pin it?"

He slipped his fingers beneath the folds of fabric draped across her breasts and instantly her nipples pearled. Her involuntary reaction to his touch wasn't lost on him. He noticed. By the time he pinned the flower in place, perspiration beaded his brow.

This would be a tumultuous day.

They arrived at the Raverse around two thirty.

Jason stood on the stage like a deer caught in the headlights. "Did you see the reporter and photographer from *The Scotsman*?" Jason said. "Somehow the paper got wind of the wedding and sent someone over to do a human-interest piece. Guess we might get some decent wedding photos after all. The photographer's agreed to stick around after the ceremony to take some photos. I'd like you and Jet to stick around so I can get some of you two."

Skye nodded, but all she could think about was having a constant reminder of the man standing beside her—a man who didn't want anything to do with her. She knew exactly how Jason felt all those years ago when he'd fled to the UK. In less than two days, she'd be the one to do the fleeing.

Very soon all the guests, about fifty in total, took their seats in the theater and waited for Tammy to make her grand entrance. Talbot stood at the AV station waiting for his cue to start the wedding march.

The set for the wedding scene had been altered for the service. The Justice of the Peace, who everyone seemed to know as Duffy, stood beneath the wedding arch, which was comprised of four Grecian columns, all topped with vases of trailing ivy and voluptuous sprays of pink sweetheart roses. To Duffy's right, there was a table supporting a satin pillow with rings tied to it.

Talbot dimmed the lights and played the music. The stage manager had made several changes to the theater to accommodate the wedding. The lighting had been altered to appear more natural, and a bank of stairs had been pushed to center stage.

Tammy wore a simple satin dress—off the shoulder with a flared skirt, seed pearls down the back, and a long train. Her hair cascaded on top of her shoulders, and she carried a simple bouquet of calla lilies. Jason met her at the bottom of the stairs, and they climbed the stairs together.

They composed their own vows, which made the service short and sweet. Once the rings were exchanged, he kissed her and invited everyone to head back to the Backstage Pub for some drinks and snacks.

Everyone left the theater except Jason and Tammy and Skye and Jet.

The photographer needed more light, so Skye went backstage to find Talbot, who had already started to put things back into place for Monday's matinee. "Would you mind adjusting the overhead lights so the photographer can take some pictures?"

"Sure," Talbot said. "I'll flip them on as soon as I get these backdrops organized."

"Thanks," Skye said. "Are you going to the pub afterward?"

"Will you be there?"

"Jet and I are going to put in an appearance."

"Jet? Are you two an item?" he asked.

"I'm working on it," Skye said. She returned to the stage. The lights came up and the photographer took dozens of pictures of Tammy and Jason. Then it was Skye and Jet's turn.

The photographer was a perfectionist. He made them strike several poses, and when he ran out of space on his card, he told them to hold their position while he slapped a blank into his camera. Right before he finished, he asked Jet and Skye to switch positions.

As they moved, a warning was bellowed from the wings.

"Watch out," Talbot shouted.

Jet moved like a lightning strike.

He pulled Skye out of way mere seconds before a huge backdrop crashed onto the stage. The two-by-four base missed hitting Skye's head by a matter of inches.

"I hit the wrong button on the control panel." Talbot rushed onto the stage. "Is everyone all right?"

Jason and Tammy hurried over. Jet hugged Skye. He held her so tightly she could barely draw oxygen into her lungs. Good thing he had a hold of her because her legs wobbled like jelly.

"I'm so sorry," Talbot said.

"You should be," Jet said.

"I'm all right," Skye said, patting Jet's arm. "It was an accident."

Jason and Tammy consoled Talbot, and the photographer packed up his cameras and left.

Jet helped Skye down off the stage and sat beside her in the first row, still holding her hand. "You're shaking even more than I am," she said.

Jet closed his eyes, and when he opened them, they were tear-filled. "I almost lost you." Then he leaned over and kissed her. Even more exciting than the kiss was the fact he didn't care who noticed.

He continued to torment her from that moment on.

He couldn't go five minutes without kissing her somewhere—on the lips, her hand, even the nape of neck. They managed to order drinks over at the Backstage Pub, but never finished them.

Who could drink or eat a time like this?

They made their excuses and hurried back to the Thrift Hotel.

CHAPTER 39

Skye and Jet rode the elevator in silence. She tingled as he kissed her hand. The car seemed to move in slow motion—it took forever to get to their floor and for the doors to open. He led her down the hall to his room.

She squared her shoulders and went inside ahead of him. The room layout happened to be the opposite of hers, and considering Jet had been living in this room for quite a while, it appeared reasonably neat. Light shone on a stack of magazines on the bedside table.

He pulled her into his arms and kissed her long and slow. He trailed his lips along the line of her chin and neck. "Would you like to freshen up?" he whispered.

She nodded. "Don't go away," she said as she disappeared inside the bathroom. She checked her reflection in the mirror and straightened her dress and hair. She wondered if she should slip out of her dress and walk out either naked or in her panties and bra, but she didn't want to do anything that would put any pressure on Jet. She'd let him set the pace if it killed her. She squeezed a dollop of toothpaste on her finger and slid it across her teeth.

When she went back into the room Jet had taken off his jacket and tie and unbuttoned his shirt. Her eyes fell to his chest, and she couldn't help licking her lips.

He studied her. He didn't say anything, and he barely moved a muscle. He acted like he would tell her he'd changed his mind again.

Oh, no.

This time she wouldn't let him dismiss her, not without a fight. She turned off the bedside lamp and noticed two things—a package of Vardenafil and girly magazines. Obviously, he'd begun some sort of drug therapy. Skye remembered reading the worst part of this particular treatment was the self-doubt. If the patient thought they were going to fail, they often did.

Skye intended to do everything in her power to help him succeed. She slid his shirt over his shoulders and down his arms. "Leave everything to me."

She tugged off one sleeve, then the other. He tried to say something, but she silenced him with her finger.

"You're too uptight. You need to relax. C'mon." She grabbed his hand and pulled him over to the bed. "Lie down on your stomach. I'm going to give you a massage."

Jet did as she asked.

Skye kicked off her heels and sat down on the bed beside him. She began high on his vertebrae.

She circled each protuberance and kneaded the surrounding tissues. She worked her way down his spine giving each bone equal attention. She took her time, and very soon she felt the tension drain out of him.

He felt warm beneath her fingers.

His skin glowed like pale ale, smooth and creamy. Muscles rippled beneath her kneading fingers.

Up until now she never considered a man's back sexy, but it quickly rose up the ranks and became her new favorite thing. Her every touch sent waves of desire rippling through her. The pressure she used was a slow build, and she couldn't believe how the exertion affected her. She'd become incredibly hot—the room felt like a sauna. Jet's breathing had steadied, and she guessed he floated in that contented place on the verge of sleep. Since she didn't want to disturb his peacefulness, she flung her dress over her head and tossed it onto the floor.

She felt like a wanton harlot riding him in her bra and panties and was anything but relaxed. Wound tight, her skin itched to be touched and her muscles burned.

He momentarily tensed, so she leaned close. "It's okay," she whispered. "I needed better leverage. I'll let you know when I'm done."

She worked the larger muscles in Jet's back. She leaned into her massage, and every once in a while, the tips of her breasts would brush against him. They hardened, almost painfully. It made her want to taste him, so she dipped her head and trailed soft kisses up and down the column of his back.

Which caused him to instantly stir, and he rolled beneath her. "When did you get undressed?"

She shrugged. "When I got hot."

"You've always been hot," he said. He sat up and kissed her.

Skye thought she would dissolve in his heat. He ravaged her lips, her neck, her shoulders, and finally his mouth dipped to her breasts.

"Please." She moaned. "I need to take it off." She reached for the clasp of her bra, but he stopped her.

"No. I want to do it." He slid his arms around her and undid her bra. "You're beautiful," he said, and her nipples hardened once again. Then he began his torment all over again. This time when he suckled her breasts, she felt an incredible pressure building between her thighs. Soon it overwhelmed her. "Jet," she moaned. "I think...I mean...I'm going to..."

And suddenly he knew exactly what to do. He held onto her and tipped her onto her back. He reached down and removed her panties in one sweeping motion. Then he touched her between her legs. He kissed her and slid his fingers in and around her swollen flesh.

She threw back her head and squeezed her eyes together. Light traveling at galaxy speed exploded into a trillion stars and rocked her entire universe. She felt like an atom that had just been split. When the atmosphere finally settled, she opened her eyes and found him staring at her. "I can't believe that just happened," she said. "Here I've been trying to help you get it on, and I turn and burn in less than a minute. I'm so sorry."

"I'm not," Jet said.

"I know, but you didn't even...I mean...you know."

"We need to get a few things straight. I'm not going to lie to you. I've been pretty frustrated. My specialist said he'd successfully reattached all the nerves to allow for an increase in blood flow. He said my problems were all in my head. And he was right. I didn't feel impotent. I felt all the symptoms of sexual arousal—sweaty palms and increased heart rate—but I spent too much time worrying about my performance. When I came back from Kilmarnock, I tried the drug therapy."

"I noticed the magazines."

"They did nothing for me."

"I'm sorry."

"I'm not. The close call at the theater tonight snapped me out of it. I realized that life is too short not to go for it."

Skye felt sick. "I thought you might have success if I helped you along. I didn't intend to have it go this far unless you..."

"Got hard?" Jet finished her sentence.

She nodded. "I'm sorry."

"Stop saying that."

Jet reached for her.

When he slid his tongue into her mouth, her mind ceased to function. Another million sensations bombarded her. Her skin tingled. A hot wire began tightening in the pit of her stomach, and suddenly she felt a tremendous pressure building at her apex, only this time it wasn't her. She pulled back and noticed the bulge in his trousers. "Is that what I think it is?"

He nodded.

"Oh, my God. When did you know everything was working?"

"I knew the moment I saw you, yesterday."

"Why didn't you say anything?"

"What? And spoil your fun?"

Skye slid her hand down to touch him.

He grabbed it before she got the chance. "Are you sure you can handle it?"

Skye giggled. "Very funny."

"That's not what I meant." Jet's voice cracked under his obvious duress. "My scars, they're not pretty."

Skye became very serious. "I love you. I can handle it. Make love to me, Jet."

"Not so fast," he said. "Anything worth doing is worth doing right."

And he inflicted the sweetest torture of all. He suckled, kissed, and licked. He worshiped every inch of her.

Skye gave as good as she got. She rubbed, caressed, and fondled his chest. She ran her tongue from sternum to naval. On all fours, she unzipped his pants and pulled them off.

Suddenly, she could no longer ignore his disfigured legs. Ridges of skin rippled across his thighs like tilled earth, and despite being forewarned, she couldn't stop herself from gasping.

Jet tensed. He knew his scars were wicked ugly and made most people queasy. He tried to sit and cover himself, but she pushed him back down.

"Don't," Skye said. Then she did the sweetest thing of all. She rained kisses all over those scars.

Jet couldn't wait one second longer to be inside her.

Tears stung the back of his eyes again. He'd witnessed the revulsion on his physiotherapists face when they first saw his legs. The fact that Skye didn't get grossed out, the fact that she actually kissed him, made him think they had a chance to make this relationship work.

He reached for her and rolled her onto her back. With one steady push he entered her to the hilt.

She felt as tight as a glove. Each stroke took him to her very core. Very soon, both of them had passed the point of no return. "I love you," he said as they clung to each other. And they rode through the eye of the storm together.

They made love for hours on end. He let her rest between bouts, but he'd already formulated a plan.

He knew he couldn't lose her. He'd marry her, but first he had to sort out all the unknowns in his life.

Serious unknowns.

He might have to consider a reassignment and a possible fertility issue. Family was something he'd never had but desperately wanted, so he needed to ask if she'd consider alternative means of fertilization or adoption if they determined he'd been rendered sterile.

One way or another, he'd convince her to stay in the UK.

CHAPTER 40

Skye dozed off several times throughout the night. Whenever she'd roll over, Jet would begin kissing her, and very soon they were breathless and making love all over again.

She'd never felt more alive or loved in her whole life.

And she'd never been more uncertain as to what to do next. In another day she'd be racing back to the States to check on her dad, when all she really wanted to do was stay in Jet's arms.

That's when she heard the knock.

Next door.

The room walls were so thin she knew it had to be coming from her room. Then came another knock, this time louder.

"Pssst. Skye? It's me, Jason."

Jet sat up. Obviously, he heard it too.

Both of them sprang out of bed. She grabbed Jet's shirt and he pulled on his pants before both of them padded to the door.

"Jason," she whispered. "I'm over here."

Jason checked the number on the door against the slip of paper in his hand and hurried over to her. "The bloke at the front desk gave me the wrong room number." That's when he spotted Jet standing behind her. "Ah, nevermind."

A woman across the way stepped into the hallway. Skye pulled Jason inside Jet's room. "What's wrong? Did you and Tammy have a fight?"

Jason turned toward Jet then Skye. "I think you better sit down."

Okay. Skye and Jet sat on the end of the bed.

"Your mom called. She couldn't get through on your cell. It's your dad," Jason said. "He's had a heart attack."

It took moments for the words to register. "What? No," she jumped to her feet. "That can't be. I still have a couple of weeks."

Jason gave Jet a sideways glance. "I didn't want to deliver the news over the phone, so I came straight over."

"Is he...?"

"No, he's alive, but you need to get home as soon as possible."

She sprang to her feet and collected her clothes from the floor. "My flight's not until Tuesday afternoon."

"I know, but the airlines make exceptions for emergencies like this. Get dressed, throw everything into your bag, and I'll drive you to the airport so you can get on the next available flight."

Skye faced Jet. "I've got to go."

"I know," he said. "I'm going to the airport with you." He snagged his shirt and his jacket, and all of them raced into the next room.

Skye grabbed a pair of jeans and t-shirt and went into the bathroom to change. She came out a few minutes later carrying all her toiletries. Jet and Jason had gathered her personal items, which she shoved into her bag and zipped. With one final glance around the room, they left in a flurry.

Jason's car sat at the curb. Jet tossed her bag in the boot and all of them climbed in.

The roads were wet on the way to the Edinburgh airport. Rain drizzled. The back and forth of the wipers put her in a trance. She'd been trying to figure out what had happened. Lang said knowing the future made the certain uncertain. In this case the time frame had advanced a couple of weeks, and mercifully, her dad was still alive. She had to focus on that.

The early hour translated into light traffic. Jason drove straight to the airport and dropped her at departures.

"I'll park the car and meet you inside," Jason said.

"No, you won't. This is your wedding night. You're going to go back home to be with your bride," Skye said.

"But—"

"No buts. Jet will stay here with me."

Jason jumped out of the car and glanced at Jet, who'd already manhandled her bag. Jason hugged her. "Fine. I'll go. Let me know what's going on as soon as you have a moment."

"I will," Skye said.

He kissed her on the top of her head and, with tears in his eyes, hopped back into his mini and sped away.

Skye and Jet went into the airport and explained the emergency to the ticketing agent, who changed Skye's ticket to the next available flight leaving in two hours.

Once she checked her bag and had her reservation in hand, she shrugged. "You don't have to stick around here and wait with me. You've got to go to work today."

"I'm the boss. If I can't be late, who can? Besides, I'm not going anywhere," he said. "C'mon. I'll buy you a cup of coffee and something to eat."

Jet ordered a couple of breakfast specials at one of the fast-food joints, but Skye couldn't choke it down.

"Is that why you were going home? Because your father wasn't well?"

Skye nodded. Tears sprang to her eyes.

"Why didn't you say something?"

She blinked several times to stave the tears from overflowing. She couldn't very well tell Jet that her aunt foretold it in her journal. He'd think she was certifiable.

"Tests were scheduled. I guess it was too little, too late. I only hope I get there in enough time to say good-bye."

"Come on, now." Jet put his hand over hers. "You don't know that. You have to be positive. Believe me, I know what I'm talking about. I couldn't help my friend Busy because he gave up. Your dad needs you to help him through this. He's depending on you."

"Do you really think so?"

"I know so."

She checked her watch. "They'll be boarding soon. I should go."

He saw her to the security check. Before she entered the line she stopped. "I know you said you weren't interested in a long-distance relationship, but that was before we…"

Jet folded her into his arms. He dipped his head and kissed her ever so sweetly. "You're going to be preoccupied for the next little while. You won't even have time to think of us. Now go."

She caught up in the wave of people. She didn't want it to end this way. She told him she loved him, and he returned the sentiment. As she approached the security check, she spun around to mouth the words *I love you*, but he'd already gone. Maybe he lied.

With the travel and time change, Skye's plane landed in Albany at nine the next evening. She collected her bag and dialed her parents' number.

"Hello," her mom's voice sounded stretched to the breaking point.

"Mom?" She didn't want to waste any time, so she continued. "I just landed in Albany. I'm going to grab a rental, and I should be home in an hour or so. How's dad?"

"They've stabilized him. Thank goodness you're home. He's going to be having some tests tomorrow and decisions will have to be made."

"We'll talk as soon as I get there."

Skye rented a compact and jumped on the highway to River Glen. She fought an overwhelming feeling of utter helplessness. Bessie's hospital stay rushed back. Would she lose her father too? She couldn't handle another unhappy ending. One in twenty-four hours was enough. Not even. She did the math. Thirteen hours ago, nestled in Jet's loving arms, her contentment burned. Now it seemed her heart had been sliced in two.

Her life swerved so quickly she should have had whiplash.

Before she knew it, she'd exited the turnpike and drove through the tree-lined streets to the house where she grew up. The door was open, and her mom came running the moment she went inside. Skye hugged her, and in that moment, she dissolved into tears.

"He's still okay, isn't he?" Skye asked.

Her mother nodded. "I didn't mean to frighten you. It's just...well, I'm glad you're home." She dabbed her eyes with a limp tissue balled in her hand. "Come and sit down. I just made a pot of tea."

Skye left her bag at the door and sat down at the kitchen table. "What happened?"

"He collapsed while doing his stress test at River Glen Hospital yesterday. I'm just so thankful it happened there where they were equipped to handle it. Doc Brailey said he was a ticking time bomb."

Skye breathed a sigh of relief and silently thanked Aunt Bessie. "What's going to happen now?"

"They stabilized him yesterday morning and transferred him to the Mohawk Valley Heart Institute. He's slated for an angiogram at eleven tomorrow morning."

"What's an angiogram?"

"It's a procedure where they insert a fiber optic catheter into the groin and move it up the vessel into his heart to take pictures. If they see a narrowing of the arteries, they'll open them with a small balloon attachment and shunt. It's called angioplasty."

"That doesn't sound so bad." Skye searched her mom's face. Betty Andrews never could hide anything from her daughter. "But..."

"Not everyone is a suitable candidate, so there's a possibility they'll have to call in a surgeon and do open heart surgery."

"Oh," Skye said. "It's always good to have a backup plan."

"That's exactly what Doc Brailey said."

Skye and Betty awoke the following morning and convoyed—Skye in the compact and Betty in the family car—to Utica. Skye returned the rental and then drove them to the Mohawk Valley Heart Institute.

It was after ten when they arrived. A nurse escorted them to the pre-op area. Both Skye and Betty leaned over the bed rails to give her father, Ross, a kiss right before an orderly whisked him away. The doors to the OR opened causing the air inside the sealed room to whistle like a vacuum.

Skye put her arm around her trembling mother and patted her on the back.

"I'm frightened," she said.

"I know, Mom. So am I." Skye noticed a sign for the waiting room at the end of the hall beyond the nurses' station. "Let's go and sit down while we wait."

A nurse glanced up from her paperwork. "There's coffee down the hall too. I'll buzz you as soon as he returns."

"Thank you," Skye said.

The waiting room contained two large sofas and a couple of oversized chairs where family members could curl up and sleep. It had a coffee machine, a bar fridge containing various juices and soft drinks, and a bathroom with a shower.

Skye read the plaque on the wall. The waiting room operated on the honor system. Hospital volunteers maintained and stocked the fridge and filled the cream and sugar containers. Patrons were asked to make a donation for using the service. Skye dug into her purse and dropped a donation into the box and poured a couple of coffees.

Then they sat down and waited.

The two of them sat very still. Skye glanced over at her mother, who dabbed her eyes every so often with a soggy wad of tissue.

One hour seemed like days.

Both Skye and Betty took turns pacing the floor. They kept staring at the clock moving at a slug's pace when a doctor in green scrubs, still wearing his OR booties, hurried into the room.

"I'm Dr. Goodheart," he said, holding up his hand. "I know—kind of hard to believe the name considering my line of work. I just finished the procedure on Mr. Andrews."

Skye could barely muster a smile.

"Is he all right?" Betty asked.

"Your husband came through the procedure very well. He'll be in recovery for about an hour before he comes back to this ward. I stented two plaque filled arteries. There should be an immediate improvement in his breathing."

Skye listened to the doctor and sensed he hadn't told them everything. "But?"

"Your father has a leaky valve in his aorta."

"What does that mean?" Betty asked.

"It means when the heart pumps, there is some leakage. A back wash of blood if you will."

"Is it serious?" Skye asked.

"Not at the moment. But I think it must be closely monitored. He'll need to see a heart surgeon. One that can discuss his options."

"Why didn't you fix it?" Betty asked.

"I'm not a surgeon. My specialty is angioplasty."

Skye listened very closely. "When do you think he'll need this valve replaced?"

"It could be months or years, but eventually, the valve will deteriorate to the point where surgery will be necessary."

"How will we know when it's time?" Betty asked.

"Ross will know. His quality of life will be greatly reduced."

"So it'll be a waiting game," Skye said.

"In the meantime," Dr. Goodheart said. "You two need to be positive. We've found that positive reinforcement greatly reduces the patients' stress and recovery takes less time."

Jet's words rushed back to Skye.

Betty shook Dr. Goodheart's hand.

"When can he go home?" Skye asked.

"He has to remain immobilized for the rest of the day until the entry site closes. Where do you live?"

"River Glen."

"That's not too far away. You should be able to take him home tomorrow."

Skye thanked him. She shook his hand. Dr. Goodheart smiled and folded his arms across his chest. "If you have any more questions or concerns, don't hesitate to call."

Skye liked the doctor. He released her hand very slowly, and his eyes lingered on her as he left the room.

Skye hugged her mother who'd succumbed to tears.

"C'mon now—Dad's going to be fine."

"I know he is. But for how long? You don't know what I went through. How scared and alone I felt. I'm not sure I'm strong enough to go through it again. And next time it'll be worse."

Skye noticed her mother's face. She'd aged since Bessie's funeral. Lines of worry were etched on her forehead. Her mother and father had always been strong and healthy, and Skye didn't know what to make of her mother's insecurity. Was it simply a knee-jerk reaction to her father's heart attack? Skye couldn't deny they were getting on in age. They had been taking care of Aunt Jane in her old age for years, but suddenly their own mortality had come into play. And her mother was frightened.

She'd made a snap decision. It felt right. "It's okay, Mom, you don't have to do it alone. I'm moving back to River Glen."

"You are?" Betty dried her eyes and smiled. And for the first time since Skye arrived home, she saw color return to her mother's cheeks.

CHAPTER 41

Very soon, Skye fell into a routine in River Glen, New York. She liked being back in the small town, where everyone still wore a friendly smile and knew everyone by name.

She'd moved into her old bedroom at her parents' house for the time being, until she found a place of her own. Time had not altered the house where she grew up. The couch in the living room still needed new cushions and the pencil marks that recorded her growth were still etched on the doorjamb in the hall. But despite the fond memories, she knew she'd been on her own for too long to go back to living with her parents. She needed her space as much as they needed theirs.

The decision to move, although fast, had been an easy one. Her experience with Bessie and her trip to the UK had shown her how tired she'd grown of the big city's nightlife. Not only that but she also didn't want to suffer the same guilt she felt with Bessie with her parents. They were more important than living in the Big Apple. She refused to go back to being an ostrich. She didn't know how much longer she'd have her parents around, but she'd make the most out of their time together.

Before she knew it, three weeks had passed since she left Edinburgh and Jet.

Three weeks of abject silence.

She ached deep in her bones.

Skye had called overseas on two separate occasions, but the army gave her the run around both times. They told her Jet transferred out of the museum at Edinburgh castle. Perhaps he'd already been reinstated to active duty. She had no idea where he'd gone and had no way of contacting him. With the new privacy laws, the military didn't give out information on personnel unless you were family.

Jason couldn't find anything out for her either and told her to stop gnawing on that bone. If Jet wanted to reach her, he would call her. Obviously, Skye wasn't high on his priority list.

The time had come to forget about him. Be resigned to being single for the rest of her life. Every time she thought about him, she choked up. She had to be the most dysfunctional person in the country when it came to relationships. It seemed when she loved someone, they weren't interested, and when someone loved or was interested in her, she couldn't have cared less.

She proved the theory yet again when Dr. Goodheart called a couple days after she and her mom and dad returned to River Glen. He called to ask her out to dinner. Skye went, at her mother's insistence, but it didn't take long to realize she hopelessly loved another.

Her father made progress. Ross worked hard at rehab, and both of her parents were attempting to eat healthier. His appointment with the heart surgeon had been a tad disconcerting, but he'd decided to take it day by day. When Ross's quality of life got to the point where he couldn't walk into the kitchen without being winded, he'd schedule surgery.

In the meantime, her father needed to figure out whether he wanted a mechanical valve or a pig valve. Both had benefits and detriments. The mechanical valve was considered loud, but would last forever. The porcine valve, although quieter, could be rejected by the body and only had a life span of approximately ten years.

Decisions, decisions.

Nothing had to be determined right away. Ross had time to figure out what he wanted, and in the interim, he had a new lease on life. Every day he got up, took his meds, ate his breakfast, and went for a walk. Walking had become part of his regular fitness routine.

And Skye had picked up the slack. She helped Mort's Moving get Aunt Jane settled at Rolling Meadows. Her house had become too much of a burden for the ninety-three-year-old—too many stairs and too many rooms to keep clean. Aunt Jane had to be very selective and chose only a few things to go with her—her bedroom suite, a sofa and chair, and her kitchenette.

Skye told Aunt Jane she would visit her this morning, after her weekly game of gin rummy. Skye stood in the back, and while she waited for the last hand to be played, she got thinking about Jet and became lost in thought.

"Skye?" Aunt Jane called from across the room. "The game's over."

She snapped out of her trance. She bent over the card table and kissed her aunt's cheek before she sat down beside her. "Did you win?"

"Not even close," she said. "I'm glad you came. I've got something to discuss with you."

Skye gave her aunt her full attention. "What is it? Are you feeling all right?"

"I'm fine dear. I just wanted to talk to you about my house."

"What about it?"

"Your mother told me you were in the market for a rental property."

Skye nodded. "There isn't a lot to choose from."

"Would you be interested in renting my house? I don't want to sell yet, in case things don't work out here, but I don't want it sitting empty either. Someone has to tend Uncle Bart's roses."

"That's really nice of you, Aunt Jane, but I'm not sure I can afford it. Currently, I'm unemployed. I need a job too, but it's slim pickings out there. Especially for an actress."

"I don't want to get rich, dear. My social security and pension cover my expenses here. All you need to do is pay for the utilities and the taxes. Then in six months, if you still really like the place, I'll consider selling it to you."

"In that case, you've got yourself a deal," Skye said.

Aunt Jane cupped her ear. "Oh, no thanks," she said. "One game of gin rummy is my limit."

The following morning, Skye picked up a copy of *The New York Times* and glanced at the headlines.

An article on the second page caught her eye. "Crime Lord Recluse Dies in Sleep." She read on. "The coroner estimated Aldo Genovese died at least four weeks ago in his Newton estate home a few miles from downtown Boston. When the mansion was emptied, over one hundred thousand dollars was found in a trunk in the cellar. Serial numbers confirm the money was a fraction of the proceeds from the famous 1950 Brinks' job." Skye put the paper down. Everything Skye had seen in Bessie's journal about Aldo's ties with the mob had been true. She closed her eyes and did the math. Aldo died around the same time she interred Bessie. Lang told Skye the Luckenbooth brooch had special powers, and Skye hoped with all her heart that Bessie and Aldo were reunited at last.

Since Skye moved to River Glen, she often thought of the sacrifice Bessie had made.

It seemed Jet had made the same pact. Maybe if Bessie and Aldo had been reunited in the afterlife, she'd have something to look forward to. Suddenly she had to find out.

When she got home, Skye dug Bessie's journal and Lang's brooch out of her bag. Lang's brooch had more weight than Bessie's, and the color of the stone, though weakened, seemed to have a slightly different hue.

Skye found the page where she'd left off, she closed her hand around the pin, and when she opened her eyes, she landed inside the Presidential Suite of Boston's Ritz Carlton.

Bessie bounded out of the bedroom.

The antique furniture—the tufted chairs and sofas—had been replaced with modern leather, low profile furniture. The polished wood floors had been covered with finely woven silk area rugs. The Louis XIVth desk remained, as did the original oil paintings.

On the center table sat a fruit and the cheese tray, similar to the one from bygone years. Bessie rolled the neck of the champagne bottle in the silver tureen of ice. Everything seemed in order for her special guest—her one and only true love. She'd waited a lifetime to see him again.

He'd be arriving any minute. She straightened the room and gave it a final once-over when she spotted her reflection in the full-length mirror leaning against the wall.

Her steel gray hair and skin etched with wrinkles and age spots had disappeared. Her chestnut hair and honey complexion glowed. The off-white kitten sweater and skirt hugged her curvy figure. She hadn't worn stockings or high heels in fifty years, but when she looked down, her legs were covered in the sheerest silk, and her shoes were the same ones she'd ruined on that fateful night when Aldo's father altered their destiny.

Knock, knock, knock.

She took a deep breath, smoothed her hands over her stomach to tame the butterflies, hurried over to the door, and opened it.

Aldo stood in the hall wearing his trademark zoot suit. Handsome and whipcord smart.

"You're here," Bessie said.

"There's no place I'd rather be," he said. "Aren't you going to invite me in?"

She'd been so taken aback she'd forgotten her manners. "Of course. Please come in."

Aldo stepped inside the room and stopped. "Is all this for me?"

"I thought you might be hungry."

"I'm starving."

"If you open the champagne, I'll make us up a plate."

Aldo pulled the bottle out of the urn filled with ice. He used one of the towels to dry it off. He unwrapped the wire around the cork and twisted it just enough to send it into the stratosphere.

Champagne effervesced and overflowed. He held the bottle over the urn until the froth abated and poured two flutes.

Bessie grabbed a bone china plate and filled it with an assortment of berries and cheeses and sat down on the sofa.

He joined her. "What should we drink to?" he asked passing her a glass.

"Let's drink to second chances."

"I'm all in," Aldo said. "I've certainly had my fair share, thanks to you."

"I don't understand."

"Your brooch," Aldo said. "I never went anywhere without it. It was my very own barometer. It showed me what would lead to disaster and what wouldn't. If it became red hot, I knew I had to extricate myself from a situation very quickly, or the repercussions would be dire."

"It did its job then," Bessie said. She sipped her champagne and ate a strawberry to bring out the flavor.

"After Don Vito passed, I became very selective and chose my jobs very carefully. I had no interest in being a figurehead like my father. I had more than enough money to live a comfortable life, and there were plenty of wise guys chomping at the bit to take over the reins. Unfortunately, my wife didn't understand why I passed on becoming the kingpin."

"I knew you'd take the righteous path."

"That makes one of us then," Aldo said, draining his glass of champagne. He got up and brought the urn with the champagne in it over to the coffee table. He poured them both a little more. "I tried to divorce her several times. She threatened to kill herself if I left her. I rushed her to the hospital twice to have her stomach pumped. She died a slow and painful death with cirrhosis of the liver on our fiftieth anniversary."

"I don't remember reading anything about it in the newspaper."

"I didn't write an obituary. Her parents were dead, and she had no siblings."

"I'm sorry," Bessie said, her eyes tearing.

Aldo's brow creased. "And that's why I love you. You had every reason to hate her, and yet you still have the compassion to shed a tear for her."

"She'd been an innocent pawn in all this too. Her father did the very same thing to her as your father did to you."

"I guess."

Bessie cut a bit of cheddar and ate it. "Why didn't you have any children? I know you wanted kids. At least you said you did way back in the day."

"That's a long story," Aldo ate a handful of grapes "I was really angry after we split up. My father kept pressuring me to sire him some grandchildren. I had a chip on my shoulder about the size of the Rock of Gibraltar. I wanted to make him pay. I told him no one should bring kids into a loveless marriage, so I went and had myself sterilized."

"You what?" More tears filled Bessie's eyes. "That's horrible."

"If my wife had granted me a divorce, would you have married me?"

"No," Bessie said. "Not because I didn't love you. My vanity came between us. I was certain you'd never be able to love me again."

"Why?" Aldo said.

"Around the same time you had your surgery, I had a mastectomy. I didn't think you'd want half a woman."

"That's ridiculous. I loved you and would have considered myself the luckiest man in the world whether you had one breast or two."

"I know that, now. It took years and years for the darkness to fade. When I did figure it out, I had very little time to put my affairs in order. I needed to make sure my niece didn't make the same mistakes with her beau."

"Ah, yes. Skye Andrews. We met at your service of remembrance."

They fell into a comfortable silence. They drank some champagne and fed each other some fruit. In a short while, she noticed a glint in his eyes.

"Once my wife passed, I spent a good deal of time spying on you." Aldo's smirk said he didn't think she knew. "I sat and stared at you from the back pews of the New Westminster Church."

"I know. The collection plate was always heavier on those occasions," Bessie said, draining her glass.

"Wait," Aldo said. "You knew about me?"

She did. She giggled.

Aldo reached over and ran his finger along her cheek. "I've missed your laugh and your playfulness. You're every bit as soft as I remember."

She lifted her hand to hold his. Neither knew who moved first, but in the next moment, his lips were on hers. Initially tender and tentative, he deepened the kiss, and it became wanton. Food and drink forgotten, she slid her hands beneath the lapels of his jacket and slipped it over his shoulders.

His lips plundered hers. He loosened his tie and slid it out of the collar before undoing shirt buttons.

She stood and held out her hand with the idea of leading him into the bedroom. Then in typical Aldo fashion, he got up and tipped her into his arms and carried her.

Prior to Aldo's arrival, Bessie had scattered rose petals across the bed and floor. The deliciously sweet and fragrant room intoxicated her. She continued undoing buttons where he left off. Once she shucked his shirt, she reached for his belt and unfastened his trousers, dropping them in quick succession. She ran her hands across the hairs on his chest and dove lower. She stroked him. A pearl of moisture on the tip made her hand slide from tip to root.

Aldo stood perfectly still watching her. He breathed in and out—his eyes widened with her tight grasp; his eyes darkening with desire. "In my dreams, I've made love to you a thousand times."

"Me too," she said. The admission shocked her. "There hasn't been one day where I haven't thought about this."

"Then I'm going to have to make this better than your wildest imaginings," he said, reaching for her.

"No," she said. "I want to undress for you."

He drew ragged breaths, and his eyes latched onto her hands as she pulled her sweater off. She reached behind her back and undid the fastening of her bra and let it fall to the floor with all the other garments. Unlike her body in life, she had two perfectly shaped breasts—both puckered and aching to be touched. She hooked her thumbs into the waistband of her skirt and shimmied out of it, lowering the angora inch by maddening inch.

Aldo stepped toward her. "I need to touch all of you," he said. He lifted her into his arms and placed her on the bed. When their lips met, they closed their eyes and let their emotions have a field day. "You smell and taste exactly like I remember."

"You've got a very good memory then," she said.

"Some things you never forget. Especially when it comes to the love of your life."

She let him remember her with his lips. He brought her to the brink of her control and would start the delicious torment all over again on a different part of her body.

Both of them were breathless by the time he finished his strict attentions.

"Make love to me, Aldo."

"I thought you'd never ask," he said. He positioned himself at the apex of her thighs and entered her very slowly, stretching her swollen tissues inch by agonizing inch. Then he withdrew and began the gradual penetration all over again.

An incredible pressure built to a crescendo.

Like their very first coupling, she wanted to laugh and cry at the same time. Her body felt fragmented—like it would shatter into a million pieces at any moment.

He threaded his fingers between hers and they held onto each other for dear life as they crested the wave of the tsunami together.

Wrecked, they rolled onto their sides until their breathing normalized.

He closed his eyes and dozed for a few moments.

Bessie took advantage of his cat nap and ducked out from beneath his arm as quietly as possible.

He sprang into a sitting position and called after her. "Where do you think you're going, young lady?"

"To get some sustenance to rebuild our strength," she said, returning with a plate of fruit and cheese. "So we can start all over again."

Aldo laughed and pulled her back into bed. "Okay. And this time we shower together. There's no way I'm letting you run out on me, ever again."

"Fine by me. This time we have something better than the rest of our lives."

"Oh, yeah?" he said. "What's that?"

"Eternity."

CHAPTER 42

T he Saturday edition of *The River Glen's News* contained a small ad from the Kershimer County Board of Education for a dramatic arts high school teacher. Skye didn't know what the job entailed, but she emailed her résumé straight away. By midweek, Superintendent Humphries called to arrange an interview.

Skye took Mr. Humphries a collection of her production programs and various stage photos taken of her over the years.

"Quite impressive," he said, flipping through her book. "Unfortunately, you don't have any teaching qualifications. I'm meeting with two other candidates, and I'll get back to you."

The idea of teaching appealed to Skye on so many levels. She remembered how it felt when she coached Tammy at the Raverse. She had a lot of knowledge she could share with young actors.

Over the next couple of weeks, Skye moved into Aunt Jane's house. The tidy little clapboard house painted a rich caramel color had white gingerbread trim that encircled the house like a lace collar.

Aunt Jane had meticulously maintained the house since Uncle Bart passed away—she replaced the roof last year and had the exterior painted. When Bart was alive, he'd renovated the kitchen and the bathrooms; and upgraded the plumbing and electrical. The windows and doors were the only things left that required replacement.

Skye had always loved the place. She had many fond memories of Uncle Bart in the garden tending his roses, and Aunt Jane, clad in her apron, making her secret family recipe for Scottish shortbread.

Skye found a secondhand store and replaced the bedroom suite and sofa. She had her eye on a new kitchen table and chairs at Morgenstern's, the local furniture store. Everything else of Aunt Jane's remained.

Skye paired a modern sofa with a richly appointed set of Victorian ladies and gentleman's chairs. A turn-of-the-century grandfather clock stood in the front hall and kept time, chiming once on the half hour and once for every hour. Waterford crystal lamps sparkled on top of burled walnut side tables.

Skye didn't want to change a thing, except the color on the walls. Aunt Jane had preferred off white, but Skye thought the place would come alive if she added more vibrant hues.

Since her arrival in River Glen, Skye had been using Aunt Jane's K-car. Aunt Jane had hung up her keys on her ninety-third birthday, and the car had been sitting in the garage unused. Bit by bit, Skye had transported all the boxes that had been in storage in her parents' basement—Skye's old yearbooks, university texts, notebooks, and of course all the keepsakes that Bessie had left her. It had taken a while, but she'd emptied them all. The knickknacks were now proudly displayed throughout the house.

She couldn't believe how emotional she'd become lately, but then she'd never had a broken heart before. The tiniest little thing seemed to set her off. An ornament that Bessie had left her, or a photo of Skye helping Uncle Bart in the garden, would cause her to dissolve into a fit of tears.

As much as she tried not to think of Jet, he'd often creep into her thoughts. Especially when she crawled into bed at night.

She wondered if he ever thought about her.

She thought about all the things he'd said to her that night, as he pushed inside her. He said he loved her.

Skye had never spoken those words to anyone but Jet.

How could another human being use those words if they didn't mean them? And how, with his problem, could he have made love to her so many times?

That's when she realized exactly how long she'd been home. Seven weeks. Skye hadn't seen Jet for seven lonely weeks.

She'd been so preoccupied with her father's health and getting her life back on track in River Glen she hadn't noticed the glitch in her menstrual cycle. She'd been three weeks into her cycle when she'd made love with Jet, and they'd had unprotected sex several times that night. It had been irresponsible, now when she thought about it.

No. It couldn't be.

It's not like she ever really knew when to expect her period. Skye had always been very irregular.

She padded into the kitchen and counted days on the calendar. By her calculations she was, give or take a few days, about five weeks late. Big deal. She'd been late before.

She put it down to stress. Burying Aunt Bessie and then learning about her father's heart attack would shoot holes in anyone's schedule.

And she didn't feel pregnant, except for the occasional crying jag. And with everything going on in her life, she deserved to revel in a little self-pity. But just to rule out the possibility, she added a pregnancy test kit to the list on the fridge door.

She got an early start the next day.

She visited briefly with her mom and dad and dropped in on Aunt Jane. Then she went to the Super Bee and shopped. Early afternoon, she returned home. She carried her bags inside and before she set about the task of putting everything away, she grabbed the test kit and disappeared in the washroom.

In a little over a minute, "she" became "we."

A baby.

Skye was going to have a baby.

She squeezed the plastic wand in her hand and hugged it to her chest.

She wasn't upset. Shocked, not upset.

A baby.

Her heart started to pound, and an immediate overwhelming contentment warmed her from the inside out.

Until her inner pragmatist began itemizing a list.

How was she ever going to manage?

Now, more than ever, she needed to find a job. Skye's savings were nearly depleted. Aunt Bessie's estate had covered the cost of her overseas trip, but moving to River Glen had drained what little money she'd managed to save over the years. She hadn't touched the inheritance Bessie had left her and wouldn't now. She might need that particular nest egg when the baby arrived.

And what about Jet?

She should really tell him about the baby—just because he'd washed his hands of her, didn't mean that he'd abandon his child. She'd notify him if she could bloody well find him. Both she and Jason had come up empty handed. Maybe she could contact John Smilie. Maybe he'd have information about where Jet had gone.

Her mom and dad wouldn't be happy about her being pregnant, but they'd come around. And she knew her mom would be happy to watch the baby if and when she found work.

Skye's mind started to race. For the second time since she arrived home, she consulted Bessie's journal. The gemstone in Lang's brooch had dulled and cooled, so she didn't have a clue if this would be the last time she could use it. Since there were several pages left in the journal, the trick would be trying to figure out where the past met the future.

Of course, maybe she should simply concentrate on the last few pages.

She shoved the pregnancy test wand into the pocket of her jeans and went upstairs to collect the journal and brooch out of her night side table. She sat down on the edge of the bed and squeezed Lang's brooch to warm it even further. Then she opened the journal to the final pages. She needed to find out if they had a future and prayed their next meeting wouldn't be in the afterlife.

"I've got an errand to run," Talbot said.

Hans Gruber stood with his hands on his waist watching the actors on stage running through the play one last time before calling it quits for the day. "Huh?" he said. "Whatever. It's only a rehearsal...we'll manage." He didn't even face the stage manager when he spoke.

Talbot didn't care. He had a knack for making himself invisible. A bonus over the years. No one ever took notice of his comings or goings.

He already knew where Tammy lived. He'd engaged her in a conversation when he got the job because he needed to rent a flat.

He took a cab to a small corner bar about two blocks from her complex—an appropriate foil. He didn't want anyone to remember dropping someone in front of the Georgian Terrace flats. Talbot paid the fare in cash—not wanting a paper trail—and hoofed it to her place.

Not many people were milling about at this time of day, and when he was sure no one was around, he went around the back, broke her bathroom window, and climbed inside.

The tidy little flat had a kitchenette, bedroom, bath, and sitting area. She'd decorated the place in Bohemian colors. The sitting area had a variety of cushions all tossed and stacked on the tongue and groove pine floor. Good kindling.

This was going to be too easy. Tammy had numerous pillar candles scattered all over the room. He went into the kitchen and grabbed a knife. Then he proceeded to cut all the candles so they were no more than an inch. He found a small cubby above the fridge that contained some whiskey and vodka. He pulled the bottles down and emptied them all over the pillows in the sitting area. Then he placed a candle nubbin on top of each and every one.

He could barely contain himself as he lit them.

He loved it when a plan fell into place. He was climbing out the window when billowing smoke began filling the bathroom behind him. He sauntered down the street to the corner and sat down at the stop to wait for a bus. When a double-decker pulled to a stop in front of him, he waved it on because he didn't want to miss seeing the fruits of his labor.

The fire brigade arrived in short order, and not long after, Jason and Tammy pulled to the curb beside the fire truck.

Of course, Tammy was distraught, and Jason had to console her. Jason would be so busy with Tammy he wouldn't have any time to spend with Skye. And Tammy, the third wheel, would put a stop to any hope Jason had of getting together with Skye.

Skye squeezed the Luckenbooth so hard the stone never had a chance to cool. She gritted her teeth and dove into the next page of Bessie's journal...

Jet's hands encircled Skye's waist. He stood behind her unmoving. Both of them had struck a pose and patiently waited for the photographer to change the data card in his camera.

Jason in his tux and Tammy in her satin dress stood behind the photographer while he finished taking their wedding photos. All of the guests had filtered out of the theater to the Backstage Pub.

All except Talbot.

Talbot remained on the premises to make sure that everything got put back in order for the Monday matinee.

Talbot skulked in the wings. He stood transfixed—staring at Jet, his fist pounding against his leg. His eyes were narrowed and the left one twitched. His lips were pulled into a grim line. "Who the fuck does he think he is," Talbot said. He checked the stage and noticed that Jet stood on top of the mark for the apartment set. His eyes flitted to the catwalk and back down onto the stage, and his lips curled into a smile. Like a shadow, he reached over to the keyed control panel and flipped the release.

Suddenly Skye and Jet switched places.

"Watch out!" Talbot screamed.

Jet pulled Skye to safety mere seconds before the apartment set careened onto the stage.

Suddenly, Skye's glimpse into the past flickered.

Oh, no, not now. Lang's Luckenbooth was nearly spent.

Skye grabbed the journal and brooch and ran into the bathroom. She used her blow-dryer to heat the stone.

Then she flipped to the very last page. Suddenly, a picture of Jet and her, naked and entwined in each other's arms in the upstairs bedroom, came into focus.

"Are you hungry?" Jet asked.

"Starving," Skye said. Playfully, she nipped at his bare chest.

"Keep that up and we won't eat for another hour."

"Promise?"

"You're killing me. I haven't eaten anything in the last twelve hours."

"Okay, I'll be good," she said.

"How about I whip us up one of my prize-winning omelets?" Jet asked.

Skye chuckled. "Your omelets won prizes?"

"The men in my unit said they were better than anything they ever got from the mess tent."

"Well then, what are you waiting for? I'll meet you downstairs in the kitchen after I brush my teeth and straighten my hair."

Jet pulled on his jeans and helped Skye up. She collected her clothes from the floor and headed into the bathroom. She heard him race downstairs and root around in the kitchen.

When she joined him, his head was buried in the fridge and he clanked and slapped items from the depths like treasures from a cache. "Eggs, milk, green peppers, onions, feta cheese, asparagus. This is going to be a culinary delight."

Skye pulled Aunt Jane's cast iron frying pan from the cupboard and set it on the stove. She pulled out a knife and cutting board. Then she washed the vegetables.

Jet began slicing and chopping.

The telephone rang and Skye grabbed it. "Hello."

"This is Mr. Humphries from the board office."

"Yes, Mr. Humphries."

"Do you have a few minutes?"

"Absolutely."

"I'm calling to offer you the teaching position."

"That's terrific."

"There's one condition."

"Oh?"

"The board has requested you enroll in a teaching certification course. There are some online, and you can obtain the practical aspect during the summer break. Would you like some time to think about it?"

"That's not necessary. I'll take the job and gladly enroll in the certification course."

"Wonderful. I'll call you in a couple of days once I have the course outline. You can come in and sign some paperwork, and I'll give you a tour of the school."

"I can't wait."

Skye hung up the phone, and out of the corner of her eye, she saw Talbot standing in the open door with a gun in his hand.

There was a flash and a deafening crack, and Jet jerked violently before he fell to the floor—a river of blood puddling beneath him.

A split second later, the scene winked out.

CHAPTER 43

Lang's Luckenbooth was dead, and from what Skye had seen, so was Jet. Her heart raced and she struggled to swallow the lump in her throat.

No way.

She would not let anything happen to Jet. Not now.

He'd come back.

Or rather, was on his way back to her.

Probably right now.

She ran out of the bathroom in a near panic. She sat down on the edge of the bed to go over the sequence of events. She had to commit every detail to memory. In her mind, she repeated Lang's words. *Knowing makes what is certain, uncertain.* She would have already buried her father if she hadn't called and told him to get to Doc Brailey's for a physical. She'd been successful with her father; she only hoped her luck would hold with Jet.

His life depended on it.

That's when she heard a knock at the kitchen door.

Could it be?

Her heart started to pound. She hurried downstairs. She could tell a man stood outside, but she couldn't be certain about his identity through the lace curtain. She unlocked the dead bolt and opened the door.

It was Jet.

"Surprise!" Dressed in street clothes, Jet's faded jeans and cotton shirt stole her breath.

She launched herself at him. She wrapped her arms around his neck, her legs around his waist, and her lips on his. He staggered momentarily and then pushed inside. He kicked the door closed and carried her across the threshold.

He didn't stop in the kitchen. He pushed through the living room and dining room, stopping and starting, until she pointed the way. By the time he got her upstairs and into the master bedroom, his breathing was labored. He set her down and they tore off each other's clothes.

She didn't have to ask him if he'd taken a pill because she felt him hard and ready. She grabbed him and hauled him on top of her and he entered her in one swift stroke.

Then they began the powerful climb.

He slid in and out. Each time he took her closer and closer to the edge. An unbelievable pressure built. He drove her upward. Pushing her higher.

"Tell me," Jet said. He closed his eyes and grit his teeth.

"I love you," Skye said, nearly at the apex.

"I love you too," he said, driving into her so completely that she felt like they were conjoined.

And both of them exploded.

He held her through their convulsions, and when it was over, he rolled beside her.

Skye could barely keep her eyes open until he got her attention by fondling and kissing her breasts.

"I had no intention of letting you leave England after we made love, but I would never come between you and your family by asking you to stay. Family comes first. Your father is recuperating nicely, by the way."

Skye's eyes sprang open. "You've seen my dad?"

"I had no clue you'd moved into your own place."

"That's because I haven't told anyone yet," Skye said.

"Jason gave me your home address, and once I introduced myself to your father, he directed me over here."

"You had way better luck than me. I called the castle trying to find you, but the army wouldn't give me a crumb of information on your whereabouts. Wait a minute. You talked to Jason?"

Jet nodded.

"The bugger," Skye said. "He never mentioned you'd come to see him."

"Don't hold it against him. I asked him not to."

"Whatever for?" Skye sprang into a sitting position. "I was worried sick."

"Because I wanted to give you some time to figure out if you meant what you said."

She narrowed her eyes at him. She didn't think he'd paid any attention to what she'd said. "And what was that, exactly?"

"You said you loved me."

Skye took a deep breath. "And you said the very same thing to me."

"That's why I resigned my army post, sold everything, and came here to be with you."

"You resigned?" Skye said. "I thought you wanted to get back to active duty."

"I thought that's what I wanted too. Turns out I want you more."

Tears stung her eyes. "You do?"

"Baby, I want you so bad I'm already rock hard again." Jet's words were more powerful that any aphrodisiac. She clung to him, and they made love all over again. This time when they were finished, she cuddled close.

"I'm so happy," Skye said.

"Me too. And very hungry," Jet said.

Oh my God.

Showtime.

She nipped at his bare chest.

"Keep that up and we won't eat for another hour."

"Promise?"

"You're killing me," Jet said. "I haven't eaten anything in the last twelve hours. How about I whip us up one of my prize-winning omelets?" Jet asked.

"Your omelets have won prizes?"

"The men in my unit said they were better than anything they ever got from the mess tent."

"What are you waiting for? I'll meet you downstairs in the kitchen after I brush my teeth and straighten my hair."

Jet pulled on his jeans, and he helped her up. She collected her clothes from the floor and headed to the bathroom. She heard him race downstairs and start rooting around in the kitchen. She tiptoed over to the cordless and hurried back inside the bathroom to make a phone call.

When she joined him, his head was buried in the fridge and he clanked and slapped items from the depths like treasures from a cache. "Eggs, milk, green peppers, onions, feta cheese, asparagus. This is going to be a culinary delight."

Skye pulled Aunt Jane's cast iron frying pan from the cupboard and set it on the stove. Then she pulled out a knife and cutting board and started washing the vegetables.

Jet began slicing and chopping.

The telephone rang and Skye grabbed it. "Hello."

"This is Mr. Humphries from the board office."

"Yes, Mr. Humphries."

"Do you have a few minutes?"

"Absolutely."

"I'm calling to offer you the teaching position."

"That's terrific."

"There's one condition."

"Oh?"

"The board has requested you enroll in a teaching certification course. There are a few online courses, and the practical aspect can be obtained during the summer break. Would you like some time to think about it?"

Quietly, Skye disconnected the phone, but still held the receiver to her ear. The moment she saw Talbot's reflection in the door of the microwave, she dropped it and paced over to the stove. She picked up the frying pan, spun, and with all her might, frisbeed it at Talbot's outstretched hand.

The gun went off just as the pan struck.

Jet launched himself on top of her and both thudded to the kitchen floor.

Chapter 44

"Jet? Speak to me." Skye struggled to breathe with Jet's full weight upon her. She wriggled to try to slip out from beneath him.

"Stay still," he growled in her ear.

Thank goodness. He wasn't dead.

From behind them a voice boomed. "Stop right there or I'll shoot."

The voice didn't belong to Talbot.

Jet must have been curious too because he rolled off of her and sprang to his feet. She scurried to her feet. Both she and Jet stood by as a burly cop with a brush cut pressed his knee into Talbot's back. He reached for one arm and then the other, shackling both in cuffs. He secured the prisoner and picked up the handgun that had skidded across the floor. He emptied the gun of bullets, engaged the safety, and shoved it into his waistband. Then he came toward Skye and Jet. "Are you two okay?"

Skye could hear sirens converging outside.

"Better late than not at all. Things went south and I couldn't wait for backup," the cop said. He waved to his reinforcements, who approached the door.

Adrenaline and anger kicked in. Skye marched over to Talbot, who was awake but dazed. "Why Talbot? I thought we were friends. You've been stalking me for years."

"You know this guy?" The officer asked.

"Since college." Skye thought for a second. She began itemizing a list. Her missing costumes. "It was you. You stole my wardrobe."

"I have something from every character you've ever played. I used to follow you to make sure you weren't molested on the way to the subway too," Talbot said.

"I always thought you were odd, but I never knew how sick you really were. You left Boston and found me in New York. I was the understudy in *Ruby Slippers* and became the lead when Jessica Simpkin broke her leg."

"She only got the job because she was fucking Jeremy Steel. They should have given me a commission for getting rid of her. The show would have tanked if you hadn't taken over the lead." Talbot said. "You were a way better actress than her. I had planned to get rid of Amy too. But you came home early and got caught in the crosshairs."

Talbot had cut the fly wires and the windowpane sprained her wrist and gave her ten stitches in her head.

No point in stopping now. Skye kept chipping away at him. "I'm not sure why I didn't piece it together when you showed up at the Raverse. Then you torched Tammy's flat so Jason wouldn't start up with me again."

"Jason's always been in love with you," Talbot said. "Even in university."

"You tried to get rid of Jet in Edinburgh, and I should have known you'd come after him again."

"Me?" Jet said.

Skye nodded. "The photo shoot after Jason's wedding? He never banked on you and I switching places when he pulled the release on the set."

Jet narrowed his eyes at Talbot.

"I never would have done anything to hurt Skye," Talbot said. He ogled Skye with puppy dog eyes. "I love you. I showed up at the Thrift Hotel to ask you to come to the wedding with me, but he beat me to it."

Jet pounded his fist on the counter and Talbot jumped.

The knock she heard at her room door—Talbot was the man who exited the hall via the emergency exit stairs. Skye's skin crawled. She scared him away when she called out Jet's name.

Talbot was delusional. He didn't know the first thing about love. "I'm curious, Talbot," she said, trying not to let her revulsion show. "How did you find out I'd gone home to River Glen?"

Jet's head popped up. "He heard me talking to Jason a couple of weeks after you left."

"Why couldn't you just leave Skye alone?" Talbot asked him. "She left the UK to get away from you."

"I left the UK because my father had a heart attack, you sick prick. I'm in love with Jet."

"I've heard enough," the cop said to Skye. "You're very lucky you called 911, or your friend here would most likely be dead."

Jet's head snapped around and his brow creased. "When did you call 911?"

She hated lying to him, but she really didn't have a choice. "You came downstairs to make your world-famous omelet, and I saw Talbot hiding in the bushes from the bathroom window upstairs. I grabbed the extension and called 911."

The cop pulled Talbot to his feet and addressed Skye and Jet. "I need you two to come down to the station to make a formal statement."

"I'll grab my purse," Skye said. "We'll come right away."

"You've got absolutely nothing on me," Talbot said.

"Keep telling yourself that," the cop said. "Attempted murder is not nothing. You'll be going away for a very long time."

Skye and Jet followed the police and cruisers down the street and across town to the station.

Skye sat down and wrote out a detailed account of what had happened. She gave the officer some numbers of the troupe in New York so some of the facts could be corroborated.

Jet issued a formal statement of what happened the day he met with Jason. In the meantime, the police processed Talbot. They photographed and fingerprinted him, and since he hadn't spoken a word since Skye told him in no uncertain terms that she didn't love him, the police scheduled a psychiatric evaluation.

A couple of hours later, Skye and Jet returned to her house on Shady Knoll Road. She parked her aunt's old K-car in the drive around the back of the house and headed into the kitchen.

The vegetables were still spread out on the cutting board half chopped. He hung up the phone that had been dropped. The skillet had made a dent in the old wooden floor and left a black streak where it skidded to a halt against the wall.

Jet picked it up and weighed it in his hand. "Nice job. You've got one hell of an arm."

He put the frying pan on the stove. He placed his hands on her shoulders. "Why didn't you tell me about Talbot?"

Skye spun around. "Honestly, I didn't put it all together until I saw him brandishing the gun." Hopefully he wouldn't press her where she'd seen him. She didn't want to start their relationship off by lying, but she knew that he might not believe her story about a magical brooch that could translate a forgotten script into film clip-like images.

"Clearly, we really need to start working on our communication skills."

"You're right," Skye said.

"But first, I'm going to make us that damned omelet."

Chapter 45

Jet chopped the vegetables and sautéed them in the very same frying pan that saved his life. He whisked the eggs until they were creamy and poured the mixture into the pan.

Skye pulled a couple of plates out of the cupboard and set the table. She filled the kettle and set it to boil for tea.

The phone rang.

She went over to the counter and picked it up. "Hello?" She paused for a moment. "Yes. I'm so sorry, Mr. Humphries. My phone hasn't been working properly for the last few hours."

Skye shrugged. The phone hadn't been working because in all the commotion, it had been left off the hook. Anyone calling through would have gotten a busy signal.

"Thank you for your confidence in me," Skye said. "The certification course is something I'd be interested in completing regardless. Let me know when you have the course outline. I'll drop around and pick it up. Maybe you can give me a tour of the high school while I'm there."

Moments later, she hung up.

"Good news?" Sloan flipped the omelet in the pan.

"The best. I found a teaching job."

"That's terrific."

"Do you have any idea what you'd be interested in doing? Now you're a civilian and all."

"You mean other than getting married?"

Skye's eyes found his. "Are you asking me to marry you?"

"If you'll have me."

Skye hurled herself into his arms and rained kisses on him. He captured her mouth and virtually everything but her soft body pressing against him disappeared. Desire flared hot and sharp in his groin.

She pulled away abruptly. "I need to talk to you about something."

"Sounds serious," Jet said.

"It is. I need to know how you feel about kids."

Damn. He intended to have this conversation with her a little later because he didn't want to put a damper on the mood.

He noticed her wrinkling her nose. "Is something burning?"

"Shit." He let go of her and grabbed a towel to slide the pan off the burner. "We'll talk all you want later. Right now we're going to sit and eat this damn omelet before anything else happens." Jet carried the pan over to the table and put half on her plate and half on his. Then they both sat down and ate. Once their plates were empty, he reached over to clear the table. "You seem tired. Why don't you go and shower or take a nap? I'll clean up here."

"Are you sure? I'd love to go and soak in the tub."

He raised one eyebrow. "Only if I can join you when I'm finished."

Skye went upstairs and ran the water in the bathtub. She unbuttoned her blouse and placed Bessie's journal and Lang's brooch beside her blow-dryer on the bathroom counter.

Skye didn't want to think what her life would have been like without Bessie's visions. Both of the men in her life would be dead—Jet and her father. Not only that but there'd still be a crazy man stalking her. Skye kissed her finger and pressed it to the journal. She switched off the water and filled the tub with soothing salts. Then she stripped her clothes and sank into the silky water. The warmth dissolved the tension in her and she dozed.

When she finally opened her eyes, Jet sat on the floor, leaning against the tub. "How long have you been sitting here?"

"Not long."

Skye saw him turning something over in his hands. "What's that?" she asked.

"A talisman," Jet said. He faced her. "When I was a little boy, I was afraid of everything. One day, Father John pulled me aside and gave me a highly polished black stone called Jet. Have you ever heard of it?"

"Jet? As in your name?"

"Yes. Father John was the same priest that gave me my nickname, but that's another story. Anyhow, jet isn't really a stone. It's fossilized wood from millions of years ago."

"That's pretty cool."

"Father John said it was magical—that it would protect me. I carried that hunk of wood for years. When Busy died, I gave it to his mom. I asked her to bury it with him. I'd failed to keep him safe in this life, but I hoped my talisman would keep him safe throughout time." He angled his head. "Do you believe in life after death?"

Skye nodded. "If you'd asked me that question a couple of months ago, I would have said no. Now I'm certain there is."

Jet angled his head, his voice distant. "Busy came to me in a dream a few nights after you left the UK. He told me to stop being such a fool. He told me to go after you."

"I'm glad," Skye said. She knew there never would be a better time to tell Jet about Bessie. "Do me a favor," she said. "Go to the bathroom window and tell me what you see."

Jet got up and did as she asked. "I can see part of the driveway and some of the walkway leading to the back door," Jet said. "Hey. That can't be right. How did you see Talbot from up here?"

"I didn't see him from up here. Bessie told me he was out there just like Busy told you to get your ass here. Both of us have people in the great beyond taking care of us. I will forever be in Bessie's debt. Not only did she tell me about Talbot, but she also told me about my dad's heart attack. The both of you are alive today because I listened."

Jet handed Skye the talisman he'd been rubbing between his fingers.

"What is this?" She stared at the flattened piece of metal in her hand. It wasn't a coin; it resembled a melted chocolate kiss.

"It's the bullet I dug out of the wall inside your kitchen cupboards. It missed me by a couple of inches."

The shock of hearing those words made it slip through her fingers and she dropped it into the water.

"I'll get it," he said, arching his eyebrows mischievously. His eyes lasered hers while he unzipped his pants and shucked his shirt. He climbed into the water behind her.

He kissed and kneaded her shoulders, and very soon both of them were breathless and writhing. She straddled him. He kissed her as he entered her. They kissed as he pressed in and out. He made love to her so sweetly tears burned her eyes. Afterward, they remained entangled in the tepid water.

"There's one more thing I need to talk to you about," Jet said.

"Only one more thing?"

"This is serious."

She lifted her head. "I'm listening."

"I know how important family is to you, and someday, I'm guessing you want to have children. So do I. But, I'm not sure having kids is even possible. I left before my specialist completed all those tests. If I can't, I wondered if you were open to exploring other options."

Crap. With everything that happened, she'd totally forgotten to mention she was pregnant.

"I don't think that's going to be a problem," Skye said.

"It's a very real possibility."

Skye reached over the side of the tub and tugged her jeans toward her. She pulled the plastic wand out of her pants pocket and handed it to him.

Confusion etched his face. Then concentration. Then awe.

"Is this what I think it is?"

Skye nodded her head.

"You're pregnant?"

She nodded and wrapped her hands around his neck. "Just so you know, I want a boy and a girl—so we'll just have to keep trying until we get that particular combination."

Jet kissed her so sweetly she knew he'd do anything she asked.

"It sounds like a dirty job," he teased, "but someone has to do it."

ABOUT THE AUTHOR

Diane L. Kowalyshyn writes heart-hammering, high-voltage thrillers—adventures that run on action, intrigue and romance. Before publication, her first novel, CROSSOVER, earned a Master of Fine Arts degree. She is an avid sailor who has survived her fair share of squalls and relied on the pulse of a lighthouse beacon to find safe harbor. When she's not writing, or on the water, she's exploring exciting new locales. Her books are available worldwide in trade paperback and ebook. Visit her at http://www.dianelkowalyshyn.com.

OTHER WORKS

Crossover
Double Cross
Crossbones
Skadegamutc: Monster in the Mirror
Catch .22